GREEN, GREEN MY VALLEY NOW

Green, Green My Valley Now

RICHARD LLEWELLYN

NEW ENGLISH LIBRARY
TIMES MIRROR

For my Mama,
and all her beautiful sisters

First published in Great Britain by Michael Joseph Ltd in 1975
© 1975 by Richard Llewellyn

*

FIRST NEL PAPERBACK EDITION MARCH 1977

*

NEL Books are published by
New English Library Limited from Barnard's Inn, Holborn, London EC1N 2JR
Made and printed in Great Britain by Hunt Barnard Printing Ltd., Aylesbury, Bucks.

45003087 3

This work was written under the aegis of the Welsh Arts Council, and I wish to thank the Chairman, Colonel Sir William Crawshay, D.S.O., T.D., the Director, Aneurin Thomas Esq., and Meic Stephens, Esq., Assistant Director, and all members of the Council for their help.

At the end of May 1974
From the house of Hermione and
Clifford Evans
In Cloddiau
Near Welshpool
Ty Cofion!

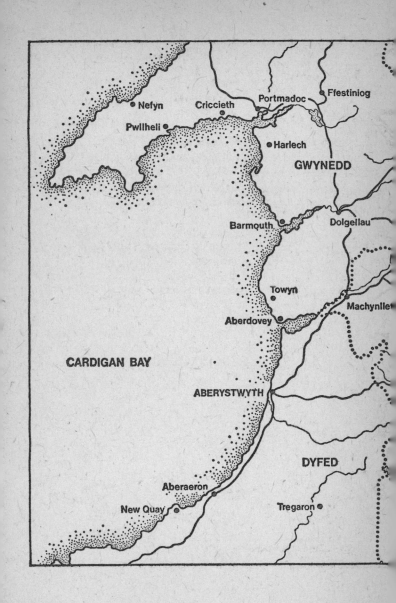

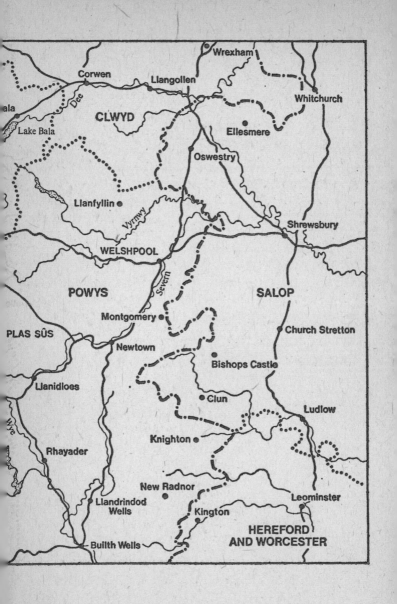

I SUPPOSE if something big is to be felt when you leave a place you love, then something bigger it should be when you go back, though standing here, all I feel is a drift of wonder beyond words or any telling.

At the head of the valley, I am, and looking at shapes I have known since a boy, the mountain over there, and the mountain at the end, but where the other mountain once was, behind our house, is only plain sky, and the river is running clear and wide down the middle, and grass grows along the banks, or in a sudden I have gone mad, for when I left the last time, a few black puddles was all, and slag, then, in a bit of a glitter, as if devils danced to see such ugliness coming from the will of men.

The pit has gone these years, with our house and all the other houses on the hill, flattened and buried under the slag. The chapel, too, and the football field, and the little patches of vegetable gardens so tidy in long lines, always with splashes of colour in summer, and I remember going down to have many a free bunch for the tables in the tea tent when the chapel gave parties, and a few for our house, as well. Mama liked flowers in the house, and especially in the kitchen to lighten the load of work, though I believe she never once thought of what she did as work. My father and brothers worked. She only kept the house, and cooked and washed and scrubbed for a dozen, though if you had said so, she would have turned the eyes, the grey warner, and said, '*Taw sôn*, boy. Be off with you, now then.'

Different ideas about women there are these days, but I am not sure why, or when the times changed, though mind you, they must have been coming long before they were with us. If it is said the reason is that women have come smart to the front because they began to work with men in the First World War, well, our women worked in the pits long, long before, and good as any man, and earning with the best. Mind, they never worked the coal-face, because it takes good shoulders and gut muscles to swing the pick. Many of the other jobs were theirs, though, and no complaints, and they left the pits only when oil began to take coal's place, and men were put from work, and mines shut down. Awful years, those were, my mother said, though I remember them only thin, a bit here, and there a bit, and yet I always see my father sitting in the big chair, staring at the kitchen fire and saying, 'The men are coming out,' and my mother folding hands, and turning her back, and saying, 'O, Gwil,' and him saying, 'Yes, my love. Nothing, no *nothing* to be done. *Noth*ing.'

I was in puzzles to know what the men were coming out from, or how, but I dare not ask in case my mother told me to *hisht* and have my nose from there. She was strict about questions none of our business. But I learnt soon enough from my brothers, and a surprise that was, too. A strike, Gwilym told me, in whispers, as if it was rude. But a strike, in English, is from hammers, and I wondered what would they do with them except to smash something. Funny it is, the way a small boy will look at things. I was sure, at the end of a lot of thinking, that they would smash the heads of the old English, and bold, one night, I asked Owen.

'Go from here, boy,' he said, and laughing. 'Do you think we are a lot of old murderers, then? A strike, it is. From struck. We have struck work from the list of what is to be done until wrongs are righted. More pay, for one. Be

10

off, now, and put your eyes strict to those books. You will need what is in them.'

A splendid prophet he was too, for my life has been bounded by the hammer, the chisel, the saw, and the plane, only because of Mr Gruffydd, and those afternoons in the timber yard, learning the use of tools and the goodness of wood. Only good food will sometimes come prettier to the nose than fresh-cut logs and planks. Women, and babies, and flowers, well, yes. But they are in a different order, and not to be compared.

I well remember Donato Urrisbiscaya, my Basque partner in Patagonia, and a good old boy, too, coming in that night through the freeze of a snowstorm, and leaving the carts of Cordoba pine in the warmth of the carpenter's shop, and the amaze, next morning, to go in to the heat of the fires we had for the metal furnace and the gluepots, and smell the wonder, the rich truth of mountain pine, giving us thanks for a warm night. Pity to cut them, too, but we saved one beauty, and lopped the branches to knots, and fitted pegs in the long wall, and lifted her on. Still there when I left, she was, and still giving us an aroma for kings. So much we felt for her, that when Plethyn John, the carter, brought in the loads of cedar from over the Andes, in Chile, and enough to build the Temple of Solomon and to spare, we asked him to pile it against the walls over in the main barn, not to take the pride from her, because that cedar held the smells of heaven, and we always had morning coffee in by there, only to dream, and on Sundays we read the Bible, certain that the Temple had much the same aroma, and taking comfort from the notion.

Curious it is what happened to the Bible. When I was a boy, Dr Johnson there was, and Shakespeare, and Dickens and a couple more, but the only book, the one solid wall in our lives was the Word, and few to argue. Today, coming up the valleys, I was shocked beyond any word to see so many chapels shut, and more than a few being used as warehouses and shops. What my father would have said I am not sure. But last night at the hotel

11

in Cardiff, my agent told a story among half a dozen of us, about a preacher, and not very nice, and if I like a good joke, I think it unhealthy to poke vicious fun at men unable to defend themselves, and I said so.

You might have thought I had given them all a good dab in the nose. Everybody began to speak at once. I was listening to one, and the other, and all of them, and they were all saying that Chapel and preachers and the Bible had been our downfall as a Nation, telling us to be meek, when we should have been on our feet and fighting for proper rights.

'Good God, you have been away too long, with you, yes?' Mostyn Price shouted, with spit almost in my eyes. 'The bloody Bible is poison. Love ye one another, is it? Who loves us? The English? Listen, Mr Foreigner. Let me tell you. We were the niggers of the Empire. Now we are the Asians of the Commonwealth. Same level. And no bloody Commonwealth. Now, for you!'

'Lowest and least, and coming less,' Powis Humphrey said, glass to his chin. 'We want our own senate and lower chamber, and a president, then. Thirty-odd fools to represent two-and-a-half million people? An absurdity come ripe and going rotten.'

'Only look at the pits,' Gilbert Jones said. 'If the boys were all working and they'd put in the plants those years ago, would we need any oil from outside?'

'Plants, yes,' Cynan Morse said, over a good swallow of ale, 'But they ruined the business long before that, see?'

'Ruined how?' Powis asked him, a little question, high in the mouth.

'Well, making it fixed wages, and overtime, and double time, and this time and that,' Cynan said. 'The old way was best. Every man cut all he can, and pay him, flat, for the weight of it. Now you will have all the coal you could want, and nobody going short, and everybody warm, like, and making a bit of cash!'

'The millennium come again,' Idris Evans said, with fingers spread on the swollen waistcoat, and looking at the colour of sherry through the bar's lamp. 'I don't think the oil boys, and the banking boys and the stocks and shares boys will ever allow it. Oil is money by the billion. Billions make millions in interest, and loans and property deals. What billions are there in coal? No business at all. Have you thought of shipping? All those tankers idle? Coal is the *last* resort. *That's* why they won't pay the miners.'

'Phase Three and a three-day week, together, will break the unions,' Cynan said. 'That's the objective. Depending how long it lasts, of course.'

'It depends on the stomach of *all* the unions,' Douglas Gough, my solicitor, said, running an elbow on the bar. 'The Tories won't go far before there is *real* trouble. I've just come down from the north. Glasgow, and down. It's in a *rumble* everywhere. A touch will do it. Miners, engineers, mechanics, civil services, the lot!'

'Talk,' Cynan said, and swigged contempt.

'I'm afraid so,' Idris said and nodded at the barman. 'Fill them up, please. Yes, yes. A good revolution would clear the air, indeed. But it won't come. Too comfortable, see, with the squintbox and football, and enough for a pint or two. Leave it now. It won't come better. Only with a bit of time, like?'

How many times I have stood silent to listen to bar chat since I came back, I have lost count. Everybody knowing what was wrong, but few able to tell how to put it right, and less with the spirit and energy to try. And always that dispirit to finish. It was that, the dispirit, which daunted me.

The same it was at the other end of the world in Argentina, in the town of Trelew, Patagonia, and up north, in Mendoza, and across there in Cordoba and Buenos Aires. The same in Chile, and Uruguay. In all those I had businesses, and employing many thousands in building roads and bridges, and then in construction of areas for public housing and by the block for offices and shops. If there was good profit to begin, there was less as the years went. But costs went up – nobody was sure why – and wages had to go up – and everybody knew why – and contracts had to be

13

renegotiated, and that was months of denial and delay. Everything was in the hands of the military, everywhere, and the last on earth to know about business. They were in stupors to look at figures, a balance sheet would frighten them, and they even turned from the advice of their own accountants, a dull old lot, to be sure, but sense enough to tell profit from loss, and to advise extra credit to meet overheads, and more importantly, the weekly payroll.

'Now, Señor Morgan, let us be patient,' Colonel Lopez Bravo, of the Finance Department said, that Friday afternoon in Buenos Aires. 'I have an account of your personal finances in front of me. You have more than enough to meet payrolls for many a year. You know the country is in a situation, let us say, not less than desperate. Argentina has been good to you. You never became a citizen. You have extraordinary responsibilities. Are you so helpless? Why can't you use all this money to pay your men?'

'If you will be good enough to look closely, you will see that enough cash is there to meet another five weeks,' I said. 'After that, what? Bankruptcy?'

'You would not be the first,' he said, and went about lighting a black cigarette as a drawn-out ritual, sucked in, and a *p'wah!* to loose a cloud, and the stink I have got with me, now, *ach y fi, a'r diâwl.* 'You must realise that we must all do our share. You have cattle. Sheep. Wheat. Sugar cane. Vineyards. Timber mills. Shipping. Many other activities. They all make money. I have the figures, here. Surprising, I must say. But you can't meet a payroll?'

'Cattle and sheep have nothing to do with construction of buildings, or bridges, or roads,' I said. 'Contracts are that, and nothing else. The nuclear project and the dams have nothing in common. But both contracts, and all the others, were based on costs summarised at the time of signing. Those costs today are more than a hundred percent higher. I want the contractual prices raised to conform. Otherwise, work will stop.'

'That would be a disaster,' the Colonel said, easy. 'For you, certainly. It would not be regarded as a friendly act. In these times we are all expected to make a sacrifice!'

14

'Except you, of the military,' I said, equally easy. 'I notice your pay goes up whenever you want. Sacrifice?'

'Cost of living,' he said in another *ph'p-p'wah-'nk!* 'We are not all millionaires. Remember, that an act so damaging to the country could have serious consequences. For *you!*'

'They are, already,' I said. 'Nothing more damaging than to know you will have to shut down in a few weeks unless someone makes a proper decision.'

'We have power of expropriation,' he said, looking at the cigarette. 'To that sort of deliberate sabotage of the Country's best interests, I don't think the General Staff would be more than most unsympathetic!'

'Men have to be paid, and pay takes money,' I said. 'Consult your superiors. They must be warned in time. Either the contracts must reflect the prices of today, including wages, or they will lapse for want of liquid cash. That's all!'

'It may be "all" for you, señor,' he said, and slid down in the chair, smiling. 'For us, it is the beginning!'

Thus it was that I saw, as a blue streak of cloud in a grey snow-sky, the idea behind the interview. Of course, others had told of it, and word had got about, but it had never touched me or any part of my business.

They intended expropriation, with a sale to the highest bidder, and niggardly compensation to me, so that all should appear in order, propriety served, justice done. But it did not end there. The highest bidder would be someone picked by them, so that the smallest sum would buy the largest property, and afterwards, the guardians of National Discipline, Law, and Order, that is to say, the Services, of one sort or another, would 'buy' what was going of my property for minimal amounts and thereafter lord it over square miles of prime land cleansed by the sweat and cash of somebody else. Send the peons and their families from there, then, and put in Service pensioners. Easy.

The story was old, and full of the breath of bad faith, and the same everywhere, for civil servants are not less greedy than other men, and with lawyers having their –

not small – cut, all was in splendid order, papers drawn, stamped, many times sealed, all according to the Law.

And true owners, by birthright, or by sweat and cash, denied, cheated, robbed.

But this was long after the time of Peron. There was not that excuse.

I went direct from there, and without any pretty good-byes, to banking friends of mine, and told what had happened. They were far too powerful for any soldier to interfere with because they dealt on the international market, and soldiers need armaments, sailors need ships, and airmen need aircraft. I told what had gone on, and within a couple of hours I had thrown aside all I had worked for in Argentina and Chile, but for a fair price, in dollars, marks, francs, lire, sterling and schillings.

It exactly suited me. I was sick to see a wonderful country torn apart by dogs in disguise.

Sûs and I had been married almost two years, perhaps the happiest of my life, or, to tell everything plain, after the long, dark years since my first wife Lal's death, I seemed to be in golden clover with me, and thankful to God.

Sûs's childhood nurses, either Tehuelche or Mapuche, taught her little of courtesy and less of table manners, but she learned quick enough from me, though if she came crosspatch about something, she went back to them, and I had a good laugh, and then she punched her fists on my chest and shouted Indio curses not of the most delicate, and I laughed more, and soon her arms were round my neck, and she laughed, too.

And she could cook. The dishes of the Indio, whether grills, roasts or boils, and not nearly so simple as they might sound, were childsplay to her, and she also had the Welsh kitchen of her Grandam at fingertips, so that our table at any time of the year was fit for kings. Only give her an excuse, always for our birthdays, and she got the peons to dig a twelve-foot-across hollow in the ground, and under her eye they put down long stone setts in circular rows, but tidy, and at the end she had a shallow, concave, stone wheel. On that they piled logs that burn a white heat, and

16

give good coals, and let it flame high for a day, or until the stones were hot as the fire. Over them, scraped clean of ash, they put a thick carpet of green branches giving a steam of wonderful fragrance, and on that, again, the turkeys, chickens, ducks, geese, vegetables, fruits, and all the other things good that will cook. Over that, cabbage leaves to cover, and more branches over, stems out, thick, and then a canvas to cover the wheel entire, and a thick topping of earth to hold in the steam. Three hours after, take off the canvas, rolling it back with the earth, out with the branches, yellow now, and the cabbage leaves, yellow, too, and then choose what you will eat of that goodness, of a taste not in any other way of cooking, and invite your oldest woman guest to have first choice. Generally, it is the goose, and they are not in blame with me, for I never had goose, or anything else, to come near it, either for taste or texture, so tender and yet so firm, and full of the natural juice.

The part about her that I loved was a direct manner of speech. A lie was never in her, and none of the prevaricator, or excuser, in fact, nothing of shilly-shally. What she had to say was out, flat, and push a thumb, everybody. Of course, it is a habit that can bring trouble, too, and many a time I have had to wish that she had a little more diplomacy, if that is a good word for smoothers, or white lies, and I always knew that one too many of them, and there we are, fat with a good black one. For that reason, I always stood quiet to let her say, and I have never been sorry. Even the time when we crossed to Chile, and the Customs men opened our baggage, and I had to hold her from clawing them. A good job none of them had a word of Tehuelche, or we would still be in the lock-up. Thieves, she was shouting, dirty thieves, born thieves and wearing uniform to hide the dirty blood of the unclean womb that threw them. Of course, the more she shouted, the more they unpacked and searched, thinking we had contraband, I suppose, but they were sorry for a waste of time and when we left, a more unhappy line of hangdogs I never saw.

'You could have saved that,' the bus driver said, and

cross, because the search had made him late. 'A few pesos for each. A kiss in the hand. That's all!'

'A boot in the backside, yes,' I said.

'*A'r cŵt, yn wyr!*' Sûs bellowed, what I had said in Welsh, but ruder, and a couple of Welsh speakers at the back screeched out laughing, and they were in a cackle almost till we reached Puerto Montt. Lesie and Jane Rowlands, they were, and they invited us to their house in Punta Arenas, south, a beautiful farm, too, with a couple of hundred thousand sheep, a herd of pedigree black cattle, and more down there in Tierra del Fuego.

He had come to the country as a wool factor, and he had been grading the new clip and buying stock in Argentina.

'It is coming thankless,' he said. 'They are so nationalist, I am in doubts if to go back. There's no need, mind, I have got plenty here. But even here is getting worse. Not long, and all foreigners will be out. A lot have been put from their farms. Down here we are lucky to have the Army and Navy near. But none of us have got long. Sell up, and go home, that's us!'

'Sooner the better,' Janie said, 'I don't want to be here another second more. The poor de Macchi's were enough'

'Burnt in their farm and every animal stolen,' Leslie said. 'But they were a long way north, and lonely. Not the only ones, either. Kill and rob. It is new to us. It never was before, yes?'

'Why is it?' Janie asked. 'Everything at peace, and then robbery and murder?'

'They aren't taking home enough to feed their families,' I said. 'Money is the curse. The same over with us. I've been lucky. I always paid my people on the cost of living. That way, I was unpopular with a lot of people. Putting up wages is a crime to some. But I never worried till now, just. I sold out. I am going to sell out everything in this country, too. We will travel a bit, and go to Wales, and find somewhere, and settle to a bit of peace for a change. The last few years haven't been good. They will be worse.'

18

'No kidnappings here, yet,' Leslie said, pouring whisky. 'Enough?'

'Thank you,' I said. 'Have no doubt they will come. The same type of brute is in every country. If they can burn and murder in cold blood, kidnap is a girl's game!'

I well remembered the shock of that blanket over my head in the five o'clock dark of morning, and the point of a knife in my back, if I was lucky to be wearing the broad gancho leather belt. I was tied Indio style, ankles to wrists at the back, and bent double, thrown in a truck, and off we went, and a bumpy old way it was, and my wrists screaming pain, and in the house, the rest of me.

Well, the boys were stupid. They should have known I would have a watchman about a place of that size. In fact, I had three. Tehuelche crossbreeds, but good, and long in my service, loyal, yes, to Sûs because she could talk to them in their own language. She was in bed, of course, after giving me breakfast – she would never allow the maids to touch anything – and she loved 'cooching' – she called it – down in the warm and sleeping another couple of hours. She woke soon enough, and out, then, with all eight Indios, and the dogs.

Nobody lives on earth better than the Indio as a tracker, and no dog is better scenter than the Doggo Argentino, bred to find, and fight, the wild boar, or anything else.

The tracking, then, was simple as following a path, so Sûs told me, after.

They went in a straight line, and no turn-offs or doubling back disturbed them, even to crossing a couple of shallow brooks, because the Indios rode across, found the tracks, and off again, and they came up with us at about four in the afternoon, but I was last to know, still held in the truck, and numb everywhere.

Suddenly, the sounds of fighting, and men screaming, and why not, because the dogs, without a sound, were in, and biting between the legs, and nothing would have their jaws loose. Then I heard Sûs's voice, that I thought a dream, and she was up in the truck, and cutting me loose, and I have never heard or seen such fury.

19

Well, of course, by the time she had rubbed pins and needles all over me, the Indios had punished the boys in their style, with a flogging that left their backs and other places without a strip of skin, and a knife-blade from the forehead, down the nose to the chin, and across the cheek one side, over the nose, to the other, and they broke their shoulders, elbows and wrists, and both thumbs and all their fingers, their knees, ankles and toes, and if I had not begged Sûs, they would have taken out their eyes. We left a moaning heap of limbs in shapes to pull the heart, and Sûs told them please to come back, and they would have a lot better. The dogs would have eaten them raw, but Sûs called them off, and for a wonder, they obeyed, and sat. If the unlucky ones lived or not, we never heard, and there was nothing in the papers.

'Why did they do it?' she asked me, later. 'For what good reason?'

'Money,' I told her. 'They would hide me, and ask you for a million pesos, or more.'

She laughed in the throat.

'Never!' she said. 'Not one centavo. You are not old meat to be bought. I am not. Die, but I would *never* buy you!'

'If it would save my life?' I asked her.

'For some money, no!' she said, and angry, and coming loud.

'But money is only paper,' I said. 'A life is a life!'

'Life is worth more than paper!' she shouted. 'How can you speak of life and paper, equal? A million horses *no. Never!*'

In many ways, in riding a horse, or in speaking what she thought, Mistress Sûs was an Indio of Indios, hating injustice, unfair dealing, slyness behind the back and all to be called dishonest. That is to say, of the Indio true-bred. They never lose their spine. The lower type of crossbreed, of course, copies our ways, and too often comes out a liar and a thief, and we judge him, and give him a bad name. But most of *us* are the underhanded, and he takes us as an example, pity it is.

20

Anyway, Sûs was beyond patience to be out, and only ten days later, the house was sold, and we were packed and gone. I thought we might stay in Rio de Janeiro for a week or so, but no. Her ladyship had to be in her Grandam's country, and in the house of her Grandam's birth more than a hundred years before, what is more, but she had the address, and once in London, getting to Wales was easy, and finding the cottage was only asking question after question, because the place had changed hands a couple of times, and each time another name. But the solicitor found it from the Police, and up we went in a hired car, off the main road, along a lane of drying ruts, between hedges heavy with blackberry and honeysuckle, and at last the cottage peeped at us between two beautiful holly trees and weeds grown over our heads.

'It hasn't been lived in these past thirty years,' the solicitor said. 'It's supposed to be haunted, I'd better tell you!'

'Good!' I said. 'Get a haunted price for it!'

Well, I must say, I was surprised at the price of the cottage and the thirty-six acres of excellent ploughland, and an orchard of apple, pear, cherry and plum gone wild, and a pond for ducks and geese. It was not a quarter of what I expected, and Douglas Gough, the solicitor, said it was because it would need a lot of money and time to put a bit of shape in it, and most people had neither.

'It could cost a couple of thousand to build the road, first,' he said, polishing his glasses. 'Then clearing of woodland, and drainage, another five hundred, easy. If you are going to have a garden, as Mrs Morgan drew it for me, another thousand, at least. A slate roof is a pretty penny, these days. And restoring the rafters, replacing the floors upstairs, no, I don't think you had *such* a bargain, indeed!'

'They shall take it to pieces and build new,' I said. 'When it is finished it will be as it was in fifteen-whatever-it-was, plus the comfort of this time. Mrs Morgan's great-grandfather left the place in eighteen-sixty-five for Patagonia. He's buried there, with all the family except her. This place is my gift to her. I don't care what it costs. It will be beautiful, that's all. And if we speak of price and

21

bargains, or in one little word, business, well, the moment it is finished, it will be worth at least twice what I paid. Yes?'

'I've got to agree, there,' he said. 'But the initial outlay will be cruel!'

'Not to me,' I said. 'Every penny spent will be a gift!'

He lifted his hands as if dealing with a madman, and indeed I was. I had my heart in it. I would have given anything to take her down to the Valley, and build a house for her, but there was no profit in showing her slag heaps up to the sky, and trying to explain that when I was a boy everything was green. She could see what was there, as she did the first time, and look at me as if I was a liar. For that reason, and perhaps because of shame that I had come from such a poor place, I said nothing. The snob is always alive in us, and in me it was full-strength, whether I scorned the memory of my good mother and father, or not, no matter.

I was a fool of silence, and no conscience.

If my lady ever thought of it, she never said. She only revelled in the farm. I have never known the real meaning of the English word revel until I saw her take that wild-grown place to herself, and try to see it as she wanted. Every morning she was up there to watch the men draining and putting in new culverts, and following the hedgers to see how they cut bracken and brambles from the fields' stone walls, and cleared ditches, and piled the cuts in a big heap in the middle, and burning, then, until we looked like an old volcano up there. But it was soon ash, and spread about, it gave the soil extra, and in a few weeks we had fields to be proud of, and when the men came to cut the growth, we had a stock of bales enough to feed twenty head through winter.

But we were far from happy about a place to stay, and still we were looking for an architect. Several had been to see us, some with sketches, but Sûs liked none of them, and I was not the one to tread on instinct, or intuition, whatever it is that says a flat No in the little voice nobody hears.

Neither of us liked hotels or inns. We were used to space, and a bathroom of our own. For years, Sûs had bathed in a tin tub in the house of her Indio nurses, and I had a tub out in the kitchen, with water boiled in kettles on the stove. In that place, at that time, we were both lucky, each of us unaware that the other existed. But when she saw a real bathroom at my house on the edge of the lake at Little Looking Glass, from the moment, no more tin tubs or kettles. The house in Buenos Aires had a bathroom for each of us, so we were used to privacy, and the hotel's public bathrooms and small shower spaces were not to her liking or mine, but if there is *nothing* else, then put up with it, and look for *some*thing else. Sûs missed her kitchen, and I longed for her cooking.

If I think, now, it could sound as if we were a fine pair of hoity-toits, but indeed we were not, and we might have gone on like that, except that one night, the hotel bathroom above us flooded, and our ceiling almost came on top of us, and water in cascades to soak. Sûs laughed herself silly downstairs, wearing two dry blankets and towelling her hair, and soon everybody wet laughed with her.

'Better off in a tent,' somebody said, over the sound of buckets filling from squeezed mops, and then, it was, I had the idea.

'Come you,' I said to Sûs, that morning. 'London, us!'

She liked London, the streets and shops, museums and cinemas, and opera, because she loved the voices. Theatres not so much. She spoke purest Welsh – far better than mine – and about five Indio languages, all of them quite different one from another, but her English was little or nothing, simply because she had no love for the English, but only a hatred, put into her, I suppose, by her father's people, and the rest.

I know we suffered as a Nation over hundreds of years, and nobody knows how many tens of thousands of our people died in the torture chambers and dungeons of the castles, or how many women were raped or how many children grew to be used as slaves, or little better, or what numbers of us lost our patrimony to Romans, Saxons and the brothers of the Norman bastard, and their sons, and on, until, with time, they called themselves English.

We were never other than Welsh, and like the Irish, we never lost the idea of a government of our own. For that reason, Sûs's great-grandfather and all the others landed in the desert of Patagonia, only to speak their own language, worship as they wanted, and live in freedom, with their own people about them.

Walking through London's streets, I told her that most of the people she could see were English, and if they did any killing or torturing, they would be severely punished, but she only half-shut her eyes, and shrugged as if no odds, so I knew I had a bit of time to go before she would listen.

We went to a tent maker in the City, a fine place full of rope and canvas, and a good smell of the sea about it, and I bought four big marquees, like the tents we had for the chapel teas those years ago, but better, with a double roof, and a place for the chimney, and a flooring of boards.

From there we went like a couple of children in a taxi, to a place that sold kitchens, complete. We had spent hours at night with the catalogues, and Sûs knew what she wanted, and the girl took us to the exact one, and indeed it looked very good, much better than ours in Buenos Aires, and Sûs said she could eat it every bit, to the handles.

From there to the furniture, and again Sûs knew what she wanted, and in minutes we had bought a couple of leather armchairs and a big couch, and carpets for the floors and walls, and lamps, and goodness knows what other, and the girl said it would all be sent off to be collected at our railway station within the week.

Kitchen pots and pans, then, to a little shop in Soho, all in copper, and if you saw the collection she chose, you could think she was cooking for the Tribe of Shem, but she was right, and everything came handy. After that, china and porcelain, and then tablecloths and linens, and bedding and blankets, and in the middle of choosing blankets, Sûs looked at me big-eyed, mouth open.

'The bed!' she shouted, to clear the shop. 'Where is the old bed, with you?'

Well, another place to get the bed, and then we had to change the sheets and blankets to have the proper size, and about then, we thought, enough for one day. Enough past enough.

Then it was, so selfish we are, that I thought of couples all over the world, and tight in the pocket, and what they would do to be comfortable without enough money. That thought had never been with me before. I wondered why the notion could come at that moment. But it was clear enough. I had been spending hundreds without thinking of tomorrow, because plenty was there for many tomorrows, though the boys and girls of families without enough money would go short, or do without altogether. And babies, then? What did they do, and how?

Sûs was far from taken with the notion.

She had lived the austere life of the Indio, which can be rich enough if that is what you want, but she had lived in my style at Little Looking Glass and in Buenos Aires. When she said she could go back to the Indio way, I believed her, for I knew I could live more than well in my first house down there in Patagonia, rough to say the least, a few leagues from Trevelin. So much so, that I was often homesick for the lakes, and the tall, redwood alerces, and the blossom of amancay in shine of gold on the hillsides, and the flights of ibis, and the strange, heart-gripping call of trumpeter swans flying over, and wild cattle bugling from the hills in time of love.

So much we have to be thankful for, yes, that we could cry for. But the Indios are there always.

'If you can have, *have*,' Sûs said. 'If not, *wait*!'

'Small profit for living,' I said. 'Are people born only to wait, and have nothing?'

'If they have themselves, they have got plenty,' she said, in surprise. 'Has an Indio got more? Does he want it?'

'These are not Indios,' I said. 'They *need* more than Indios. Another life, it is. And children to feed and clothe and school. For that, they work. But the money is never enough.'

'It would never be!' she said. 'The more money, the less work they want, only to enjoy the money. Like the worst of the Indios. Work, have money, and then buy wine and be drunk three weeks. Then work again. But the more money, the less work!'

'Wait, now!' I said, knowing she had struck at least half a bell. 'Not all are like that, are they?'

'More, much more, than the good ones,' she said, as a truth. 'The good ones will buy cattle and sheep, and a bit of fencing, and good horses, and put up houses of logs with a roof of alerces tiles, and four or five women to look after them, and having a new dress every shearing, they live better than the best, no?'

'Wait, you!' I said. 'What has that life to do with what is here? They are at the other end of the world, girl. Nothing is in common with them!'

'Except work!' she shouted. 'Every man can earn with work, isn't it? With work is money. With money, he buys. The same here as there, yes?'

Well, what to say, indeed, would have Gabriel himself in a tangle of fits.

'Look,' I said, and patience in the drip. '*There*, is horses, and cattle, and sheep, and wool, and whatever, isn't it? But *here*, except for a few, it is machines. Machines make industry, you know that?'

'Well, yes, *Dûw Anwyl* I do!' she said, sweet to put your teeth in crinkles, knowing something was coming. 'Like your wonderful mechanics in Cordoba? Smashing the machines that earned the money? Making you close down? The same in Mendoza? In Buenos Aires? Industry, is it? What do they care? Money they want. But they smash the work. Did you ever see any Indio smash cattle or sheep?'

'Steal and slaughter, yes,' I said.

'Hungry, yes, they will,' she said. 'But how many?'

'We are on the wrong way,' I said. 'Indios live in their world. These people live in another, entirely different. They want other things, not horses and cattle.'

26

'And less time for work, but more money, isn't it?' she said, and nodded. 'Go, you!'

She spoke with the voice of another world, more honest, whether to themselves or to other men, working all the hours of the day, not because they were told, but because they wanted to, and not for any stated sum of money, but for what would come. Very well, and perhaps those days are gone, and with them, the men and women of that time, and in their place, a rabble, each with a union card, and National Insurance, and a squintbox, and a radio, and some with a car, a washing machine, a mortgage on a house, all of them bound in an idiocy, and no thought for what is to come, believing they know, but that is worse, because they never do, and when the strikes come, or whatever, they are caught, flat, with nothing.

Sûs took no notice of the day's news. I read the papers to her, but nothing made her feel, except men or women being hurt, or children brutalised, or aircraft crashes, or people knocked down on the road. For all those, yes, she had feeling. But for politics, nothing. The French, she had words for, not very nice, because everybody knew what Gallimard, the barber, once in Trelew, said of his country. It was not fair to repeat because he was a political exile, but from what I have seen since, it is right what he always said, and it will do.

Unless you have everything signed, and the money in the bank – *your* bank – never trust a Frenchman. Even to his own countrymen, he will eel his way with the words they want to hear, but he will do anything else, to his own profit.

We often talked, but it was always a bit of a puzzle to us how a country could live with fat fools at the top. Any ordinary business would be bankrupt, but because it was a government, nobody could say *Stop!* and nobody could examine the books, and the shouting went on, and nobody wiser.

' '*ch y fi*, old politics!' Sûs said. 'I have got my own. You, the house, and the farm. Come, now then. The rain has stopped. Let us go up. I am in itches to be there!'

The squares of red brick in two tiers for the tent floors, and the narrower passageways, were drained and ready, and the tents came by truck, but only because the men spaded out the deep clay ruts in the roadway, and laid branches, we got it up there, and a weight those tents were, indeed. There is nothing better than to see a good workman set about a job. Sûs called me for tea and rum in the stairwell, and by the time I was out, the tents were up, and roped down, and the carpenters were putting up wooden walls to break the force of the nor'easter, and the others were laying the floorboards.

Well, Sûs, with her rubber boots off, was dancing one to another, and singing at the pitch of her voice, and the men laughing, and singing with her, and we had a good, rough choir there, indeed, and I knew, then, I was almost home.

Douglas Gough had come a good friend. He knew everybody, and anything he wanted, he got. He had the permit to build the road, and the work contracts, that I signed, with a cheque to show willing.

'Now then,' he said, pressing the case shut. 'In the car outside, I have got Lys Machen. She's an architect. Had the gold medal for her year, and a lot of prizes since. She specialises in restoration of old buildings. She is back from a big job in the United States, so when I heard, I phoned her, and here she is. Shall I bring her in?'

'By all means,' I said. 'Pity to keep the girl in a car all this time. In with her!'

Well, Lys, I suppose, was mid-thirties, a tidy figure, white hair, and not a beautiful face, but beauty was in her, and it shone out. Sûs took to her as a sister, and in moments I left them, and went to town with Douglas to see the road contractors. By the time I got back, the house had been sketched in charcoal on big sheets, and we saw it as it would be, but far better, and that spare touch with the line made me sure.

'This stair should be removed to the back, leading off the kitchen, and I've got a more suitable staircase of the same period, with a wide handrail, and nicely worn,

28

carved balusters,' she said. 'I know where there's a large dresser, perfect for the kitchen, and there's some period farm furniture coming up for sale in about ten days, settles, armchairs, tables, and so forth.'

'Buy anything you think is right,' I said. 'We will go to any sale. But what we *don't* want is rubbish!'

'There's plenty of that!' Lys said, and laughing. 'Plenty of fakes, too. But I don't think they'll catch my buyer. Too long in the tooth, and part of the trade. And by the way, there are Welsh artists, painters and sculptors. You could use a few pieces in these big rooms?'

'Anything good, we will buy,' I said. 'As long as it is not this dab and slop. No shape to it!'

'I understand that,' she said, and smiling. 'I don't think you'll be disappointed. I suggest parquet in the hall and through the drawing-room, in the corridors and the bedrooms. Slate flagstones in the kitchen, scullery and larder, and in the garden as far as the well. Then bricks for pathways from there on?'

'Good, you!' Sûs said. 'There is a clever old girl you are. Let me see it!'

'I'll have the plan, and most of the sketches ready in about ten days,' she said. 'Meantime, if you wish, the men can take the stairway down, scrape the paint off the rafters and the roof beams, and strip the beams and plaster outside. I suspect dry rot. It should give them plenty to do till I'm ready. And Mr Gough can prepare my contract?'

'With greatest pleasure,' I said. 'At the right time, you are here!'

Well, they were quiet days, and they came quieter, because the roadmen were a couple of months taking measures and putting in sticks, and using the theodolite, and then nothing for weeks, and at last a superintendent to show drawings of the road bed, and drainage, and the macadam surface, and the circular pathway to the front door and out, well, anyway you would never think there was such a lot of work in only an old road.

In that time Lys's blueprints gave the masons and carpenters a lovely lot of measures, and Rhodrick, the foreman, said he never saw better.

'No chance to go wrong here,' he said. 'I thought we would have a lot of trouble with that retaining wall, but see what she has done? Brains, yes!'

We went to several sales, and stayed away five days, but what we bought had Sûs in a real shine with her, and Lys's buyer said every piece was genuine, not less than two hundred years old, cabinetmakers known by name, and famous, and considering the times, every one a bargain.

'They are gutting the country, here,' he said, a little man, high voice, and a long lock of thin black hair falling over the nose. 'A few years, and nothing will be left. Nothing to tell what sort of workmen we were. Or if we had craftsmen in wood, or anything else. It will be another time like the Roman pillage. They took everything. Saxons took everything else a few years later. Don't speak of the Normans. They were worse than Hitler in Poland and France and Italy and wherever. Now it is pillage with money. The people are too ignorant, too selfish to know. Two beautiful armchairs, see, and tassels on the arms, and look, now, at that brocade, will you? Perfect for looking at the telly. Hours, years, of comfort after the day's work, look. Give me that old table in exchange. O, yes, take it, and thank you, sir! The poor blind fools don't know the table is worth a couple of hundred times, and more, than the armchairs!'

'If you find anything you know is good, let me know,' I said. 'Or buy it. You can trust me. Who's doing the pillaging?'

'Americans,' he said. 'Shipments at a time. And a lot of fakes. There are still good carpenters. A cabinet maker, worthy of the name, would never put his hand!'

The parquet went down, the slates in the kitchen were laid, and parquet again in the big withdrawing-room, and we could walk steady about the place, as Mr Rhodrick said, like Christians. All that time, the raftering under the roof was scraped and oiled, and the big beams running across, and the thick doors slid on the hinges, and one morning, when they took away the high wall of brush-wood against the side walls and the back to stop the winds and rain, we saw we had a house about twice as big as we had thought, and a surprise that was, too.

New rafters of aged wood came up for the kitchen and withdrawing-room ceilings, and a lot left over, and when Lys came that Wednesday, she pointed to places in the outer wall of the withdrawing-room, and said it had once been spacious, probably for wool carding and spinning, but it would make a lovely study, and she had the panelling and bookshelves, and the desk, and a lot of other things, all of the period.

'Go you!' Sûs said. 'He shall be comfortable. Is there a fireplace, with you?'

'A real beauty,' Lys said. 'I saw it, and bought it. An old farm that must have been a manor. Terrible lives, those people must have lived. The fireplace and a couple of other really rare items were under eight foot of bones and rubble. Something else, too. But it's secret. My buyer will talk to you!'

In those days we lived in the tents, nobody happier, or with more of warmth. The sitting-room, with carpets from Welsh looms, in soft colours on the floor and round the walls, seemed to put arms about us. Next door, the dining-room and kitchen, different, brighter colours, with the wash-up in the smaller tent, off. The bedroom then, with only the big bed and side tables with lamps, and after, a good, big, bathroom, and everything working splendid.

Sûs was happy as a singing bird. On that big shiny stove, of glass and enamel, she cooked many a good dream, and Douglas Gough said he wished he had met a Patagonian before.

'Plenty there,' I said. 'Go, and pick!'

'My wife is bigger than me,' he said. 'She would kill me!'

By that time we had a couple of blood horses, and every morning we went bareback over the fields and along the hedgerows to see what needed to be done, and there was always plenty. Behind us, there were twelve good fields going up to the crest of the hill, but I had never seen an animal in them, and I asked Douglas if there was chance of sale.

'That's about twenty—twenty-five acres,' he said, looking up there. 'You'd then have about seventy acres? It's worth trying. The owner's a recluse. Lost his wife, and shut himself in. This is years ago. We'll see if a price interests him!'

It did, indeed, and we met in another solicitor's office, and I signed, and wrote the cheque, and the ex-owner came in while the girl was on the way to the bank. To see him, I was sorry. He was mauve in the face and hands, with a ragged wool cap and hair poking out, and a black, torn raincoat, and bindings round the legs, and boots just able to stay on his feet.

I looked at Sûs, and she knew.

Methylated spirit. We were back with the worst of the Indios again.

'Good farm, it is,' he said, and O, a dull, dull voice. 'I hadn't got the heart, no. Nothing worth. If you do want to buy the farm, yes, with me?'

'I will buy,' I said to Douglas. 'Please to get the figures, and I will go over, and decide.'

An early Tudor cottage, it was, but in such a state of ruin that you would wonder how even an animal could live there. The cow barn was almost to the knee in dried manure. The stench of ages was about the place, and where he lived was a pile of sheepskins that cried to be burnt, the wood ash of years of fires, and piles of tins and bones and paper everywhere.

'No need to look to the Indios,' I said, to Sûs. 'We have got enough with us!'

She said nothing. She had seen it all before.

I bought, for far less, the cottage and eight more fields, each larger than on the other side, all of them in sad state, but with a bit of work, something to see. I got the men on to the place, and they were happy, for they thought they were finishing, but no, more work they had, at least a couple of months more, and they put their backs into it.

Lys went up there, and you would not believe the difference in four days of work.

'Look,' I said. 'This could make a good farm manager's house.'

'And you look!' she said, and the pale grey eyes shining a smile. 'Properly restored, you could sell this as a flawless period cottage. I'd say, Henry the First or Second. I'll have to dig a little. You have no idea how rich our country is. Especially here, in these lonely parts. Roads used to go all over, until the Normans took the lands. About the time of the Plantagenets and Tudors, things settled down. But not on these hillsides. The roads went through the valleys. Only cattle came up here. And drovers, to buy. Drovers die, places were forgotten, labourers go where there's money. So the best cottage can fall into ruin. It takes people like you to restore. And by the way, you know that inside ten days, you can be in your own house?'

Well, if you had seen Sûs. She danced from room to room, and I followed, and we saw it was dry everywhere, and everything old, but new, and shining.

We sat on the floor of the bedroom, and planned an asado for all the workmen and their families, and everybody helping, even to the telephone girl and the men running the wires to the house, and the roadmen, and the plumbers and electricians, and the rest. Almost a hundred, there were, and we planned five appetites to a sheep, and so twenty sheep and ten more to allow for the unexpected, and all the little things for the grill, sausages, and livers and such, and we chose the space beyond the barn for the fire because all the trees made a warm windbreak, and we needed two barrels of red wine, and other bottles as well.

That afternoon, the black cattle came, and we put them in the lower fields near the river, and later the black-necked swans and the geese uncrated, and three dozen ducks of different sorts, and before they were all quacking for the pond, here came a big truck with the poultry. The cockerels would take your mind in a marvel of colour, and the hens were as pretty, if plainer. Everything was ready for them, and they clucked into the run as if they had known it always, with nesting boxes ready, and ricks of hay and bales for them to do a bit of pecking in, but no batteries. I like a hen to go free, and do what she likes, and sit in her place, then, and lay a beautiful egg, with an orange yolk, and a brown shell. All our hens laid brown eggs. A lot say that white and brown eggs are the same.

Not me.

I like a brown egg.

The surfacing of that road leading to the house became a burden during the night in the weeks going by. At first we wondered what the noise was, a lot of talk and giggling, and then we found out. The locals were parking cars both sides and having a love feast. I am not the one to spoil a bit of fun, but when many of the cars stayed till after four in the morning, and everybody calling jokes, and starting the engines, I thought I would end it. There never was a more irritating sound than some fool running a motor for minutes on end, and doing a bit of shouting, then.

I had a five-barred gate of solid timber made, with a lock.

Peace, then, for almost a week, and a truck backed into it, and the gateposts were broken, and the gate sagged. I went into town and bought a good heavy iron gate, and set it in reinforced concrete, and again, peace, but not for long.

Douglas Gough came up one afternoon with some coloured papers.

'You're being summonsed for closing an ancient pedestrians' right of way,' he said, and put a map on the table. 'This map's dated sixteen-fifteen. There it is!'

'I'll open a gate for pedestrians,' I said. 'Those in cars weren't pedestrians. Never. A nuisance. There have been twenty-odd cars out there, both sides, especially on a week-end. And noisy. All hours. And no room to pass up the middle.'

'Yes,' Douglas said. 'They are not as discreet as we were. Well, we *had* to be. Or get a name. Those today? They don't care, they shout from the rooftops. Anyway, I'll represent you. A two-bar stile will do nicely. And Mostyn

34

Price has worked out the premiums on the house and contents, the buildings and animals, and he'll be up this afternoon. Of course, the premiums are stiff, because the house is far from the town fire brigade, and water is a serious problem.'

'The men are working on a pump, now, to serve five hundred foot of hose from six hydrants,' I said. 'I have got banks of foam extinguishers in various places. I also have two night men to clear up, and milk the early morning round. I believe I'm fairly safe. Apart from that, a director of Mr Price's company will be here for the weekend. A word from a little bird?'

'He'll be grateful,' Douglas said. 'He told me the farm was defenceless. It would burn to a crisp!'

'Let me see the crisp,' I said.

The premiums were not up that afternoon, but two days after, and surprisingly mild after what I had heard, and there seemed more of respect in the turn of Mr Price's head, and I invited him and his wife to the asado.

'What is an asado, then?' he asked.

'Whole sheep grilled, and beef, and everything else,' I said. 'Come and see!'

'Mr Morgan,' he said. 'I think I must tell you this. People are talking of you as an old foreigner. And your wife. This asado business will only underline!'

I laughed at the beams.

'My wife's great-great grandam was born in this house,' I said. 'I was born in Glamorgan. Do you speak Welsh?'

'No,' he said. 'I have to do business in English!'

'My wife speaks the purest form,' I said. 'I don't speak as well. At least, I can understand. Which is the foreigner?'

'Oh, well, you know what people are,' he said. 'I'll put it round, don't worry!'

'And put it round I have a kennel of guard dogs coming in,' I said. 'They don't waste time with arms and legs. They go for the balls. Understand me? Put *that* about!'

'You mean they are *dan*gerous animals?' Mr Price said, with a little pale-blue of alarm in his eye. 'No warning, then?'

35

'None,' I said. 'Until your balls are chewed on the floor. Then it is a bit late!'

I had taken two half pages in the local paper over the month, addressed to anybody with relations or friends in Patagonia, and inviting them to an asado in our style, if they could show proof.

I was knocked flat, and I gave thanks I had asked Evans the Butcher to supply ten extra lambs. I had to send in the truck for more. More than a hundred and seventy people had letters, papers, photos, albums, and most of them, Sûs knew by name. She was in tears, there, and I not much better. Well, it was an asado to put a mark on the wall. Sûs showed them how to cut, and indeed, that meat was even better than in Patagonia, because the Welsh pasture has more of rain, more of bounty, and that lamb will have you smacking your chops and looking to the sky. Blackcurrant tart, then, three-fingers thick, with butter pastry, and coffee, brandy, and cigars after.

'I see you know how to live, Mr Morgan!' the magistrate, Mr Soper Reynolds, said, a fat little man, bald, thick horn-rims, and five or six chins. If he moved, there was one less. Move again, two more. I never saw where they went.

I took time to chew.

'This is common with us, either in Trelew on the Atlantic side, or over in the Andes, to the west,' I said, coming a bit careless with the truth, but not all that much. 'There are small asados for the family, and then for the family and friends, and then several families will give an asado like this. No trouble. Everything is there!'

'But expensive!' he said.

'We don't think expense,' I said. 'With friends, never. We don't have to buy the sheep, to start, they are ours. The wine we have got in the cellar. What, expense?'

'Where, may I ask, did you find that marvellous bread?' he asked, looking at the baskets almost empty.

'My wife made it,' I said. 'Her Grandam baked it in this house, in the same oven, more than a hundred years ago. Why? Would you like a loaf to take?'

'O, I couldn't be a bother!' he said, sure he would be.

'It will be in your car,' I said.

From the moment all those people left, I felt that something had 'loosened', even if I was unsure exactly what I meant. People seemed more friendly, we have no lovers' lane nonsense, and if we went into town, people waved, or came over and invited us to a picnic luncheon, or a pot-luck dinner. We always found that the picnic was a little grander, and pot-luck must have taken hours to get ready. Well, in case something goes wrong, people like to give themselves some sort of excuse. We knew it, and we were grateful. It was always good, and we were coming a lot more open and warmer with the people, and yet.

There was always, somewhere, a holding back, either from them, or from us. I often thought about it, and talked to Sûs, and she felt the same.

'Yes!' she said, loud, in the not-to-be-argued voice. 'Often I am laughing with them, and in a terrible moment I see the teeth and claws, and I wonder why. Look. No more going out at night, is it? I like my own time by the fire to do a bit of needlework, or crochet, or knitting. Nobody can give me anything as good. Have we said yes?'

She had the Indio love of her own fire.

'The scent of my fire is sweeter than the perfume of another man's woman,' trolls an old gaucho ballad. True it is, too. I had always lived lonely. At night I did my figures, or drew what was to be done for tomorrow, always by the fire. Sûs grew up, I suppose, five hundred miles or more north of me, neither of us knowing the other was in life. But we had the same love of a fire. Everything we did was with a fire, because without, there was nothing with any taste, no warmth in life, or any comfort. It was almost, I suppose, that a fire was one of the family, and tended with good care, for in that country, without a fire, you can soon die, and painful.

'We have said yes,' I told her. 'But sometimes we will have to go out. Or they will think us a couple of old savages, and anti-social.'

'Let them think, and push every thumb they have got!'

she said, and giving the wool a good pull as if it had part of the blame. 'Sitting about a table, and chewing, and talking old nonsense, what is that? A good half, I never understand. English is old grit in my mouth. *A'r diâwl!*'

'Not all like that, girl,' I said, but a bit weak. 'Not all English, either!'

'More shame,' she said, crochet hook flitting in the eyes. 'They are like low class Indios. Only copying those above. And who are *they*? Low. Buying the fashions in Buenos Aires to swank, and coming back, then, to live in a den!'

'Wait, now,' I said. 'You are too hard!'

'Go and look at the dens!' she said, bright grey in the eye. 'I had long enough to see!'

'Not all of them,' I said. 'They are worried in case another flood will take them all out to the Atlantic, again. Why should they build, and furnish, if they will lose everything?'

'They have got that big dam at the top of the river, at last,' she said, in her little voice, which was warning enough. 'The engineers say it will hold against everything. Others say it won't. But if it does or doesn't, they will still buy things in Buenos Aires to swank, and come back to live in a den. Our people in Buenos Aires have all got a good house. Or an apartment. It is the city making a difference. People in a city never notice old swank. Only the low Indio, and them of us like them. Swank, and live in a den!'

No use to talk, because what she said had the bells of fact in it. But the words were not from the air, and that Thursday, Mr James Prosser, Douglas Gough's managing clerk, was at the front door in his morning coat almost tatters, with a big envelope, and I saw the stamp of the Argentine Consulate.

'Mr Morgan, Mr Gough is in court, so I had to come,' he said. 'This is an action by two British citizens, one Nelya Peninah Morse Elias, and her husband, representing seventy-eight children of one Vrann Corwen, and seeking shares of three estates, interest on principal, and damages!'

'Good,' I said. 'Tell Mr Gough to attend to it!'

'Sir,' he said. 'But it comes into court next week!'

'Whenever,' I said. 'The case was over rather more than fifteen years ago. Nothing has changed!'

'Could you please give me basic facts?' he said, and took out a pencil.

'Basic, yes,' I said. 'There were three sisters, Lal, Doli and Solva Corwen. They were co-heiresses to the Corwen estate, then the estate of their mother, even larger, and Lal, the eldest, married a Mr Matithiah Morse, and on his death, became heiress of that estate. I married her, and after two years, she died. I succeeded to her share of the estate. Doli, the middle sister, died, and again the estates were apportioned. There has never been any question. Who is the complainant?'

'A man mentioned once,' Mr Prosser said, pulling the skirt of the coat to sit. 'Elias, the name is!'

'Elias, Snuff, we called him,' I said. 'The shadow, and shape, and the substance, of a rat. Do you know, Mr Prosser, there are Welshmen I detest so much, that even to think of the word, I can vomit. Have you met them?'

He nodded the small, gentle nods of abundant truth recognised.

'Sorry I am to say it, but yes, sir, I have met them,' he said. 'Not many, indeed, but more than enough!'

'Good,' I said, feeling I had a friend. 'Because of shifts in the Argentine government, and soldiers coming in, and a change in judges, perhaps he feels he can overturn the decisions of so long ago. Ask Mr Gough to get in touch with the British Consulate for advice. I shall not waste a thought on it!'

I had made over my shares of all three estates to Sûs, the fourth sister. But I was sure she was unknown to Elias. When she was a baby, her mama had sent her into Indio territory with her maid of years and other girls, and there she had stayed till I found her, and a miracle that was, too. But except for the family house and lands at Maes Corwen, the estates had been sold, and changed into the cash of various countries, and the buyers had been living there ever since, and Sûs had the money in investments, and in cash in the bank. Except to make a nuisance, I could see nothing to give Elias, Snuff, a hope.

We forgot that a rat, knowing what it wants, will gnaw and gnaw. We have got to kill it, first.

But in those days of late spring, we had a wonderful life. Up at six, with coffee, and out to look at the animals, and the ducks and geese and swans, and the chickens, because people forget that chickens like a friendly word and they will lay better, and the flowers coming up in the garden, and we had thousands of daffodils and narcissus, and still we could find snowdrops and crocus, and we were worried for the day when they would be gone till next year. But then the primroses came, and the violets, and I think no man has written poetry beautiful as primroses and violets growing in the stones of a hedge. Yet only one look, and I think I know why a poet would try. There are wild and gentle things to say that are not in the pens of ordinary men, and so, a lot of beauty goes fast asleep in the mind. Well, thank God, too.

Elias gave us nearly twelve months of paper, and a heavy tramp of small worry, though, in the end, all for nothing.

'It must have cost him a fortune for a fine display of spite,' Douglas said. 'Anyway, it's finished now. Not much cost to you, and no more commission of nuisance!'

But that was underestimating Elias.

Midday, one Sunday, the girl answered the door, and came back to say there was a big man talking funny Welsh, and I put down the paper, and went out, and I had to look again.

Ithel, son of Vrann, half-brother of Lal, and of course, Sûs. I had always found him a good one, and by the time we had him at the table, Sûs and he were talking Tehuelche fifty to the dozen.

'Ask him who sent him,' I said.

I heard the name Elias, and Sûs's face came straight.

'Elias paid his fare to make a case,' she said. 'He wants what is owed to him and his brothers and sisters from what his father left. The law is with them, isn't it?'

'Keep him talking,' I said, and went to telephone Douglas.

40

'Ah,' he said. 'Yes. A little awkward. Mr Elias, again. On no account pay this man any money. It's a precedent. You would have all seventy-eight on the doorstep, one after another. How did he enter the country?'

I called to Sûs.

'A cattle-boat from Buenos Aires,' she shouted. 'He doesn't know what a passport is!'

'He *must* have some papers?' I said.

'What is old papers to him?' she said, and laughing.

'Wait a moment,' Douglas said. 'This is serious. If he entered the country illegally, you could be charged with harbouring. I'll be up there with the Police. Ten minutes!'

Well, of course, it went blank against every tradition of Indio or our own Patagonian hospitality, and I had to be very careful with Sûs, but when I told her we could both go in prison, and Elias had counted on it, she became one of reason, and I told her to tell Ithel what was to happen, and like a frightened little boy, he asked her what they would do to him, and she said they were not like the Gendarmeria, and be at rest, they would treat him well, and put him back on the ship, and off home.

'You haven't given him any money?' Douglas said, coming through the door, with an Inspector and a sergeant and two policemen. 'Or promised him any?'

'Nothing,' I said. 'Sûs, go you with the policemen and him, and translate!'

Douglas and I had a drink, and he warned me to expect more visitors.

'Obviously, money means nothing and he's out to harm you,' he said. 'What sort of fellow is he?'

'Smart in business, very wealthy, and a rat,' I said. 'And pure Welsh, sorry I am to say it!'

'Supposing you give the Inspector ten pounds for food, and so forth, till he's delivered to the Argentine Consul in Liverpool,' Douglas said. 'Don't let him see the money pass!'

'I am more than sorry to treat him like this,' I said. 'We are used to other ways.'

'You would have ample time to be sorry,' Douglas said.

'Ten pounds under the table, no more!'

The Inspector said there was no doubt he had jumped ship, and in strict legal terms, we had no right to give him a moment's shelter, or we would suffer severe penalty. He would be delivered to the Argentine Consul in Liverpool, and that would be an end, except that the owners of the ship he came on would be fined, and warned.

'I don't understand how he got here,' Douglas said.

'You could look through those papers, sir,' the Inspector said, holding up a flat leather Indio pouch. 'Here's this address. The rest's in Spanish.'

'Let the Consul deal with it,' Douglas said. 'I think you'd better take him away!'

Well, the look Ithel gave us when the policemen each took an arm and nodded to the door would have cracked stones. Sûs went into tears and ran upstairs.

'A heavy day,' I said, to Douglas. 'We are not used to such treatment for a guest!'

'Nuisance, yes, and sent to be,' he said. 'Thank God it was not more. You will have to be well on your guard!'

The Consul rang us next day, and said it was a scandal, and nobody in the office spoke Tehuelche, and they could get nothing out of him.

'The poor man has been sent all this way on a chase of wild geese,' I said. 'But in Buenos Aires you will be able to find out more. You will possibly hear the name Elias. A wool dealer. A millionaire. Hides. Refrigerated meat. Coffee. Tea. Cereals. An importer of everything. His business is in a big building on a corner of Lavalle and Florida. He has warehouses in the docks. He boasts he has the Army, half the Government and all the Customs in his pocket. Money will do everything, he says!'

'I know the type,' the quiet voice said. 'We shall see!'

But it was small comfort to Sûs and me.

Ithel was her half-brother, if what Lal believed was true, but we had treated him as less than the meanest. Our hospitality was in question, and Welsh or Patagonian or Indio were all one, and all of them were hurt. The true-bred Indio will give you his horse and saddle, and his shirt, and share any bone with you. But worse. We had turned away a half-brother of Sûs, and I was looking for some way to send him something to relieve conscience, and stop her sudden tears, but it was difficult, because everybody knows everybody else's business in those lonely places, and word is soon heard. A whisper and Elias would hear it. Behind it all, I saw the sly blue eyes of Nelya Peninah his wife, that mare of the lost of no brains, no morals or scruples.

But that morning, looking at the nesting geese, and ducks peeping from the reeds, I remembered Dugald McGrannoch, and I thought I knew how to help Ithel. Dugald had many years of a hard life, and his wife had died, but he married an Indio, and happily, and of course, all the good Indios, because of her, came to help in round-ing up, and shearing, and fencing, and all the work to be done on a sheep farm. When I left, he was in a good way with him, and he told me that at last he was putting money in the bank to send his sons to school in Scotland, and the girls would go to a convent near Buenos Aires.

I wrote to him, saying nothing of Elias, but only to put out word with the Indios to tell Ithel to see him, and give an address for me to reach him. Six weeks later Dugald sent me a ten-page letter, with every small detail, and I could see he was in a far happier way. Except that Elias bought his wool clip, and banked the extra money at a small percentage. Two-and-a-half. Instead of something like twelve or fifteen. And not a mention of Ithel. What to do then, I was not sure. Sûs, again, gave me a pointer. Hywel Roberts, of a pioneer family, was a Lloyd's agent. I wrote to him, and suggested he might make a round of all the smaller men, and tell them what advantage there was in good insurance, and investment of extra money at proper rates. A month later I had a letter thanking me for the suggestion, and he would look into it. I read between the lines. Elias was a power. He had plenty of men to do as they were told, whether to steal cattle and sheep, or burn a barn, or any other crime to hurt a man, and warn others.

I felt helpless. And it was at the other end of the world.

People were different. Words, there, meant something else. There were tens of square miles of space anywhere, and not a living thing. Perhaps two-and-a-half per cent was a fair price for being left alone.

Sûs, again, gave me the idea. Solva, her elder sister, had married Oracio, an officer of First Gaucho Cavalry.

'*Don't* tell me you can buy him or them!' she said.

'Right, you,' I said. 'Splendid idea. *You* write to Solva and tell her that dirty rat has bought the Army!'

Only then I found out that Sûs had no reading or writing. Her name, yes, but illiterate, except in the eyes, and heart. What is that?

Well, I wrote.

Solva's letter was short, because, like all the Corwens, she had a love of reading but not of writing, yet there was plenty in it. She wrote from the middle of Buenos Aires Province, a lonely place, but she loved it, and she had five children, three boys, one named for me, two girls, and no surprise if somebody else was on the way. She had spoken to her husband, the General, and he had said only that he would look into it. And love from everybody, and be sure to come and see them if we were ever there again.

In Argentina, Generals looking into things can be very dangerous, and the effect was not long in coming.

I had a package of clips from *La Prensa*, and *Clarín*, and *Buenos Aires Herald*, reporting the arrest of Elias for bribery of public officials, misuse of public funds, and other charges unspecified. 'It means he will be in prison for the next two or three years, at least, till the case comes up,' Solva had written across the white space. 'It will teach him to boast he could bribe the Army. I have never seen my husband in such a temper. Love, S.'

Well, if we thought we would have a bit of peace after that, we had reckoned without the Mistress Nelya Peninah, of the same cut and breed. She was at the door one Friday morning, in black, and looking as if she was dressed in all the clothes of her grandam but passed through moth and no brush.

I was sure she was not coming in, so out I went, and shut the door.

'Like this you will treat me?' she said, in whispers. 'After all I have been through? My houses sealed against me? My bank account closed? Not a rag to wear? And no money? Oh, Huw. When were we enemies?'

'There is nothing for you here,' I said. 'Go back the way you have come!'

'That Indio has changed you!' she screamed.

'I don't know any Indios,' I said. 'But I know a few policemen, and they will be up here, now, in a moment, and you will go with them.'

'I am free, and a free country!' she screamed again, from the lungs. 'I am here for justice. I will have the law on you!'

'By all means, but off my property!' I said, and thankfully, I saw Lys Machen's car turning in the driveway.

'Kindly telephone the police,' I said, and let her in, and when Nelya lunged, I pushed her off. 'There's a trespasser I want to get rid of!'

Nelya screeched all the worst words, but in Welsh, and Lys turned to her.

'Even a guttersnipe of a man would think again before saying what you spat from your muzzle,' she said, in perfect Welsh, and a surprise to me because I had never heard her use other than English. 'Think shame to yourself!'

She went in, and Nelya seemed shocked in silence. Perhaps she had forgotten that many people in Wales speak their own language.

I heard the telephone ring-off, and Nelya fell against the wall to start a howling of tears, and laughing, then, and more slobber, though I can stand plenty, as hail falls on rock.

'Why have you come here, exactly?' I asked her. 'What do you want?'

'You put the charges that got my husband to prison!' she screamed. 'Take them off. Let him be home. Millions he is losing. Take the seals from my houses. Let the banks open to us. What have we ever done to you?'

'No charge of mine put him in,' I said. 'Nothing I can do will let him out. You know that. What can a foreigner do with any court in Argentina? If you, his wife, can do nothing, what can I do?'

The police car came as a blessing. The sergeant and a policeman listened to her, and wrote, and the sergeant asked for her passport. It was at the hotel.

'Right,' he said, and opened the door. 'We'll go down there, first!'

Well, you would never believe the screaming struggle she gave those two. She was always a big girl, and now, like a maniac she used strength, and they were ducking like boxers to come from the reach of her nails, but then they got rough, and she was in, and no nonsense, and screaming the last reaches of hysteria.

'She won't bother you any more, sir!' the sergeant said. 'We'll look into the passport situation, and make charges of trespass and resisting a warning to leave!'

'Don't press charges in my name,' I said. 'Anything except!'

But still Lys and I had to appear as witnesses in Court, if it was only to answer yes and no to a few questions, and not look at Nelya, and go from there, a bit flat, in her curses. There was trouble with the passport, and the Argentine Consulate in London wanted to see her, and she said she had no money, so I asked Douglas to look into it, and we all had a shock. Her husband had bank accounts in most European countries, and a fat one in London.

'Not one brass farthing!' Douglas said. 'But what did she expect to get from you?'

'To get her husband out of prison, I suppose?' I said. 'With the Army on top of him, what could *I* do? They *are* authority. Not like it is here. There, they rule!'

'Poor woman!' Douglas said. 'They had to give her a drug and take her all the way by ambulance. The medicos at the hospital think she's deranged. Insane!'

'We have always thought so,' I said. 'But there, the signs

are not seen for what they are. I suppose we are all a bit cracked?'

'No surprise to me,' he said. 'I've *seen* enough, indeed. Some of the things I've done should have put me in a padded cell. Anyway, you *are* going to the Council meeting on Friday?'

'For what?' I said, in surprise.

'You will probably be asked to stand for this part of the County,' he said. 'You have a fine property, freehold. Well found at the bank. They couldn't want better!'

'I am not a bit interested in politics,' I said.

'It's not quite that,' he said, and pushed the glasses across the bar. 'They know you were a construction engineer.'

'Not quite!' I said. 'I was a contractor employing engineers. But I could have taught a few of them, indeed!'

'Very well,' he said, impatient. 'Don't you see they need that kind of experience on the Council? They have to decide contracts, prices, priorities, local housing, roads. They need experienced men. What is the use of a lot of old grocers and ironmongers? Are they able to so much as *read* a contract? Come, now then, and do your duty!'

Well, that meeting was one of the funniest, but not a laugh in it, and perhaps the most tragic I was ever at. They were all men of good conscience, well aware of duty and responsibility, but afraid to say yes, and nervous at no. Public money they were spending, and they would be judged on results, and because they were all local men, they were naked to attack, and not of the gentlest.

I was given good welcome, and I sat at the end of the room with several others, and listened. All I heard seemed sensible and quietly proper, until there came a complaint from a farmer that the new drains on the hill above his farm were unable to accept the flow of rainwater, and his house, barns and fields were flooded worse than before, and he would sue the Council for loss and damage.

'Not in the ground three months, and no good!' a little man said, at my end of the long table. 'I said it should be six foot piping. No. You voted three. *Now* look!'

'You know nothing about it!' somebody said, further along. 'Say what you know!'

'It is put plain enough for me!' the little man said, louder. 'A mistake was made, and it will cost us hundreds, perhaps thousands. But please to look up the vote. Mine is against!'

The gavel tapped.

'The engineer's report states that a widening of the road above also widened the ditches up there, and the excess water was not taken into account because at the time it was not known about. It's in the next County!'

'Lack of co-ordination!' the little man said. 'Let not your left hoof know which window the right is going into!'

'No need to drag the Scriptures into this, is it?' somebody else said. 'And especially when there is no necessity. Gratuitous!'

'Drains, we were talking about!' the little man said, losing his temper fast. 'Some of you are blind with a lot of old words, here. Why didn't the engineer look about him? Why didn't he find out what water to look for? Or where it could come from? Shall I tell you? The master plan for that job was drawn in the bar of the Crossbow and Bolt, and I have got witnesses!'

'That is a slander!' somebody shouted, standing.

'He can sue, but he won't stop the fact from coming out, see?' the little man said, quieter. 'I have got plenty of witnesses, *and* the publican *and* his wife. Come, you. *Sue!*'

Gavel, again.

'Another study, and an estimate,' the calm voice said. 'A show of hands?'

'Wait you, now then!' the little man said, and sharp. 'I had this before. We voted a Yes. Yes to what? The same engineer? He couldn't drive a bloody sewing machine. For me, *no!*'

'Wait, now,' somebody else said. 'If Mr Beynon is suing, we should wait for what the Court decides. The money we have got in hand could buy a small bus to take the children to school. Winter is on us. It is coming very hard for them. Nothing could be spent more useful!'

Everybody nodded agreement, and a show of hands gave a Yes, and the Chairman adjourned.

'Well,' Douglas said, when we were out, and had places at the bar. 'What did you think about that?'

'They can all speak their minds, and afraid of nobody,' I said. 'They are all well aware of responsibility. They have all got a good, hard head. I see nothing wrong. To the contrary. There's a great deal others might borrow. With advantage. But they were wrong to let the engineer be accused in his absence, weren't they?'

'Well, perhaps,' he said. 'But if he drew a plan in a bar?'

'I have drawn many, and in Indio wine shops, too,' I said. 'Nothing wrong with a bar. It is where the idea comes. Draw it. Keep it. Ideas come once. Remember them, because God never gives them back!'

'You are right,' he said, quietly. 'Should I put your name forward for a place on the voting list?'

'I will have to speak to my wife,' I said. 'She is the boss!'

'Right, again,' he said. 'I have got one of the same!'

'No!' Sûs said, with a flat of the hand before the words were cold on the air. 'Look, they call you an old foreigner, never mind what *they* are. I am a foreigner, too. Never mind I speak better than any of them, even the school teachers. Shall I tell you what it will be? You have been used to deciding. You have been used to saying no. Or yes. None to argue. What will you do among *them*? Shall I tell you? They will drive you mad, boy. You will come home, here, and smash everything in the place!'

'I haven't yet,' I said. 'I don't think I would!'

'It would be past time for thinking,' she said. '*No* is the answer!'

No, it was, and Douglas smiled, and seemed satisfied.

But there was no satisfaction for me.

I knew I owed a civic duty I had never paid, because every man owes a duty to every other for helping to build the world he lives in. If there is something to be done extra, he should do it, especially if it is professional knowledge he can give, and for nothing.

So I started to worry, and Lys noticed, when she came with her little surprise.

A marble sarcophagus, it was, and beautifully carved, with pagans, and virgins running loose in nothing, but it went up on four raised steps, under a canopy held by four pillars, down at the foot of the rose garden, and anything more beautiful you would have to wish for.

'If anybody asks questions, it was here when you bought the place,' she said. 'A little digging, and there it was. Now, then. The other cottage is a real trove. It will take another year, at least, to clear the entire mound, but I'm sure it's going to be the find of the century!'

'Of what?' I asked her.

'The original Celts,' she said. 'We still don't know who they were. Where they came from. How they got here. One school says Achaeans, from Greece. Another, tribes of Israel. Others, the Aryans coming from India, across the European plains. Well, they all have something to say. But no real proof. And here we are. I am me. You are you. Where did we come from? It would be nice to find out, indeed!'

I was coming to like Lys more and more.

Something about her was warm to me. She was gentle, and in a way, hungry. How a man tells that, is in the senses, but senses are not held in trust. We can all be wrong, especially when nothing is said.

'You seem a little out of sorts,' she said. 'Is something worrying you?'

'Nothing,' I said. 'Only that I was asked to stand for the Council, and I refused, but I feel I dodged a duty, and I am far from happy in myself!'

'You don't know how right you were!' she said, and laughing. 'It's a local council of local people. They know every inch here from boyhood. If you were elected, would they listen to any suggestion from you? If you don't know the place, how can you know what's wanted? No. It was the proper decision. And something far more important might be coming along. Do you know anything about Plaid Cymru? Dedicated to Home Rule for Wales?'

'I've heard of it, yes,' I said. 'Seems a bit dreamy to me, though.'

'Dreamy, yes, until we have enough of the right people,' she told the sarcophagus. 'I'll bring some papers next time. See what you think!'

I didn't ask questions. I had no interest. I thought it some student game or other to make a nuisance, and a good reason to go in the pubs on Saturdays and drink it up. No harm in it. With us, when I was young, it was Rugby, or boxing, and anyway, healthy, and profit to everybody thirsty, and the brewers too.

Sûs only lifted the needle when I told her.

'They could have had it long ago if they had wanted,' she said, flat. 'They are like us in Chubut. Everybody talk. Nobody doing. The sight of a soldier was enough. Do you want it plain? We have not got the character. Leave it, now then!'

'You weren't there long enough to know, girl!' I said. 'Did the Indios tell you?'

'We always had plenty of visitors to tell,' she said. 'And the few months in Trelew were quite enough. I saw the people. I heard them. But now there are not enough of us, and they are all in dreams of time gone. Pity, too!'

'The old ones would have thought so,' I said. 'But those two floods did the damage. Soul and spirit. Stripped of everything. Twice in a lifetime. People can't suffer so much without loss of faith and hope. That will ruin character, for a start. We are left to be sorry. It can happen again, mind. Then we shall see. I didn't like that big lake of blue water grinning at me on the other side of the dam, *that* is sure. And I don't think the dam is so strong, either. Give it time!'

Funny we should be talking about Patagonia, and dams and floods that day, because there came a storm in the afternoon, and the rain poured two solid days, and that morning I woke up to a strange noise. Our little brook was a river, ducks were swimming in the garden, cattle and sheep and pigs were all safe up on the rise, and the hens roosted along the barn rafters. I thanked God that Lys had

51

put the house on stone blocks, though many argued not. Not a drop of water came in, though all the doors were blocked with everything brought down by the flood. We found out when it was light that new culverts put in at the top of the hill were pushed out by pressure, and we saw why when we got there. They were too small for the job.

The same engineer.

We gave a hand to the roadmen, and water was smoother, but still too much, and the sky glowered grey with more rain. The engineer came to look, and light a pipe, and walk here, and walk there. Forties, I suppose, and quiet enough, and no alarm, but a bit of a tremble in the hands.

'Nothing to come near that rain since records were kept,' he said, in a little voice, and stroking red hair over his ears. 'The trouble started with the catchment a few miles up. We won't have this in solid repair for a good month, or more.'

'Who supplies the culverts?' I asked him.

'A firm in town,' he said.

'I know them,' Tom Davies, one of my men, said.

'In the truck, all of us, and off!' I said, and while the engineer put his face to say something, we were gone. I stopped at the house to tell Sûs, and give her a kiss, and under the hour we had the culverts paid for, loaded, and coming back, we stopped for a coffee. A good job we did, because the little Councillor was there. Tom Davies told him, and his eyes went to the roof and he raised a hand.

'All over the County!' he said. 'A lot of damage, there is. Not the engineer's fault, mind. But the work done was not strong enough. A waste of money. No eye for the future, see. You have bought the culverts, have you, Mr – ?'

'Morgan,' I said. 'Bought, and they will be in today. Four up the top, and two in my farm. Plas Sûs!'

'The old Corwen place,' Tom said.

'Mm,' the Councillor said. 'I knew it well as a boy. Finest blackberries in the County. Yes, well, I doubt you'll have compensation for the work, Mr Morgan, or for the culvert piping. Things have to take their turn, see. The right forms for the Ministry, and that's weeks. Mind, I congratulate you on initiative. But compensation – !'

'I'll have compensation in a dry farm, and poultry and animals at peace,' I said. 'Good morning to you!'

Out, and we had the culverts in by late afternoon, and Sûs brought up a splendid lunch and a flagon of wine, and everything went better. A bulldozer loaned by men on a flooded building site cut a trench down to the river and the job was done, and the water spouting, happy.

'It would have taken a good two, or even three months,' the bulldozer driver said, and tipped his cap for the notes. 'Thank you, sir. If I see anything in the morning, I'll put it right.'

Then we had two culverts to put in our place, much easier, and by dark, we were dry everywhere.

'Funny Lys didn't see this coming,' Sûs said, at dinner.

'Go on with you, girl!' I said. 'The place was surveyed and new drains put in weeks before she was here. An architect, she is. Drains, yes. But she had the certificates. And could the surveyor see a cloudburst breaking new County work miles away? A bit of reason, here!'

'You have got a favour with her!' she said, loud. 'I have watched you. A little stroll in the garden, is it?'

I had to laugh at that frown. Not even that, but Indio flatface, and that is worse.

'Don't talk a lot of old chaff!' I said. 'Next time she comes we shall talk in the same room with you. Favour, you say? Look at your house. Who drew everything under your eyes? The favour was to us!'

'For money!' she said, in the mouth of a wildcat.

'And every penny has brought a blessing,' I said. 'Sent from God, she was, and give thanks!'

'It was better in the tents!' she said, head down, same mouth, same voice, none of them part of the Sûs I knew. Then, it was, I noticed something wrong with the way she was looking, to the side, and half-closed lids, and tears at the outer corners, but not the tears of crying.

'We can always put them up,' I said. 'But we would

53

have needed boats the past couple of days, yes? I can see you sitting on a coop, and drenched, and floating about, hours here, cackling. An old hen, waiting to lay, is it?'

She tried not to laugh, and I had a close look at her eyes when I put my arms round her, and slowly she came loose, and herself, again. But from what I had thought about Lys, I knew she was not a hundred miles from being right, and sharp surprise that is, to find a woman can judge so much without a single thread of knowing.

Before light next morning, I woke. The room was quiet. Outside, no noise, not even a cockerel. Sûs lay away from me. I put out a hand, and she was wet with heavy sweat, and I went round there, and her face was red and she had breath hard with her. I seemed to know this was nothing for the local doctor to see. I went downstairs and called the Police for an ambulance, and woke the girls to make a warm bundle of her.

At the hospital, a brisk young doctor seemed to know what he was doing, and Sûs went in a whisper of wheels, and the doors flapped, and I waited nearly an hour before he came back.

'I've put a call in for the ophthalmologist,' he said. 'There's a condition of the eyes. He'll be here this morning, and I think you'd be safe in coming here at about eleven?'

'What is the condition?' I asked him.

'I'm not sure,' he said. 'We got the fever down. She's sleeping normally. If you come at about eleven, you'll have specialist advice. Have you a car?'

I shook my head. No word was in me.

'We've got a night taxi service,' he said. 'I'll call. Good night, Mr Morgan!'

A good night, it was, too, but Tobey, the maid, brewed something, and I was out cold till nearly eleven thirty next morning, and I ran for the telephone.

'The patient can go home for the moment, but Professor Stansthorpe would like to speak to you,' the voice said. 'Would three o'clock today be convenient?'

I was there, but the Professor was later, and he came in

a green blouse and a little cap, and he looked tired, poor man.

'An emergency case came in,' he said, taking off the spectacles. 'Please accept my apologies. Yes, well, Mrs Morgan's is not a common case. I shall have to examine the specimens and the X-rays, and consult certain colleagues of mine. Let's say, today week? This time?'

Those days passed in quivering, everlasting misery. But no sign of harm to Sûs. She was almost herself. The stuff they gave her cleared the tears, and the fever went. She was mistress of the kitchen and everything else, and I thought whatever was wrong could not be *so* serious.

Every morning I took her, rain or not, around the farm, and it was a big place, now, to look at the goslings following their mamas, and the ducklings in a pretty waddle after theirs, and the turkey poults, and the chickens coming less than balls of fluff, and lambs jumping, and the cows swollen, and the mares almost ready, and sows about to farrow, and everywhere a sharp sense of new life, unending, and good.

I knew something more than serious was wrong when I wanted her to look at perhaps the last robin redbreast of winter, on a bough not ten foot from us.

'Nothing there!' she said, in a little voice, a baby's ready to cry. 'No bough. No robin. Will you make a fool of me, boy?'

'Let us go to the house, and have a good hot cup of coffee, yes?' I said. 'It's cold, and you can do with a bit of fire, isn't it?'

I was waiting for the taxi to take us to the hospital, and the bell rang, and Lys was smiling, with an armful of papers.

'I brought some Plaid Cymru stuff, as I promised,' she said, in her beautiful way. 'The ship's table from the dockyard's bought, with eight chairs, and it'll be here next week. I'll have the carpenters in to prepare the floor. It's not on legs, as I told you. The chair legs have to be set. Leave it to them. The canvas of Morgan James?'

'Buy it,' I said, one eye on the clock.

'The stone fawn by Lucas Watkin?' she said, from the list. 'The silver collection, twenty pieces? The glass? The Swansea porcelain? And the last blue willow set in the country? It will look wonderful on that dresser, with the pewter to set it off. Did they polish it?'

'It is in glow of elbow grease,' I said. 'Cover your eyes. When did people let pewter go dull?'

'When they stopped using it on the table,' she said. 'Pewter was for eating and drinking. Scoured and polished day after day. It had almost the shine of silver. But then chinaware and porcelain came in. Pewter was thrown aside. Then it was bought as a decoration. Dull as the people who bought!'

'What are you two chatting about, down there?' Sûs shouted, over the first floor banister. 'I can hear you, remember. I don't want that woman in the house. Go, you, now, you bitch of Sodom!'

Lys stared, closed her mouth, took her bag from the floor, and gathered the portfolio, and I saw the shine of tears, but she turned from me.

'I'll never come here again,' she said, in the hallway, and I was too paralysed to leave the chair. 'I was happy to have worked —'

'Go you from here!' Sûs screamed from upstairs. 'Not wanted!'

The door shut, and the car started, and I heard Sûs crying to break the heart.

Slowly I went up there, a weight in each foot, and put arms about her, and soothed, and took her back to bed. Tobey gave her a pill, and she went to sleep holding my hands.

I called Lys, but when she heard my voice, she rang off. I talked to Douglas and told him Sûs was under drugs, and probably going into the hospital, and unsure of herself, well, anyway, I made a case, but I made him promise to tell Lys there was no need for her to feel she had any fault. She had been treated in a shameless manner, the cause was illness, and nothing more to be said.

Lys said no more, either.

56

'She was dazed and sick, she told me,' Douglas said, and very sad. 'She will *not* visit the house again. She can no longer supervise the dig up at the cottage. You probably know what she means? Her assistant and the buyer will deal with you, and the carpenters will be there on Wednesday, at nine. If you wish to see her, an appointment can be made at her office. That's all!'

And enough. I was making no appointments.

I sent flowers, instead. They came back. While I was taking them upstairs to Sûs, there was no pleasure in a sudden, horrible stab of thought that they should never have gone anywhere else, and straight I turned, and went downstairs, and put them on the fire, and telephoned an order for double, and felt as if every word screamed over the banister was true.

That morning Tobey brought in a newspaper with a story about me, telling of time in Chubut, and in the Andes, and a fortune, and Plas Sûs, and pedigree sheep and cattle, but my mind was upstairs.

Not an hour later, a reporter called, and I told Tobey to say the next afternoon, for tea, at four o'clock, and another called, and somebody else from down in the south. I made a tea with all of them, and talked of this and that. What surprised me was their ignorance of Chubut, of the Andes, or, for that matter, nothing much of Argentina.

'Very little comes from there, Mr Morgan,' one said, thirties, spectacles, steak-and-kidney-pudding-fat, nothing wrong, gentle as a rabbit, but I'll bet a tiger with a couple of pints, and a ballpen that worked for a few words, and clicked off.

'I will have to get new,' he said, raising the spectacles. 'This old thing makes up its own mind, d'you see? I wonder is the industrial age achieving a mind of its own? Not the human side. But the product we make. After all, long thought is in it. Thought produced the design, yes? The materials to make them. All a part of human thought. I have just covered the story of curing by prayer. A woman, it is. No impression on me, I felt nothing. But others did. She made things move. Unbelievable. It makes me ask. Is there something of us in the things we make? Have we permeated material without knowing it? Have we started trying to control something we don't know?'

I thought he might have had a couple of pints too many for lunch, but he was sane, serious, and thinking about it, and I wondered, why not? I had seen so much between Argentina and Chile, among the Indio peoples I had lived with. I loved them, trusted them, knew them to be good as hard stone. They, yes, travelled in the mind. They had other ways of thinking. In their own way, they were far in advance of us. Our chemist shops were full of little packets and bottles, and pills and all sorts to cure everything they didn't. But the Indio wisewoman would, indeed, cure anything except death itself, and that they seemed to know, and when they knew, they did nothing more.

Nothing. They sat at the side, and held a hand, and gave water.

Enough, and the family had time to have the asado ready, and everybody called, and in place.

Death was only death, and goodbye.

With us it was only calamity, or extra expense. With them it was of the house, at any time, when they were called by Ranginhüenüchaü, Father of all the Gods, of animals, trees, stones, water, and men and women. Then, with experience of the earth, and of other lives lived, and saved, there was other work to do. For that, they thought, there were caciques, or chiefs of men, and wisewomen, more than ordinary women, among us, to say what should be done. True, and often it was, that a man or woman would be born, unknown, and rise in light, years later. But from birth, there would be hope. Many a young woman would blossom. Nobody questioned. The moment she spoke, they knew. She became one of the small circle, and denied to all men.

But that was not the country of machines.

I was out of it. Tobey had to tell me, and I knew by her face.

'Mr Morgan,' she said, in twists of the hands. 'My mouth is bitter with me to say, but Mistress Sûs is in hard

58

old fever and nothing to bring it down, see? I'll call the doctor, yes?'

I went up the stairs a madman, and stared at that beautiful little face, so red, and the eyes swollen, and the breath in squeaks with her, and all I could do was take the little hand, and kiss.

The doctor looked once, and felt the wrist.

'Hospital!' he said. 'Immediately!'

That day I should have been at the cattle show. Instead, I won a blue rosette for the black bull calf walking up and down the corridor outside her room. Professor Stansthorpe had her in X-ray and the operating theatre for nearly three hours, and came out to me, shirtsleeves, drying his hands.

'We made an exploratory examination, he said, not looking at me. 'It's an exceptionally severe condition, strange to most of us, but I believe we have control for the moment. In addition to information we already have, I shall know rather more tonight. I don't want you to visit today. She's asleep, and I want her kept as quiet as possible. D'you see?'

I felt he was talking for the sake, and I nodded, and went.

Those days of waiting dangled with the knotted thongs of cruelty. There was no sleeping, no sitting, or standing, and eating was a mouthful and finish. The only times I was allowed in, she was asleep, with a bandage from the nose to forehead, and very still, and no sound, always a nurse with her, looking after the bottles, and tubes in the arm.

I am not sure what comes in the mind at those times. Sorrow, yes, and rage that we are helpless, and always prayer for no pain, and for her, lying there, and imaginings of her riding Bimbo, and jumping the hedges, and having a good Tehuelche swear because her boots were slow to come off, and dancing from the bath, an angel more delicate than palest rose, and the perfume of carnation with her, all those in one small moment, it seems, and so with all the moments, and sending the mind to madness.

The telephone never stopped. People wanted to know how she was, and after a bit of that, I let Tobey or Menai answer, and I roamed the farm. Friends I found among the cattle and sheep, and the poultry, and the horses loved the apples I gave them, and so did the sows, in farrow again, and the turkeys, grown big, now, came to gobble, even before I had the corn from my pocket.

'Mr Morgan, I fear I have no good news for you,' Professor Stansthorpe said, that grey afternoon. 'Your wife suffers from a disease of the eyes. There's extensive damage, and it's reached the brain. We're making sure there's no pain. In fact, her tolerance to pain is quite extraordinary. Didn't she ever show any signs of pain? Or loss of eyesight? She must have done!'

'Well, she never complained of pain, no,' I said, though I shall never be sure how I had the words. 'She was brought up by Indio nurses in Argentina. They were some of the last Tehuelche, and they were taught never to show anything. Never. With them, it is weakness. They will suffer to death, but no word!'

'Poor little soul!' he said. 'She's a remarkable girl. We've all become very fond of her. Did you ever see where she lived at that time? Under what circumstances?'

'Well, they don't live as we do,' I said, seeing the house down there by the river, mud walls, red corrugated iron roof. 'Bare, it was. Blankets about the walls. A dirt floor, but always clean. A fireplace of stones in one corner. Always a fire. And sheepskins to sleep on. She was there till I met her, a bit more than four years ago, now. Will she get well?'

'Were there any pigs kept about the place?' he asked, and dodging my question. 'Bred for food, possibly?'

'They had everything there,' I said. 'Pigs in plenty. For food, any time.'

'How were they cooked, do you know?' he asked, and writing. 'Boiled? Roast?'

'Grilled, generally,' I said. 'Spread-eagle upright on the grill irons, and the coals about them. The head could be cooked separately for brawn. The food was always good, and plenty.'

'How were these pigs kept?' he asked me, still writing.

'Loose about the place,' I said. 'Sometimes in a pen for a farrowing, and locked up at night in case of puma, or a wildcat, or jabali. That's a wild boar, but three times the size of any boar you ever saw.'

'Interesting,' he said, and looked up. 'I want to keep her here for a course of treatment. Physically, she's very strong. She has to be kept quiet. I told you there's brain damage. She mustn't try to talk. So if you just go in and look at her now and again, that must be enough. You see?'

A stroll, naked, in a freeze of sleet, might deaden some of the feeling, but I had to go back to a warm house that called her from every corner, each piece we had bought together, all the little things on the tables, and when Tobey saw me, she put hands to her face, and ran crying for the kitchen.

I am sure everybody had known long before me. If I could have got drunk, I would. But drink and me are strangers. I can tilt so much, but then I am sick, or floored, and the place sailing. So I went to sleep in the chair, and then Tobey and Menai were pulling my coat from me, and they had my boots off, and arms about, they took me upstairs, and sat me on the bed, and the eiderdown, then, and I was lost, and thankful.

'Mr Morgan,' Tobey said, that morning. 'If you were in hospital, and the Mistress Sûs had to go there, how would she go? With a good bath, and hair done, and dressed, smart as Mrs Morgan, Plas Sûs? Or like an old *pŵt* from the hedge?'

'Well, Tobey!' I said. 'Do I look like an old *pŵt*, with you?'

'A man, you are,' she said. 'A woman in the same state *could* look like an old *pŵt*, indeed!'

I had a look in the bathroom glass, and she was right.

A good scrub made wonders, and a shave, double, and I was never so thankful, because when I was downstairs, and trying to have my mind in the paper, the doorbell rang, and Tobey came to say a young lady had a message from Olwen, my youngest sister. I had thought her dead these ten years. I was out of that chair, and at the door, and yes, Olwen, but different, and young as the bud.

'Uncle Huw,' she said. 'I only heard you were here from a newspaper the day before yesterday. I'm your niece, Blodwen Tiarks!'

'Inside!' I said, and took her hand. 'Where is your Mama?'

'Gone from us,' she said. 'My father, too, last year. I don't know how to begin!'

'I will tell you,' I said, and put her in the armchair. 'Begin, now then!'

It is funny how the longest story comes in few words if two minds are together. If they are not, the tale can go without end. Olwen was a headmistress, and she married an examiner from the University, and he died, and she died, and Blodwen was left by herself, with property bringing in a little money, though not much to begin, and none now.

'I have cousins on my father's side,' she said. 'They're wealthy enough, and very kind. But I wouldn't ask them!'

'For what?' I said.

'Money!' she said, flat as her Mama might. 'I want to continue studying the piano. I want to go to Heidelberg. The best tutor's there. I'll give you the properties as a guarantee. Is it possible?'

'Not!' I said, and I saw the shadow fall in her eyes. 'It is done. You will go there. How much do you want?'

She cuddled herself, and turned away, smiling, eyes shut.

'I think five hundred pounds, to start,' she said. 'I don't know what the fees are. But it's for at least three years. That's a long time!'

'Three or thirty, in this family the same,' I said. 'Do you know any more of us?'

'There are quite a number,' she said. 'Shall I put them all in touch?'

'How are there quite a number?' I asked her, because Olwen was one.

'Aunt Angharad's grandchildren in South Africa, and Uncle Owen's, in America, and Uncle Gwilym's in Canada, and Uncle Ianto's in New Zealand, and Aunty

Bronwen's in Australia. The eldest are in school here!'

'Why don't I know about this?' I shouted.

'Did we know about *you*?' she asked me, honey coming from her. 'Mama often said you were the remotest brother any sister ever had!'

I knew about that, too. Only a fool goes near when he is kept at armslength. A millionaire, yes, a bit simpler. But an ordinary man, no money, as she had thought, only himself, and a kiss? No. To hell I had sent her, those years before. But this was her child, different again.

'Send them all here,' I said. 'I shall love to see them. How many?'

She counted, and counted again, careful on the fingers.

'Seven,' she said. 'Two boys and five girls. The two boys aren't much for the moment. They might change for the better. You never know. But all the girls seem quite, I mean, up to it. Two are biologists. One, botany. One, and myself, music. One, architecture. They are all, well, a little bit apart. Like me!'

'Explain it!' I said.

She made a large shrug and pulled breath through a broad nose.

'Apart!' she said. 'Not of the common herd. They don't hobnob. No gang of boys. No pub crawling. No weekends. Does it sound strange? It shouldn't. That sort of thing is common enough. If I found someone, I might. I haven't. None of the others, either. So far as I know. Where is Aunt Sûs?'

To hear her called that by someone almost her own age savaged my heart.

I explained in few words, and I saw her eyes change dark again.

'But I can't visit her?' she said.

'As I do, but only to see, not to speak,' I said. 'It has gone on a long time. It may go on much longer. But if she is having the right treatment, I am more patient than she must be. Where are you staying tonight?'

'I'm catching the five-fifty six,' she said, and took her

bag from the floor. 'But I'd love to stay next time. When could I have the money?'

'When you please,' I said. 'I'll call the cab. Simply give me a sheet of paper with your fares, board and lodging, fees, daily expenses, only for my accountant, it is done!'

'O, Uncle Huw!' she said, and came gentle to put her arms about me, and kiss both cheeks, soft. 'I had this extraordinary feeling exactly this would happen. Is this something that only *we* feel? I was so *certain* it would happen. But why?'

The three weekends of having those lovely girls in the house seemed to bring everything to life. Indeed, I was proud to know their grandmothers and fathers had been my brothers and sisters, and Tobey and Menai always cried when they went away.

'Even the silver do shine more, yes!' Tobey said, and in gulps with her. 'I only wish Miss Blodwen would come back. O, a princess, that one!'

If I had a favourite, I suppose she would be the one. But among such beauty, who could say for sure, I am not certain. If you have got them all round you, and arms about, and jumping up and down in a shout, well, it is like putting your nose to a big bunch of beautiful flowers and trying to pick, then.

And, o, the sad quiet of the house when they were gone!

Nothing, in any moment, so brought to me the silence, and the loneliness, of that little one up by there at the hospital. The girls had been there only once, to stand, and look, and it was enough, and so sad they were coming back, that Tobey made a special tea, with a lot of cakes, and it was like Christmas with us.

Of course, they were young, and nothing of their grandams except beauty and spirit, and I did little talking, but plenty of listening, and I began to learn how the world had changed. They talked about everything in the same way, open to the skies. But even the grown men of my young time never spoke so free. Then, they would talk in whispers in a bar, yes, about women, and going up the mountain, but not all of them, because if they were too forward somebody would tell, and they would have a session with the deacons, and warning of sin, and punishment in the life to come.

But those girls had no chapel or church, and they were impatient to talk about the Bible or anything to do with it. Christ, yes, he was on a pop record, and finish. Matthew, Mark, Luke and John all howled in the wilderness, and the Virgin Mary forgot to take the pill at the right time.

'What pill is this, now then?' I asked, and they shouted laughing, and I never had an answer because Tobey came to say dinner was ready.

The letters I had once a week from Blodwen were rich caskets of jewels for me, full of light about another sort of life beyond me, of piano lessons, and the kindness of her tutor, and her lodgings of three rooms under a roof where birds nested, and she had a hot bath only when she could bribe the girl to come up with the buckets. I wrote and told her to pay a lump sum for the baths she needed, as many as she liked, and let me know what the girl wanted, but she told me if she paid in a lump, she would never see the girl again. She had her Mama's head.

The other girls flew home for the holidays – they called them the vacation – to South Africa, and Australia and New Zealand, and Briony flew to Detroit, and with time I had letters from all of them, and their mothers and fathers, those that lived, but I found it a bit mixed to remember who married who, and what, after. Mind, I think it wrong that we forget each other. I had plenty of time to be sorry, indeed. I could remember my good brothers and sisters, yes, and who better, but their children were unknown to me from my years down in Argentina and Chile, and a world turning, and clocks ticking, and love bringing children, and them growing, and again love bringing children, and I was building roads and bridges and growing vines and sugar cane and cereals, and breeding herds and flocks for the international market, and everything on earth, except to put an arm about my own.

Wrong. But late to know.

I had letters from all of them, but not sure which one

belonged to which, which granddaughter and which mother and father. With the girls, I thought I saw a bit of one, or a spark of another. Angharad's granddaughter had that lovely hair, but shades darker, I will swear, not Titian, that bright flame of wonder to crown the head of a splendid girl, yes, and a temper to match, but yet she had her Grandam's beauty in the heart.

Of them all, only Olwen's daughter, Blodwen, was a little bit tight in the pocket, because her father and mother had not been in business, but only teaching in school. A disgrace, it is, I believe more, now, that teachers, them putting the knowledge in us, are paid as a lot of old slaves, few to speak for them, and none to champion. I had a valuer look at Blodwen's properties at Gwynaldrod, not far from me, a village gone to ruin because the young had left the land.

The cottages were small, of three or four rooms, agreeable, and rustic, without bathrooms, of an early Georgian period, and I bought on all sides, and over a few weeks, we had a village ready for development. Next, to get an architect, and I called Douglas to ask Lys to go and look. She was told nothing about me. I had a report from her, and drawings, and a plan that took in more property to make almost a township, that I was sure Blodwen would like, with a school, and a hospital, and playground and parks, and a baby's creche, and a shopping centre, and underground roads to have the surface free of traffic. The drawings and plans came in week by week with Blodwen's letters, so the two seemed to be one in my mind, and always I thought of my little one up there, so still, so quiet, but I hoped, I prayed, not lonely, though never mind how many times I went, there was nothing to tell.

Tobey gave me the first warning, not, I am sure, that she meant.

We all went up there once a week, together, Tobey, Menai, and me.

'Mr Huw,' Tobey said, when we came out, in the dark, that afternoon. 'The nurses are looking at you very sorry, isn't it?'

'What, sorry?' I said, and cold.

'Well, nurses are only nurses,' she said, looking in the darkness. 'No feeling for everybody. Rip off a bandage, pull off anything, no feeling, yes? Why are they looking so sorry for you?'

'Hisht, you, now then!' Menai said, the first time I knew she had a word to say. 'Better if you had your mouth tied, and a muzzle, then. Are you senseless, with you, girl?'

But I was made to think, and even if I wanted, there was nothing to say.

After that I watched the nurses look at me, but they looked down to speak, or away, never really in the eye.

Professor Stansthorpe always spoke to me here and there, something about maintaining the condition, or an improvement, nothing to cling, little for hope. But that afternoon he came after me in the corridor, and said to go home and wait and he would bring her inside the hour.

If he was God, I could not have looked at him better.

True, it was, inside the hour, the bell rang, and Tobey ran, and Sûs was on the step, arms out, thick dark glasses, and if you listened to the voice, herself again.

'Thirty minutes!' the Professor said, behind her. 'Let her go where she wishes. Drink a glass of champagne. Then let the nurses put her to bed. Tomorrow morning is another day!'

To feel that little hand in mine, with strength, yes, there is plenty in prayer, indeed.

Well, Tobey strolled her about the house, and talking, and I got champagne in the bucket, and after those minutes she came to sit with me in her chair, and I poured, and we drank, but she was slow to speak, and I was unsure where she looked, but it was enough she was home. The two nurses came, and she pushed them away to finish the glass, and we kissed, and they took her upstairs.

'They are both staying the night,' Tobey said. 'The rooms are ready. Will they be here long? We will want more linens!'

'Buy them!' I said. 'Enough she is here!'

Sûs had the big room. I was in the small room beside,

the nurses had rooms down the passage, and the nurse on night duty had an armchair and desk in the wide corridor, with a lot of magazines. I had a look over everything, and saw my beautiful in her own bed, at last, and nobody happier than me, or more filled with hope. And hope, I have learned well, has the strength of wet paper.

Dark, it was, and the nurse was shaking me.

'Come, quick!' she whispered. 'Come, you, now then!'

I put on the dressing gown and slippers, and went to the big bedroom, twice as big in the one small light by the bed. Sûs was sitting up, breathing as if with a machine, and I took her in my arms, and crushed to have her near.

'My poncho!' she said, in her voice, in Tehuelche. 'I shall ride for the river. The rocks call. They are with me. I cry with the trees. Huw. Stay with me!'

'I am with you, my beautiful,' I whispered. 'Stay with *me*!'

'My poncho!' she called, in the loud voice. 'I shall ride. Huw. *Huw!*'

She straightened to the feet, strong, and her face fell in the hollow of my shoulder. And I knew.

In that way, Indios die.

I held her until the nurses took her from me.

But worse moments came after.

'Where will Mrs Morgan be buried, sir?' somebody said, a whisper from far beyond.

I could see only the willows of Chubut, and the broad run of green water, and the purest blue of the Maes Corwen sky, and I could smell the waft of the wheat in blow, and roses, yes, black with scent in the garden.

In a few hours we were flying, and then Buenos Aires, and south, to Trelew, and a truck, and out to Maes Corwen, a glorious place I had kept only in memory of Lal, and then for Sûs, if she wanted to go back there. Well, go back there she did, to join four generations of her family, and I thanked God she would be with her own. I tried to find her Indio nurses, but nobody knew them, or where they were.

That lead casket, in front, and me. Indios walked before,

and behind. I knew none of them, but they all knew me, and certainly the women knew Sûs, and they sang for her, and I was glad she should go with little songs she had once sung herself.

O, an empty land.

Skies, spaces, rocks, rivers, mountains, lakes, and not one warm kiss, not one hand to take, strong. I tried to find Solva, but she was gone north.

It was not in me to look at the house of Maes Corwen where Lal had lived her beautiful day, and Sûs had been born. Instead, I paid the Indios looking after it, and got back in the truck, feeling I had left the best of myself, and along quiet lanes to Trelew, and on to Buenos Aires, and the night flight, out, away.

Out. Anywhere out. Away. Leave it. The bee buzz of an aircraft is part of me, of flight, running away from where I buried love. Heartbreak is only a word, but some of us have got it with us, and I have so often seen it in another man's eyes, and wanted to go to him and say, Yes, I know, but what is there to do?

What, indeed.

Nothing.

My father staring at the kitchen grate, and nothing, no, nothing to be done.

If you have been worrying over a long time, and thinking with hope, and without, a lot of shock is saved to you if there is enough to do that must be done in the moment. But then, when the work is over, and you have got time to think, the shock is worse.

So it was with me, but I had been through it before, and it was different only because Sûs called, not Lal, and louder, as if she had not gone anywhere except to the kitchen to make us a cup of tea, and fool I was, because often I watched the door to see her come back, and I knew I was going a bit funny in the head, and a wonderful thought that is, too.

I suppose Solva, it was, saved me.

'We have now just come back from Maes Corwen, and I can't begin to say what I would like, because I expected

69

a disaster, but I found miracles,' she wrote. 'Those Indios are apart from any I ever saw. The oldest all remember Mama, and when they saw me, you would think I came from God in fire. My husband will retire this year, and his English is not good in writing, so I am doing it. He wants to tell you this. The fields are badly overgrazed. You have far too many head, and the flock is too many for the pasture. You could sell all the bulls except four, and all the cows except thirty, choosing the pick of the pedigree. They are all championship, and they will have top price. He will see to it. With that money, you could build new cattle stalls and barns, and buy machinery. It is needed. The older Indios are near the end, and the young go to the towns. You could think of television in their houses, and a new house and furniture as a present for any wanting to marry and stay. I could attend to it. If you would let my husband manage the farm when he retires, we could live in the house, and have a special part for you when you come to see how your property is growing. My husband wants to say it can only grow, but the Indios have no idea of growth, but only to keep everything well. There are nearly eight hundred hectares on our side of the river for sale. He says land will never come lower, and buy, and have a bargain for fattening the flocks. We have a good place in the Territory, and we can bring in the market flock and fatten, with a share to you. Potatoes, cabbage, lettuce, and other vegetables can be put down to catch the market. I know I am thinking only of him, but Oracio is an active man, and I am afraid of him retiring. I have seen so many of the best retire, and day by day go down, and down, and die. O Huw, please help me. Let him go on a horse, and plan, and use his brains. Let him live. Oracio is my love. I shall pray. S.'

Well, of course, I could hear Sûs shouting *Yes!* long before the end, and so I got Douglas to write a careful letter and give Oracio the manager's place on the farm, but with restrictions. I had no intention of having the Indios moved off – NO! – or treated in any way other than they had known.

I bought good farm machinery and had it shipped, and asked for two prize bulls and thirty young cows sent to me, and four rams and sixty sheep of the pick, and when they came, they were the talk of the market. Too many know nothing of what is done in the south of Argentina. Too many have no respect for what their great-grandfathers did. About their great-grandmothers, less. But they were a golden people, of a goodness not now.

How do I know?

I have been there, and I have seen them, and talked to them, and I know. Just as I know my Mama was one, apart, and not in today. She had another way. It is not with us.

But those letters every three weeks from Solva gave me a new hold. I could see my Sûs, and her sisters, in royal quiet near the shadow of the willows, and the river's green run, and all the flowers the Indios had planted and promised to keep shining through the years. I could hear her voice.

If so much you may have, never mind to ask for more.

Blodwen's letters became milestones in distance of time, too. I had said nothing of the Gwynaldrod plan, but week by week the blueprints came in, and a lot of people were writing to find out who was behind with the money, and if they could have work. Douglas replied to them, and I made it a special order that local labour should be employed, not to bring in a lot of old foreigners.

One letter came from my little Councillor Williams.

He had a son with a small builder's business, and could he have work, because winter was not far, and if there was something, anything would do, he would not have to put his men from work, and the children would go to school filled.

I wrote a note to Douglas, asking him to instruct Lys that the man and his men should be taken on for any small job, and shift them to better if they were good. They were some of the finest dry-wallers in the country, and Lys gave them the job of building all the walls, in the schools, parks and playground, and when that was done, more to follow.

Her, I had not seen since the day.

She wrote a note, but I read it when I got back, of as much interest as flyblow, and I left it, and when we met, at last, in her office, we were strangers, and the voice of Sûs was between us. We spoke of detail, and Douglas had it all in writing, and we had a good cup of tea, and that was all.

Blodwen began bringing friends, and every two or three weeks she was there, and one Saturday, she pointed to a corner of the withdrawing-room, that we called Rŵm Draw, and said, 'There is a bare place!'

Exactly those words Sûs had said months before.

'Right!' I said. 'What will fill it?'

'A piano!' she said, hands in her lap. 'How else can I play for you? But if you get one, have the men here. It will have to go on a platform. Parquet can be uneven!'

Right she was, and the men came, and in a couple of weeks a platform was put up, of fine timber, and then the piano, unpacked, stood on her throne as an empress.

'No better in all Europe!' the foreman said, and the tuner ding-dinging. 'If you have the smallest complaint, let us know and we'll be here in a matter of a few hours, no trouble!'

Blodwen came that Friday evening. I had told her nothing, and she noticed nothing, until Tobey brought in the teatray in firelight, and I nodded to Menai to turn on the switch. Blodwen poured, and I took the cup, and in giving it to me, she looked over my shoulder.

She started to run over there, and came back to clutch me, and reached for the piano, and turned to me again, and then hands above her head in a shouting *Oh!* and ran to the platform, and sat, and turned wheels to have the seat higher, and opened with the little key, and gave it a kiss, and made a lovely little run up and down, and Tobey and Menai came to listen.

'The only reason I've always hesitated to come here were the two days I lost in practice,' she said. 'That's eight days in a month. It's a lot. My tutor doesn't like it a bit. You won't mind if I practise?'

'Mind?' I said. 'A privilege it is. Why do you think it is here? Practise, you, now then!'

The only times I have been near a piano were in the sitting room at Maes Corwen, and in bars or restaurants, but in future I will listen with more respect to people giving hours of the day to practice, and not much notice from anyone. It is only a sound, to some, but for many, a help in loneliness, and I was getting lonely, so I listened more, and it came to me as food.

Blodwen brought friends now and again, but I made it my business to be out of the house those weekends for them to have the place more to themselves. None of those friends, it seemed to me, were half the girl Blodwen was, and presently I found myself thinking of her as rather more than a niece. I found myself thinking, yes. Well, I had the thought, and that thought surprised me, as if there were two different people in me, one to say, and one to listen and be surprised.

Saturday evening, it was, and I came from my room to the stairway, and she ran from her room along to the linen closet. A small white bra, and only a V of panties, and she got a towel and slid the doors, and saw me, and laughed, coming to put her arms round my neck, and kiss a cheek.

'How do you like me?' she said, open as day.

'Anything more beautiful would have to be written in music!' I said. 'And special music, too!'

'That's pretty!' she said, and running back. 'Br-rr. I'm cold!'

But then I knew, and it is no safe place, because thinking can lead to something else.

Solva's letter decided me.

'Do you remember the Indios who worked for you in the timber mill?' she wrote. 'I have just had a message from somebody I never heard of, in the house where you found Sûs. The man came to us here, on his way to do his service with the Army, so my husband posted him where he will use what he knows of horses. The message was that Sûs said, last time she was there, she would put the girls to school. One is twelve, and the other fifteen, and they are granddaughters of one of your Indios. If you will tell me what you want done, I will do my best, depend upon it.'

I wrote back that what Sûs had wanted would be done. I asked her to find a dependable woman, English speaking, to take them home to have the rough corners off, and when they were ready, send them to me and I would have them in a good school.

It is simple to think, and write, but doing is a hard job sometimes, and I suppose they had the task of the Devil with those two, and Solva's letter had all the breath of tiredness.

'Huw, please take my advice and let them go back,' she wrote. 'Mrs Meirion Rhys is used to Indios. You may remember her. She taught school in the Territory for years until she retired, but she can do nothing with these two. They have no habits, and nothing is in their heads to learn, and Mrs Rhys is not slow with the cane, but it is all water from a duck. Last week she had to go to her sister's place near Gaiman, and went back at night and the house full of boys, and wine, and the two of them, no clothes. She brought them back yesterday, but my husband won't have them near, so I have put them with Taikan, the capataz, and his wife has promised there will be no more old nonsense. I think it a pity because as Indios are, they are quite pretty and big for their age, but there is no dealing with them. They have only a word or two of Castellano, none of English, and only a bit of Welsh. They might get a job in the Territory as servants, but it is impossible to keep them here. There are too many men about the place. You understand what I am saying, don't you? A pair of wild mares, they are, and they will jump any gate to be out. Please to put my mind at peace, and let them go back.'

But I could hear Sûs shouting *No!* through it all, and No it had to be, because a promise is that, and Sûs's promise was a thousandfold. Well, luck was with me.

That evening I met Douglas and his partners over the details of a farm I was buying next to the house, and some other matters to do with Gwynaldrod.

'Everything in order, and settled again,' Douglas said,

putting away the papers. 'By the way, do you know a Miss Weyman Lewis from Trelew in Argentina? She's an assistant matron of a hospital in Buenos Aires.'

'I know many a Lewis,' I said. 'But I was mostly over on the Andes side. Why?'

'She just finished examinations here, and she's going back, and she said she'd love to meet you,' he said. 'A cup of tea would do it!'

Well, a cup of tea we had, and a fine girl, too, tall, reddish-grey hair. I knew her father and mother on the farm near Dolavon, and in a walk about my place she was surprised to see everything up to date, and in good order, and nothing spilling.

'I don't like one thing running with another,' I said. 'Everything in proper place, except the chickens, and they peck where they like. The goodness is in the eggs. I like to see a few chickens about the place. Always cheerful!'

'You have made me homesick!' she said. 'And these ducks. We have got flights with us. Wonderful colours. I've never had a better time than here. I mean, in the country. I hope my sister is as happy. She'll be here at the end of the month. The same examination.'

'Wait, you,' I said. 'Could she bring a couple of girls with her? I mean, take care of them? All expenses, of course!'

I showed her Solva's letters, and she read them all, and tidied them, and put away the spectacles.

'I know the kind!' she said, soft. 'Left too late, and hopeless. We've tried to train them. Most of them, if they haven't got a white father, impossible. If you bring them, and they have to go back, it will be worse because this is a better life. They'll be spoiled. If you leave them there, they will spoil in their own way, and perhaps marry a peon. But it will be their life, and no interference. If they have school, what will they do, after? They can't go back to their own people. If they don't, they will always be strangers, yes? What will they do in Argentina? Or anywhere, this type? Shall I say? Or do you know?'

We will take anything except good advice.

I cabled Solva about passports and Weyman Lewis

cabled her sister, Rhian, and the girls were picked up and flown from Trelew to Buenos Aires, and a night there, and on to London, and when I met them at Heathrow I saw by Rhian's face that we had trouble.

'They are with the airport nurse in the medical centre for the moment,' she said, in the crisp Trelewese English. 'They were both violently ill on the flight. A calmative kept them quiet. This letter is for you. My friends are over there, if you'll excuse me!'

'Wait!' I said. 'What about expenses?'

'None,' she said, going away. 'Nothing, thank you!'

Only too glad to go.

With weights in both feet I found the medical centre, and the nurse looked at me as one from another world.

'The doctor's with them,' she said. 'The Argentine Consul has been called. Their papers are not in order. I'm sorry, but you'll have to wait!'

Well, I waited. Tobey was with me to help, but all she did was bring cups of coffee for us, and then the doctor came in with another man.

'This is the Argentine Consul,' he said. 'I'm the medical officer. I don't think I can permit these girls to enter. There are too many irregularities in their papers!'

'I wish them sent back to Buenos Aires!' the other man said. 'The regulations are not kept. They are disregarded. Somebody must be held responsible. They have no international health certificate. How is it possible?'

'I'm sorry about it,' the doctor said, and looked at me. 'Are you a relative?'

'No,' I said. 'I offered to put them in school!'

'School?' the Consul said. '*Those* two, *school? Here?* They don't even speak their own language!'

'Let me explain,' I said, very patient.

'The facts speak for themselves,' the Consul said. 'They are under age, one. There is no parental or other permission, two. And three, their papers are not in order!'

'I'll add another,' the doctor said. 'Their medical documentation is incorrect. They both show signs of a merciless flogging. You know nothing about it?'

'How could I?' I said, 'I was here!'

'True enough,' the doctor said. 'Well. Without a good deal of pressure, which I can't see, I won't sign a release. That's all!'

'I support you!' the Consul said. 'So many irregularities, I cannot sanction. After all, there are laws, no? For me, they leave tonight!'

'I'd suggest a night's rest here, and some medical treatment, and let them go in the morning, sometime,' the doctor said.

'Who pays the fares?' the Consul asked me.

'They have return tickets,' I said, and thinking of Sûs, and wondering what she would say, and I knew. She would have put both men on the floor, but those girls would have been from there. I was more of civilised life. Fighting laws and regulations was not in me. Who is the wiser, Indios without law, or us with, it is hard to say, Without law, all is possible, even to getting a couple of girls out of paper and rubber stamps. With law, any fool with a rubber stamp is Lord God, and well they know it.

Well, the girls went back, and I had a letter from Solva.

'They pushed off loose from where they were taken, and I'm not sure where they are now,' she wrote. 'I found out what happened from Zuri, Taikai s wife. He took his bridle leathers and beat them senseless over the bed, and two days later, the same, and two days later, once again, so they were in proper condition to go with Rhian to Buenos Aires, and he promised them if they gave any more trouble, he would beat, and they would never walk again. My husband says it is the only way with that kind, and the only way the Indios have any sense out of them. I have been thinking about women's liberation. From what? To do what? The farm is wonderful. A report from my husband later. Love from all of us. S.'

So that was the end of it. But I kept hearing Sûs and her NO!

Those girls got permits to fly because the General added his weight, that was plain enough, and so I wrote a letter to him, asking his ideas about what could be done for

Indios, generally, boys and girls. Solva wrote for him, of course, but I could hear Oracio in every word.

'If you have them as infants, *a lot can be done,*' she underlined. 'So much is proved by the Church. Many have gone to good positions. They are exceptions. The wildness is always with them. They are at home only in the simplicity of the pampas, the wilderness. A school to them is a prison, and our lessons are another way of making them into slaves to do our work. Any Indio boy or girl working on a farm earns keep and money, but in school they earn nothing, and of course their parents resent the loss. The way they think is different. I believe if we could have enough land far out in the Territory, and made by law into a Reserve, where they could build their own toldos, live as they want, and work at their own handicrafts, a good long step would be taken towards civilisation. The women could weave blankets and ponchos on the loom, and dye their own wool. The men are masters in leather work. We should nourish these basic arts. But no church or missionary activity of any type. Schools for those requiring, but only voluntary. Never obligatory. But sending one or two to school here and there is worse than useless. They are not examples, but creatures apart, not one, not the other. Remember, the wildness is always in them. It will erupt when you are least expecting. Everything here is splendid. Love. S.'

I wrote back two lines to ask why Oracio had not put the idea to his President, and Solva gave me one line in return. 'Land is politics. Why give land to Indios when the money is in sheep? Have sense, boy. Love. S.'

In such a way duty is put aside.

Yet, I had a jolt on that Monday.

Rhodrick took rams and ewes to the market for sale, and had excellent prices, and we went to the tearoom for a good pot of tea and a brace from the bottle. We had just sat, and four hobbledehoys came in, hair to the shoulder, bits of whiskers, cowboy clothes, dangles about the neck, a parcel, indeed, and began a lot of loud talk, pretending to be American, and giving me that freeze up the back I

78

always have when an idiot tries to be somebody else. Nobody is worse than a false fool. Fools there are, thank God, and they will have you laughing because they are on the note, and right, and they make you sure. But the false fool comes of the brute trying to make itself something more than it is, that they hate because they seem to know it will never be anything better.

Well, I was hit hard, because there is little use trying to help Indios in the Andes, when we had plenty of our own, and nothing to be done.

'The worst we ever did was get rid of conscription,' Rhodrick said. 'A couple of years with a Sergeant Major's boot behind you puts lessons for life. We are suffering for the want. What you have got now is loud buggers like this. No use to anybody. They will learn, mind? When they are hungry. But too late. Useless!'

There were other lessons to learn.

We had fields of early potatoes to clear, and a lot of work with cauliflowers, spring onions, tomatoes under glass, and cabbage, and labour was scarce. Rhodrick put out the word, and the same type of Indio came up, and they worked well.

That was the surprise.

The second day I had an asado for them after work, and taught them to cut from the grilled sheep, and eat from a piece of bread, and afterwards they sang with guitars, and to me, there was nothing wrong, and the wine went round and a good night everywhere.

Next night was Friday, and Blodwen came about eight, just in time for the asado, and I taught her to cut from the grill, and she learned as a daughter of Chubut, and drank wine to the cheers of Indios, but when they played the guitars I saw she was restless.

'I wish I could play for them!' she whispered. 'There's a lot of talent, here!'

'Tomorrow, let them finish their work, and you shall bring them in the house,' I said. 'Work first, isn't it?'

There were many more girls and boys, the next day, and the fields were cleared, and the boxes packed, and only

79

because of the promise of an asado, and they all brought a good knife for it, and at the end, I gave Blodwen the nod, and she told them to take off their boots and come in the house.

Well, Tobey had taken all the silver off the tables, and I began to laugh.

'A lot of old thieves, they are!' she said, and big eyes. 'Will you lose all you have got?'

'Go on with you, girl,' I said. 'Only see!'

Well, some played the guitar, and sang. I am not one for the guitar. A tickle of strings and little more, and the songs, bare words of nothing, with a chord now and again. A noise, yes. Music, no. The difference is knowledge, and that is a matter of study.

When everybody sat on the floor, and Blodwen played, that was the difference, of an age from an age.

But where was the age?

Did they cheer because she played so beautifully, or because of the effect of the music?

I was apart. I sat over in the corner. I watched Blodwen at the piano.

I was not away from her, and certainly not away from them, in their feeling and cheering, but I wondered why they shouted.

'Was it the playing, or the music?' I asked her when she was tired, that night, and she said, 'Perhaps it was a bit of both. There are so many kinds of lovers of music. One sort or another. Why trouble? For me, get it out of the piano, as you want. If you can. If it comes from an orchestra, the same? Wonderful!'

'But there is a serious question,' I told her, 'Is it the music? Or the way it is played? Or who plays it? Or who conducts? A man sits, in his beautiful plainness, and writes music on sheets of paper. Another takes the sheets, and collects musicians, and reads, and plays. Is it what the man who sat wanted? Poetry can sound different in other mouths!'

I asked her, because I wanted to know, and I think she

should have known, but she had no notion, and she said she had never thought.

'But what *is* music?' I asked her.

'It is what you hear,' she said. 'It's sound, isn't it?'

'But is any sound music?' I asked again.

'I think it is,' she said. 'They made it from machines, didn't they? And they're composing electronically.'

'So music is anything going in the ears, then?' I said.

She frowned, looking away, and smiled.

'I've never felt about it like that,' she said. 'It seems pointless to me. I buy music, and pay for tuition, and try to play as I'm taught. People want to listen, or not. What the composer feels is in the score, isn't it? As for what music *is*, there must be thousands of explanations. Not one of them completely satisfactory to everybody, I suppose. My tutor always says stop talking, and play. Are you thinking of the singing tonight?'

'Singing?' I said. 'Not a voice among the lot!'

'It doesn't need a voice,' she said. 'It's assembly-line folk. Industrial pop? Depends on feeling more than anything. It's the voice of the poor. The words of the illiterate, the back streets. But even they have their poetry. The guitar gives it shape. Keeps them on the note. You didn't like it?'

'I'm strange to it,' I said. 'I was brought up in the choir. We had to *sing*. Those tonight were in an old bumble, with them!'

'I quite liked it!' she said, and laughed. 'You aren't getting an old stick-in-the-mud, surely? But you're wonderfully old-fashioned in some things. It's rather nice. I wouldn't like it any other way!'

That little bit of talk stuck with me because I was taught to look at myself a little closer, and I had lessons from it. The first, that to think of the young of this time as Indios was wrong. I had seen them work as good as the next, and I heard them at play, and although there were not more than forty of them, I felt I could base an opinion. The young of my time were not better-natured, or better-behaved, and that was a surprise, too.

About stick-in-the-mud I had to think again, and the

old-fashioned part had me to the tailor for new suits. Those I had were years old, and I told Menai to give them to anybody.

'O, Mr Morgan, nearly new they are, isn't it?' she said, in whispers with her. 'Not a stitch out, see, and not a button loose!'

'New, I will have,' I said. 'Somebody can do with them!'

Tobey came just after, and stood in twists of the hands, not looking at me.

'Mr Morgan, I have got to tell you!' she said, as if forcing herself. 'I am getting married!'

'O, dear!' I said. 'There is a pity!'

'Well, it's time for a family, isn't it?' she said. 'I will be leaving the end of the month. Menai can find plenty to help. Or I will bring a few for you to choose, is it?'

'No,' I said. 'Menai will have to work with them. Let her choose.'

'I will be living in Caernarvon, and a nice little house, and he's got a steady job with the Council, so we are lucky, really,' she said, coming brighter. 'And those suits you gave to Menai now just? They will fit him beautiful, indeed. Shall I have them for him? For once a gentleman he will look, yes?'

'Take them,' I said. 'What would you like for a wedding present?'

'O, Mr Morgan, a telly would be wonderful!' she said, and quick, as if on the tip, and laughing. 'O, thank you, sir. A lovely telly, then? You have always been very kind, yes. What could I make special for your tea? And could I have the night off, then? My boy is taking me home, and a long way to come back, see, and the old buses do stop too early!'

Well, a small shock, but Menai had one bigger, and I had to ask her what she had been saying, and not in whispers, standing there in the doorway.

'I can't stay in the house alone, here!' she said, loud enough. 'Everybody is talking. Young girls in the house, and only you, and hippies having the run everywhere!'

'You know that isn't true!' I said.

'Try to stop the talk!' she said. 'For that, Tobey will be married. She would stay. She told me. But she can't even do the shopping without hearing what is going on, here!'

'What *is* going on?' I asked her.

She shrugged, and turned away.

'I can't be here any more, either, without her!' she said, loud, again. 'I shall have a name, and who will marry with me? Only a fool would ask!'

'Leave when you wish,' I said. 'I didn't know people thought like that in these days. When do you wish to go?'

'I am packed, now, and ready to be off!' she said. 'Will I have my money, now then?'

I had always thought her a quiet one, but she was on edge to be saucy, and more than ready to talk.

'Go and see Mr Douglas Gough for your wages and insurance cards,' I said, and looked at my watch. 'I'll telephone him you'll be there. Away you go!'

Well, another shock with Douglas, too.

'Yes, well, I've been expecting it!' he said. 'It's still very much what it was here a hundred years ago. People don't change. Clothes, shoes, that sort of thing, yes. Basically, with a few exceptions, people, no. It seems ground and trodden into them. The puritanical business, I mean. Now then, I know a couple of good women looking for just that sort of job. Send them in the morning?'

Mrs Frew, a widow, and Miss Rampole, both thirties, somewhere, with something clean and comfortable about them, I took on sight, and they were exactly what the house needed, and without any new broom nonsense, before the week was out, I knew.

I tried to tell them about the local gossip, but Douglas had been there before.

Neither of them had a doubt.

'Don't let it worry you, Mr Morgan!' Mrs Frew said. 'We are old enough to look after ourselves. This isn't our neighbourhood, so let them chat!'

'We'll let them know what *we* think if we have any nonsense!' Miss Rampole said. 'Nelly and me've worked together a couple of years doing catering, so we know most of what goes on. They have no room to talk. And by the way, sir, my name's Cress!'

I wondered what Blodwen would think, but she had no doubt, either.

'For one thing, the house is infinitely cleaner!' she said. 'Men don't notice. We go for the details. And the food is so much better. I didn't like to say anything before. But I was never easy with those two, and they didn't like *me*!'

'But it was Tobey called you a princess!' I said.

'Butter, or better, hogwash!' she said. 'At least, the piano *and* the dais are being polished correctly, as I showed them. And my bed is properly made. That's a departure!'

Only that way, you learn.

Professor Stansthorpe sent me a note to see him professionally, if I pleased. Well, I did, and after an examination of my eyes, he pushed the machine away, and smiled.

'That eye condition is extremely contagious,' he said. 'I was rather worried. I'm thankful to find no sign. In fact, for your age, your vision is remarkable. I believe you have a majority holding in Gwynaldrod?'

'Yes,' I said, sure, then, I had been called for that, and eyes were excuse.

'I hear you're having trouble with the hospital permits, Health Ministry, so forth,' he said. 'I have a suggestion. If I may? I don't want to sound as if I were trying to interfere. That area is excellently well served with hospitals in the surrounding towns. What we *haven't* got is a hospital exclusively for eyes. My team has to fit in days to come here, or go there, and it's often a damned nuisance. A place of our own at Gwynaldrod would be perfect. If I could possibly persuade you? I'll do all that's necessary with the Ministry and everyone else!'

I could hear Sûs's *Yes!*

'It is done,' I said. 'Talk to the architect. Tell her what is wanted, and I will see Mr Gough. You'll want special equipment, and a lot of things different, yes?'

'Allow me to specify,' he said. 'I'm tremendously grateful, Mr Morgan. Lys Machen's a quite extraordinary woman. Whatever she touches comes alive. Incidentally, I'm glad she's found a good man, at last!'

'Me?' I said, and coming up straight.

'Well, you, yes, as the power behind the scenes,' he said, and laughing. 'I meant the man she's marrying. You didn't know?'

I stared.

'No,' I said. 'Whatever it is, I am always the last!'

'Oh,' he said, and made a *mph!* with his mouth. 'He's the County Engineer!'

If he had taken a cannon from the drawer and fired between my eyes, I could not have felt so much. That one, strolling with a pipe, and looking at wasted work, his own, yes, a bit trembly, and *her*? I came again to think there must be something wrong with all of us. In the eyes, first, with how we see.

How I could see it, and she not, puzzled me splendid, indeed.

But everybody has to choose.

But.

Good God.

Him?

I was home late that afternoon and Cress told me Blodwen had called from Heathrow, asking if she could bring someone to stay.

'Why would she ask when she knows there's no question,' I said. 'What did you say?'

'She's calling again at six,' Cress said. 'I think it's a man!'

A poser, indeed.

On the first floor was the big bedroom, and then a smaller bedroom and bath, and on the other side a dressing room and bathroom and then the room and bath Blodwen always took. There were spare rooms upstairs, but unused. I had no thought of allowing a man in the room next to me, and I had no notion of letting him sleep anywhere else.

When she telephoned from a pub in the town – she said – I asked her, blank.

'Well, yes, he's a man,' she said. 'But he can sleep on the

85

couch downstairs. We don't want any fuss, for heaven's sake!'

'No fuss,' I said. 'Mrs Rhodrick's got a spare room. I'll ask her –'

'No, no!' she wailed. 'He could sleep in my room. What's wrong with that?'

'Plenty!' I said. 'It's going to look as if the gossip had a solid base!'

'Oh, don't bother!' she shouted. 'We'll go to an hotel!'

I wrote to explain, but I heard nothing for weeks, and then I had a letter from her tutor in Heidelberg, asking me where she was, because the term was ending, and wanting to know if she would be returning for the next. I had to write and say I had no idea, and please, if he heard anything, to let me know.

Indios, indeed.

Rhodrick looked me in the eye, that cold morning in the stables when I told him I was worried about Miss Blodwen.

'I miss her not coming here,' I said.

'Well, she's not far, whatever!' he said, and leaned on the hay fork. 'You didn't know, sir?'

I suppose I glared, daft as a brush.

'I know nothing!' I said. 'If you know, tell me!'

'O, well,' he said, as if he was tired to say. 'Everybody here's known it these weeks!'

'Known what?' I asked him, and angry.

'Where she is, isn't it?' he said, as if I was unfair. 'Down there with the hips, she is. Playing the piano for them. The hall is full, there. Night after night. Fortunes they are making, yes!'

I went outside to have the wind cold on my head, and breathe, and then straight for the house, and into the kitchen. Mrs Frew looked at me from chopping carrots, and I asked her.

'We've known it since the night she started!' she said. 'The night she didn't stay here!'

'Why not tell me, girl?' I shouted. 'Do you think I would have allowed it?'

86

'Well, we thought you *were* allowing it!' she said. 'It was going on, night after night. They'll be on the telly in a couple of weeks. The newest of the new, that's what they call them!'

'New what?' I had strength to ask.

'Well, singing in the group, I suppose?' she said. 'I haven't heard them. No interest.'

'I wouldn't go from here to there,' Cress said. 'An old noise!'

I telephoned Douglas Gough, and he said everybody was talking about the new group at the dance hall, and Blodwen, and who she was, and a real scandal at the way she was living in a caravan outside the town.

'You know what these things are,' he said. 'Here today, gone tonight. But they seem to be doing very well, I must say. The owner of the hall's a client of mine. He wants an extended contract with them, but they want more money. He can't afford it, I think the pianist made all the difference!'

'Why?' I asked him, and angry.

'A new style brings in the crowd,' he said. 'People pay just to listen. They also buy drinks. That's clear profit!'

'I'll be there tonight!' I said. 'She is a niece of mine. I must do what I can. She can't live that sort of life!'

'She's doing very well, so far,' he said. 'But be careful. They can get very rough. I mean, the people with her!'

Well, being rough is something I know a little bit about, and so I took Rhodrick and a few of the bigger men with me, in case, and paid at the door, and pushed into a crowd that surprised me. There were not many lights, and chairs were round the walls and in a couple of rows at the back, and the floor scuffled with couples, and the music came from the back, all in purple and red light, and big globes in the ceiling went round and round, flashing colours, and the voices whined on, with guitar twang, and piano chords, and the many sounds and clashes of drums.

Blodwen, in a copper-coloured dress with little beads catching different lights, had a grand piano in front, a little one at the side, and another behind her, and a harp, a beauty, beyond, and she played splendid, indeed, until she turned to the little one, and saw me, stopped a moment, and smiled, and went on.

All that time people by the hundred were dancing, but such dancing as I never thought to see. Some were like boxers sparring, even the girls, and others like apes in a crawl with them. I have danced a bit in my time, but I would think shame to be out there, in such a prance. Indios, yes, have got a dance, and if it comes strange to us, it is natural to them, and they have their own simple grace. Even a rough gaucho has his tango, and a wonder, too, and the best dancing I ever saw was on sheep farms after a shearing. But this was what Dai Bando used to call a rum shanks, and I almost laughed to think what he would say. About my father, the less said.

Blodwen played a chord, and the music stopped, and she came down the steps to me, but no kiss, and the smile of somebody leaning over a gate.

'Well, found me at last, have you?' she said, but none of the old spark. 'I thought you'd have been here before!'

'I only knew a couple of hours ago,' I said. 'If I hadn't said I missed you, I suppose I still wouldn't know. You knew I'd worry, didn't you? A letter from your tutor!'

She looked at it, and almost flipped it back.

'Finished with all that, thank God!' she said. 'We're leaving here next week. We're touring Europe, so I'll be able to call in and see him. And don't worry about me. I'm doing exactly as I want!'

'And how about your career?' I asked her, over the rattle and clink from the bar.

'It's here!' she said, and a nod at the stand, and gold and silver guitars. 'If you're worried about money, don't. I'm earning far more than I ever imagined. In a few weeks I'll come up to pay what I owe. I'd like my properties back. They'll be a lovely place to go and rest in. If ever we get time off!'

'Well, well!' I said, in no patience. 'This, instead of a

concert career? What would your poor Mama have had to say, I wonder?'

'I'll tell you!' she said, head down, and a lot of Olwen in those eyes, too. 'One of the last times we had a talk, she told me never to do anything if it meant a scrape through life. Go where there is money. Don't try teaching. You will have nothing for it. Don't throw away your life as I did. Find out where people can spend the least to have the most. Music, yes. But be careful which music. The cheapest is best!'

'She had a pupil!' I said.

'That's just what I mean, don't you see?' she said, and the drummer rapping to have the band in place. 'This was what I was waiting for. I'll always be grateful to you for what you did for me. But I'll never be able to thank you enough for meeting Jon and these boys. I was all they needed. Piano backing, and arrangements. That's why I'm earning. I'll never have to scrape. Must go. See you in a month or so!'

'Are you being married?' I called after her.

'Ho!' she laughed over her shoulder. *'Married!'*

The beard with the guitar slapped it three times, and they all began again.

'The world has changed,' I said, to Rhodrick, outside. 'The monkeys are from the cage, indeed!'

'Well, they say we are born from them, isn't it?' he said. 'What wonder if we go back?'

Disappointment is a long old word, indeed, and we know what it means, but if you nail it to the wall of your mind, and look at it, there is nothing to explain that pain, in the head, or somewhere inside you, some sort of burn you can touch, with hurt, but never to heal. Time does nothing. That feeling of loss, of a theft in the spirit of goodness put away, or a happy laugh thrown to the teeth of curs, no, time will do nothing to rid. While you can think, it is there.

So it was with me about Blodwen, and many a time I could have taken the axe and smashed the piano, stool, and the dais, every chip for firewood, and burnt them,

89

with all the sheets of music, but I was stopped by a thought of Olwen. If I had known about the scrape, I could have done plenty, but without a letter all those years, I was deaf, and Patagonia is a good place to be deaf in. But I could see my Mama nursing her, the very last, she called her, and now her granddaughter was newest of the new.

I saw reports in the papers about the band, and pieces about Blodwen and her training in classical music, and Rhodrick said he had seen them on the telly, and very good, too, and they were at the top of the ratings, whatever that was.

'Well, a lot of money, they were saying, there,' he said, mixing the turkeys' bucket. 'I wish I could sing, indeed. Damn, I would be in a good bawl, here, day and night, to fill the cap and be off!'

'Not old caps they are having today, boy,' Mrs Frew said, pouring hot water in the mix. 'Banks, it is. Caps, that was in the pubs, and a few pennies. Money, yes, it is paper for old age pensioners, and us, isn't it? Those with the work, it is cheques. Is singing work, then?'

'I will be damned!' Rhodrick said. 'What is work about singing? Open your mouth!'

'Open yours!' Mrs Frew said. 'What will you have? Old flies, with you?'

I had letters from the mothers and fathers of the other girls, thanking me for hospitality, but I knew none of them, and I was slow to answer. Perhaps I was afraid of another Blodwen, but in any event, not one of the girls wrote or telephoned, and I was happy enough to let sleeping dogs.

More people were coming to see me, but always I asked Rhodrick to show them round the farm, and went on with the carpentry. I had got a taste back for work, and I found two good men from the village to help panel the old barn, stone-built, and re-timbered, a fine place to invite friends in for meals. I wanted nobody in the house. Sûs called from every corner. Sometimes I could almost see her. Mrs Frew and Cress liked to go out at night and come in the back way, so I had the house to myself, and grateful.

Yet I knew how lonely I was on the night I had dinner with Sam and Ella Hooper. He was much older, but they made a fine pair, he red-faced, an apple, she taller, fair, always a laugh ready, and warmth seemed part of the furniture, not just in the fire of logs. He supplied most of the material for Gwynaldrod, so it was no surprise to see Lys Machen come in with, well, of course, the County Engineer. I will never remember his name. You would think buckram was between us, so stiff we were.

Ella cured it by dropping the sauce boat, but instead of temper, she laughed, and Sam said he was always dropping sauce boats, and nothing to worry about.

Just that laugh brought everything a bit softer, and Lys became almost as she had been, and we talked about the work going on, and I asked her to give another look to the cottage behind the house.

'I've got so much to do,' she said, and the County Engineer took out the pipe, but Lys made a look into not quite a small frown, and he put it back. 'There isn't a moment of the day to myself. Not even time to be married!'

'Yes, I heard,' I said. 'Congratulations to you both. I hope everything will go well with you!'

Why we say such lies I am not sure, except perhaps to be social.

But I was glad that Sûs had put her voice and a weight of words between us, or perhaps there might have been another story. In that look not quite a small frown, I thought I saw what could come after, and I was in shudders to think of all I had missed, and I suppose because of it I was over-friendly in good nights, for next morning the County Engineer was at the door.

'Lys and I thought of offering a nominal rent for the cottage,' he said, a bit high in the nose, on the step. 'It's just what we're looking for. Right in the middle of everything. We'll restore the entire property with greatest care, I assure you. At our own expense, naturally. We thought a twenty-five year lease might be in order, with an option to buy, perhaps?'

91

'Perhaps not, thank you,' I said. 'None of my property is for rent or sale, and my compliments to Miss Machen.'

'Oh,' he said, and a bit of a jiggle with the pipe. 'I see. Well. Sorry to have troubled you.'

Remembering that frown inside a look, I was sorrier for him.

The answer was not long, and we had the barn walls almost panelled, and Cress came to say three gentlemen from the regional surveyor's office wanted to see me, and I said to bring them round.

The three came in, one old, two young, and looked surprised at the work, and I sent Cress for tea.

'A lovely place you'll be having here, sir,' the old one said, and very civil with him. 'My name's Sullivan. Mr Jones. Mr Rosson. We've had information a marble sarcophagus was found here. It should have been reported, of course. These things are rare. It's a museum matter. Fine Arts. Ancient monuments, and so on. Could we have the pleasure of viewing? Not too much trouble?'

I could see the frown inside the look all the way through to the garden. But that day I was with luck, and every bulb in the world seemed to be laughing at me, tulips, daffodils, narcissus, and the plinth of the sarcophagus had great rings of them, and primroses in cushions, lovely, yes, beyond any dream.

It was enough to stop those three, and Mr Sullivan turned to me.

'Anything more in beauty than this, no, I never saw,' he said. 'Beautiful, indeed. A perfect setting, and excellently well taken care of, too. I expect you'll soon have the experts down to look at it for the catalogue, and photographs. But you'll have my solid vote against moving it. Hm?'

The two younger nodded.

'First century Roman, or before,' Mr Rosson said. 'It'll have to be thoroughly examined, which'll take time. But I'll certainly report against removal.'

'Have they got the power?' I asked them, and surprised.

'Of course,' Mr Sullivan said. 'It's a national treasure, isn't it? I don't know how it got here. If we hadn't heard from the Machen office, we'd never have known, yes?'

If I had any thought of asking Lys Machen to do more work for me, it burnt there.

It has never been in me to do anything harmful to anybody. But I had the pleasure of giving the plan for the concert hall and the market in Gwynaldrod, both small places, to a team of young men and women from the University, and something more to frown at when I chose another man to restore the chapel.

Nothing more from me, and I could hear Sûs shouting her *NO!*

Well, everything, at some proper time, falls into place, and I knew when Mrs Frew came out to the barn to say that Miss Valmai John, from Melbourne, Australia, would like to speak to me. I was out like a racer. She could only be my brother Davy's granddaughter, and I thought I saw him in her eyes, and took her to me, and she cried.

'I've been so homesick!' she said. 'Arms about you is pretty strange after such a long time. I don't know what I'm being so idiotic about!'

'Come in, girl!' I said. 'A good cup of tea, and off with your shoes, and tell me everything, isn't it?'

She told me she had studied architecture for a degree in Paris, and wanted to find a job in London.

When I heard the word, I saw the cottage up at the back, there, and put it tidy up my sleeve. Most of what she told me about her family went in the teapot. None of the people were known to me. It was like walking through a cemetery and seeing names, born now, died then, and God be kind to us, and home, then, to a good plateful of roast lamb and mint sauce, and figs to the lot.

Until it was your turn.

Mrs Frew took her up to the room, and Cress came to clear away the tea tray.

'My night to cook dinner, sir,' she said. 'Will a turkey poult be all right?'

'I should think, yes,' I said. 'See in the greenhouse for the vegetables. Rhodrick's got new potatoes, there. French beans. Lettuce. Tomatoes. Anything you want, take. Peaches, too.'

'This farm's got a name for the best,' she said, and turned in the doorway. 'Only because of bed-linens and blankets, will the young lady be staying long, sir?'

'While she's here, she's home,' I said. 'One of the family. But I hope not like the other.'

'Ah, but she's doing all right for herself, though,' Cress said. 'A lot of talk about her, but she's raking it in. That's what matters, isn't it?'

I have often wondered if all that matters is money. There are beautiful arguments on all sides, but if we are tight in the pocket, and hungry, words lose meaning except for a few saints, and I suppose their example puts the doubts in us when we try to pretend, or forget. Certain it is that I denied nothing in the way of money to Blodwen. She had herself to look after, and her Mama had grimed the idea into her. But what she was doing among the cheap and vulgar when she might have had a concert career, that, yes, more than worried me.

Valmai shook her head, slowly, surely.

'That's plain snobbery,' she said. 'Just heard from her. We haven't talked for more than a year. She always knew what she was after. Never made any secret of it. After all, what's the difference? Play for a lot of stuffed shirts, or a younger lot, more energy, more grab for light, colour, sound? They're the *real* hungry ones. Hungry in spirit.'

'I'm a stuffed old shirt, then?' I said. 'Because I wanted the girl to have a life in dignity as an artist?'

'I don't know about dignity, but she didn't think she had the talent as a pianist,' Valmai said. 'That's what bugged her. Not quite enough spin on the ball. That's why she went to composition. Writing, she was top. So when she got a few pink earfuls of these lads she's with now, she knew all they wanted was some pulling together. She can't go anywhere except up. They only had to hear her. As for being an artist, you've got to be pretty dam' good to get up anywhere and stay up. She has. I believe she's nailed there.'

94

'Good,' I said. 'If you write, tell her to come and play the piano when she likes. Never mind I don't like what she's doing. It's her business, not mine.'

'Dam' right,' Valmai said. 'I'll tell her. While we're on this, would you mind if I invited a friend of mine here? She's so like Blod' in many ways. She went for the same degree I did, but she didn't have it. She failed. I had a few days' hell with her. Well, she's a Breton, on the coast. With all that temperament. She hit the bottle. She couldn't go home. She said her Dad'd kill her. But she's a really good, sound constructional draughtsman. She can't be wasted. I want to team with her. I'm going to ask my Dad for enough money to go out on my own. The two of us, I believe we'd make it.'

'Don't worry your father for the moment,' I said. 'Send the girl a telegram and bring her here. You can both stay as long as you please. I believe I have something you can both work at. Let us find out.'

Well, the other girl was with us in a couple of days, when we were oiling the beams and panels of the barn, and the men were bringing in the long tables, and chairs, and the village women worked the wax polishers on the slate floor, and the other girls dressed the buffet at the end in copper pots with all the flowers from the garden. A party for the Sunday School children we were having for Mrs Rhodrick, the deaconness, after forty years of service.

I was dusty with the breath of timber, and oily, uncombed, unshaved, and I was called from a corner with the electricians, and I met Kyrille, and Valmai said, if I heard through some sort of musical fog of many colours, to call her Kiri, and could somebody help with the luggage and packing cases. Mrs Frew and Cress had cleared two of the spare rooms upstairs, and by the time the men carried up the last case, drawing boards and tables were in place, and the two girls were hanging up framed drawings of buildings, all in tints, far prettier than many a picture, and I said I could do with a couple for my place downstairs, and think pleasure every time I looked. Val chose two of hers, and Kiri two, and they went then, no wait, to put them up.

If I had come from the grave, and met Kiri in another life, I might have felt as I did, though not less, and if more, I would go in flame. She was tall as Val, and the same fine figure, as, I noticed in gleams of joy, those of the pagans dancing in marble, and long black hair to the waist, in the sun with some bronze in it. Her eyes were a calm grey of summer's sea, and a smile beyond, a touch of light in cloud, or anyway, so I thought, and nobody to argue, and I remembered Mama telling Angharad, all those years ago, if you think, *say*, and you will never be sorry.

The girls took a couple of days to settle in, and I was out most of the time at Gwynaldrod, that sounded a far bigger work than it was. A red telephone box was the only note of today. The village had been by-passed by a main road years before, and a lot of people had left to find work. Buildings were still up but in sad state, and all I wanted the architects to do was put them as they were a couple of hundred or more years before. Lys Machen had done a good job in clearing the ground, and the steam-rolling could not have been better. Five streets of small cots led to a square at the crossroads, with two inns long shut, a blacksmith's forge, a chapel gone in weeds, and two shops, one shut, and a grocery kept by an old woman, a bit silly with years, and sure she would never sell the shop. Only her place and Blodwen's were not mine, but the rest was almost in order, though hard to get through narrow lanes of stones and mud.

'The roads are a problem for ambulances, or any other transport except a horse and cart,' Professor Stansthorpe said, at the meeting. 'I think we'll have to apply to the County.'

'They will stay as they are,' I said. 'Tourists will be here with their cars. To hell.'

'I doubt the hospital will get permits or anything else,' he said, and the rest sat. 'We're in the twentieth century.'

'And very welcome,' I said. 'It is a lovely little place, and it will stay as it is, except I will repair the stone bridge, and replace the cobbles in the square.'

Professor Stansthorpe stood, and gathered papers.

'Won't do,' he said. 'An emergency case might not get through at all.'

'I got here today in the rain without trouble,' I said.

'I withdraw,' he said. 'Any hospital in such a wilderness would be a liability.'

'Use a helicopter and your brains,' I said. 'Goodbye, now then.'

I had a stroll through the village, not more in length than a hundred yards each way. The dry-wallers were finishing the corner outside the chapel, a little place built, from the plaque, in 1822, and in ruins.

The young man using the plumb saw me, and stood, and came in a touch of the cap.

'Mr Morgan, I am Evan Williams,' he said. 'I had the contract for the dry-walling, here. Well, except for this run, I'm told we've got nothing else. We're finished.'

'Who told you?' I asked him.

'Miss Machen's people were here yesterday,' he said. 'I told them there was a lot of work we could do, but they said no. But there *is* a lot of work, and we can do it.'

'Come to work as usual on Monday,' I said. 'I will have others here. Miss Machen is finished. Not you.'

I left him and his few men in a stare, and walked over the bridge to the little wood hut with the Machen sign, and only a small table and chair in it. Rain put cold sparks in my face, and I went in the telephone box and called the Machen office. Somebody answered, and I said to tell Miss Machen I wanted an account of any sum owed, and to take away the hut, and not to come near Gwynaldrod again, and put down the receiver.

I went along to Blodwen's three cottages, on the edge of the village. The gardens had been walled, and cleaned of weeds, and the paths bricked, but the buildings were as they had been, still in bad repair, and nothing, no materials or tools about the place to tell of work to be done.

I went back to the box, and called Sam Hooper, and Ella answered.

'I know he's got everything ready in his yard, there,' she said. 'He's surprised he's heard nothing. The County

Engineer said there's been some trouble, and Sam felt he didn't want to worry you.'

'No worry,' I said. 'Start delivery on Monday, and report to Evan Williams. He will be the building foreman. Another architect will be there. Miss Machen will have a letter from me. I'll talk to Sam before that. And the County Engineer has nothing to do, or say. Understood?'

Sam called that night and said Lys Machen had taken on too much, and had no dependable staff, and refused to delegate work to others, and she was in Scotland for the next week.

'She's clever and she's done a lot of fine work,' he said. 'Your place and this, for example. I tried to tell her months ago. No use.'

'I'm giving the work to others,' I said. 'It's a small job. A couple of months will see it over.'

'Have you got the blueprints?' Sam said.

'Rolls of them, and nothing done,' I said. 'Quantities and prices, yes. Send me what was ordered from you, and let us compare, isn't it?'

'Look out for local politics,' Sam said. 'She has a lot of friends. So has the County Engineer.'

I sent Rhodrick to take the girls to the cottage behind the farm. I had the Mayor to see, and not long after, the Member for the Constituency, both of them, for me, of less importance than any Cacique, the two in by the vote, the other by birth and trained responsibility. I got rid of the Mayor with a cheque for the school, but the Member seemed to be thinking that Westminster, the name itself, held terrors. I put him easy with a drink, and told him I had no interest in any party, and wanted nothing to do with speeches or meetings.

'But your duty as a citizen,' he said. 'Shouldn't you protect those weaker?'

'Look here,' I said. 'It is years since I was in this country. I know nothing about it. From the newspapers, enough are talking. Leave it, now.'

'I am told you have a leaning towards the Nationalists,' he said.

'If I knew who, I would lean towards him with a boot,' I said. 'Tell him so, and goodbye, now.'

Rhodrick came back laughing, and rubbing his hands, and shutting his eyes as if to taste the joke in the darkness of himself.

'Those girls had pads full of drawings, with them,' he said. 'Measuring like old carpenters, indeed. And when could they have the workmen? They want to flatten all round.'

'Send them a couple,' I said. 'Ask Mrs Frew to send up their meals, and a kettle and pots to make tea. What do you know of Lys Machen?'

He stared off, mouth down.

'Well,' he said, slow. 'She has come a long way, see? She uses people, yes, too much. And no thanks. When they have finished, out they are. And never in again, either.'

'But how can she get such a lot of work, and do nothing?' I asked him.

'Easy,' he said, and laughing. 'Sub-contract.'

'But sub-contract with who?' I asked him, sure he knew. 'What about other contracts with her?'

'Wait till the sub-contractor has got enough sub-contracts to do all the work in the smallest area, and littlest time,' he said. 'Big company, it is. All over the country. They make a nice profit? She makes nicer, see. These new dams will make a lovely bit of cash for her. *And* them. And the old mayor makes a bit. So does the old beauty of a boy in here not an hour ago.'

'What new dams?' I asked him. 'Where?'

'Where you have got Gwynaldrod,' he said, and a straight face. 'You will pay a lot of money to build, yes? And they will flood it for you. An Act of Parliament. And pay you how much?'

'They can't do it,' I said, in whispers. 'For what?'

'Water for English towns,' he said. 'Can't do it? They have done it. That beauty from London, this afternoon? He was a spokesman, yes, years ago, when they spoilt Vyrnwy. And he will be spokesman this time. A pig in bloody clover, he is, see? But no knife to his throat. Ah, there is pity, indeed, no?'

I had to think in coldness about it, and for Blodwen, and that poor old silly in her shop in Gwynaldrod, and nothing there to sell except little sweets at the bottom of glass jars, and tea-wrappers and birdseed.

Birdseed.

How many small voices of good friends gone silent, and never, no, never coming back.

So others might think. I thought not.

A little stroll I had down to the office of the *Midday Post* to find Leishon Howells, Mr Steak-and-Kidney-Pudding, and indeed, there he was, in a mix and muddle of bits of paper, and more on spikes, and thick in clips, well, you would find it hard to think anybody could work in such an old devil's push, and have his brains with him. But he had no trouble finding a big envelope full of cuttings about dams in North Wales, and the new lakes, and the fight to save small farms, and lost voices, and the fists of weakness, but no use, and the flooded land became pots of water for English towns. Anger was in the print, in the smell of the paper, coming into the air, holding my lungs in a hot fist, and tears from other eyes were in mine.

Leishon nodded, pushing the spectacles up, looking at the ballpoint, putting the papers in a roll, and back in the envelope, then.

'Impotent,' he said. 'That is the word in English. We are impotent. Without power. If enough money is voted in Westminster, and enough of them can make a profit, what is it to them about farmers? Or us? Who *are* we? A few votes, that's all. A farmer? Who is he? He can't even speak English!'

I looked through the walls in cobwebs of posters, and beyond, to the people, and the country, and across the Atlantic, to the Chubut Valley, and Trelew, and over the pampas, to the Andes, and to Trevelin, and Yr Ysgol, meaning a school, in our language, our first there, that now they call Esquel, in Castellano, meaning skeleton, and so true.

Skeleton.

Impotent, indeed.

'What is it about us?' I asked him. 'We are put from everywhere, and nothing to say?'

'Plenty to say, nothing to do,' he said. 'No power. No army, no police. Naked hands, that's all.'

I talked to Val and Kiri that night, and Kiri put down the sewing.

'The same with us, the Breton,' she said, in English as good, or better than mine. 'We can do nothing. Put carts across the road. Cut telephone wires. What is that? We want many things? We get nothing. It's the same.'

'If they tried it in Australia or New Zealand, they'd have a battle on their hands,' Val said. 'Why hasn't this country got its own government?'

'Not enough believe in it,' I said. 'Only the English have got brains, yes? Scotland, well. A sop or two. But no government. The Irish, yes. They had to fight for it. But they got it. I was given a good picture this afternoon. Black, yes. Not bright for us.'

Valmai put the sewing in her lap, and looked at me.

'Why the Irish, and not us?' she asked.

'I told you,' I said. 'They had to fight.'

'Why don't we?' she asked, picking up the needle.

'They had the help of Irish-American money,' I said. 'How much could we get?'

'We could collect,' she said. 'There are still plenty of us.'

'For bombs and bullets, no, I don't believe so,' I said. 'I wouldn't give a penny.'

'How else will you get it?' she asked me.

'Time,' I said. 'At some time the English will want something from us. Then will be the time. Not before.'

'A long time,' Val said.

'But no girls' legs blown off, and no children killed, and nobody blinded,' I said. 'We will have it as we want it. Because it has come time, and in peace. Yes, Kiri?'

'I believe so,' she said, at the sewing. 'What use to kill?

101

What for? Seven men of my family, my father's and mother's family, they were killed in the last war. For what? Everything is the same.'

'They helped to save France,' I said.

'They helped France to put more chains on us,' she said, and angry. 'What *can* we do? What *can* prisoners do? Look out of bars? As you do?'

I could see my Dada looking at the bars of the kitchen fire, still with his cap on, and nothing, nothing, no, *noth*ing to be done.

There have come times, and I have wanted to go back to the Valley, and look, and think, and remember all of them gone, but still warm, with me, even to the sound of their voices.

But some thought or warning there always was, though, not to go, not to see the ugliness, but stay away, and remember them all in a place of beauty, and peaceful.

It came to me again when Mrs Frew had a telegram, and came crying to say her Mama was ill, and she wanted to go to Pentraeth, and there were no trains or buses till tomorrow, and she might be too late.

'Pack, you,' I said. 'I will have a car, now.'

'O, but too much,' she said, tears stopped. 'A fortune it will cost, yes?'

'Go on with you, girl,' I said. 'Your good Mama is waiting for you. What is money?'

'Where is Pentraeth?' Val asked me. 'Is it worth seeing? Could we go?'

'Worth seeing, yes, to you, as an example of building in the age of industry,' I said. 'Look at the streets of houses, and the chapels, and the public buildings, if you can find any outside Cardiff. Yes. Go, both of you. A lesson for you.'

'Oh, but you come with us,' Val said. 'You can show us what we ought to see.'

'No,' I said, flat. 'Find it for yourselves. You have got new eyes. Mine only know what they have seen. I don't think they will like what they will see now.'

Well, the house was quiet as an old chapel without them, but each night Val telephoned. Mrs Frew had to stay a couple of days to see her Mama better, and Cress said no when I asked if she needed help. The girls were staying in Cardiff, and going up the different valleys day by day, and to Neath, and Swansea, and up, then, to Aberdare and Brecon, and I told Val, enough, come home, and I will take you everywhere else. Almost a week it was, but a week of years to me, and I came to know how much I missed them.

Kiri, yes, especially. The calm about her, the line between her eyes when she drew, and wiped a pen to dip, and draw again, the move of her body when she crossed ankles, the sheen of light in hands and along forearms to the lake shadows in the bend, so I thought about her, and longed to see her back again, and smiling.

But I had more than a bucket of cold water that morning, indeed. I was coming from the main barn after seeing the poultry fed, and going in the old barn to see how the tables were being dressed for the children's tea that afternoon, and I passed the tool shed, a long place for racking tools, and keeping pots, and fertiliser, with a table and benches for workmen to stay out of the rain, and a stove to make tea.

'Experience,' Rhodrick's voice came from the window. 'You can't buy it. You have got to live it.'

'Certainly,' somebody said. 'Those two have got the run of the place, do this, do that. Lys Machen only looked at a job, and we did it. No need for old talk, yes? That one, the Frenchie, coming with airs, here, and always bloody wrong, too.'

'Not wrong,' Rhodrick's voice said. 'A bit of a mistake, it's not wrong, yes? The measures are dead on, you know that. Too much digging there was before, and not marked. If the cottage falls, nothing is lost, see. It will go up again, and better.'

'The old fool is blinded by them,' the first voice said. 'I would like to have a job, and no bloody women. Women? Bits of girls, good God, and knowing nothing, yes?'

'Well, they have got a lot on paper,' somebody else said. 'The drawings are beautiful, with them.'

'Drawings?' that first one said. 'You have got to *work*. What is drawings? *Work* it is. My father built his own house. I made it bigger. With drawings? Don't be bloody silly.'

I walked in, and Rhodrick put down his cup, and rubbed the back of his hand across his mouth, and stood. Two others were day workmen, and their capes still dripped rain, and Tom Davies sat behind with Illtyd Edwards, a carpenter.

'If the rain hasn't stopped in an hour, all of you go home,' I said. 'My two assistants will be back in the next couple of days. What they want will be done, and on the instant. No old chat. And for the benefit of any listening, this is the old fool talking, and go to hell.'

'I am sorry, sir,' Rhodrick said.

'No need,' I said. 'Only shut the windows when you talk. If some of you had windows in your heads, only God knows what would be heard, indeed.'

When I went in, Douglas Gough came out of the lounge and shook hands, and a big man in black smiled, and made a little bow.

'Kyrille's father,' Douglas said. 'He's very worried she hasn't come home. I understand from Cress she's in the valleys, somewhere?'

'For the next week or so,' I said. 'He is welcome to stay here till she's back.'

Douglas spoke French, and Kyrille's father held up his hands, and talked a few moments in a deep voice. I could see he would have a bad temper.

'No,' Douglas told me. 'He must be in Paris tonight to be home tomorrow. He doesn't like his daughter living here with a man.'

'Tell him she is not,' I said, and loud. 'She has a friend here with her, and there are always at least two other women about the place, somewhere. Nothing happens here that doesn't happen in his own house.'

Douglas talked again, and Kyrille's father bent his head of chopped black hair standing as wheat stubble, with a grey winking here and there, and a couple in the moustache, and said something, and went to Cress, holding his coat.

'He went to the Constabulary, and they came to me,' he said. 'Nothing more to worry about. She's not a minor. She may do as she pleases. I told him he can cut out the French lark.'

'What lark is this, then?' I asked, and Cress pulled a face behind his back.

'A man and a woman, they think are always a pair,' Douglas said, putting on his coat. 'They never quite understood about Joseph, poor old boy, and Immaculate Conception. Well, neither did I. Goodbye, now.'

The car started, and Cress shut the door, and stood.

'I thought we would have trouble,' she said, but smiling. 'He came in here, o, looking everywhere, yes, in a hound's sniff with him, and Mr Gough asked if they could see the offices, and I said, I thought you would allow, so I took them up. Well, everything up there was tidy, thank God, too, and he looked and looked, and he put his fingers on her drawings, and he cried like an old baby with him. So I took them downstairs and showed Miss Valmai's room, and Miss Kiri's, and he sat on her bed and cried again, not much, and Mr Gough said to leave him, and let him come down. Well, he came down and tried to give me some money, and I said no, and they had a cup of tea, and you came in. Was I right, sir?'

'More than that,' I said. 'You shall have a present from me. I understand a father being worried. But not about me.'

'O?' Cress said, and looking up from taking out the tea tray, and her eyes were big, and in smiles. 'Why not, now then? Is there something wrong with you? Who can see it? Only ask for a piece, and you shall have it, isn't it?'

She went out in smiles, and I looked at her going across the hall, good big legs, going up to splendours, and a small waist, and everything else very good, too. But asking for a piece was new to me, and if I thought I knew what she meant, I was in shakes to think I could be wrong, because although people seem to talk in the same way and with the

105

same words, times there are in this day that you cannot be sure if, or if not. Well, if or not, the bell rang, and Lys Machen was on the step, hand on the jamb, looking down, and she seemed to me not sure if to come in, or run.

'Mr Morgan, I had to see you,' she said, but not coming in. 'Evan Williams told me you were in Gwynaldrod the other day, and he told you I didn't want him to work any more. It's untrue. I have to be fair to myself. It wasn't even someone speaking for me. I know nothing about it. It was Gilbert George.'

'The County Engineer?' I said. 'I have no liking for him. Now, there is something far more important. Is the village of Gwynaldrod going to be flooded?'

She looked up, but not at me.

'If I can help it, *no*,' she said. 'I've done very little there until I know. It may be two or three months. The decision will be in Parliament. We have nothing to say. Another matter. About the sarcophagus. My office had nothing to do with informing the Regional Surveyor, or anybody else. I must also tell you that I am not marrying Mr George.'

'Well,' I said. 'Shall I say I'm sorry? Because I won't.'

She looked at me, grey, from the side, wide with light.

'Why not?' she barked, as a vixen.

'Because, let me tell you now, I don't like fiddlers with empty pipes,' I said. 'An excuse for something to do with the hands. To cover a search for mischief, isn't it?'

She lifted her shoulders, and turned out to the darkness.

'With signs, nobody can tell,' she said, and sad. 'We are not in the time of witches. You have two girls working here? One is a graduate of the Sorbonne in architecture? I would love to meet her.'

'You have a nice hold on the local line,' I said. 'Who is the little bird?'

'Some of us read the publications,' she said, in a bite. 'For you to say. Goodnight, now.'

Off she went in tap of heels, and the headlights shone, and she growled away, and while she turned into the road, an owl cheered hip-hip-hoo-hoo-hooo, rrrp!

So many times in my life I would like to end with a hoo-

106

hoo-rrp! but it is too simple. We have got to go on, even if we are not sure how, and I can see my father staring at that grate, and nothing, no, nothing to be done.

Mrs Frew came back very quiet, in black, so there was no need to ask, and Cress was on tip-toe not to make a noise, or say something to remind her, so the house was even more like an old chapel, and I wanted to throw something to smash, and shout, dance, sing, anything to bring the healthy blood back in the air. The two girls saved me, and no siren on her rock ever sang sweeter notes for lonely ears than the horn on that little car. Valmai and Kiri came in and run to meet me, and I had kisses from cool cheeks and cold noses, and Val curtsied to the new car, small to make you wonder how two big girls could fit, but they did, with the luggage, and presents for Mrs Frew, and Cress, and a hamper of smoked and fresh salmon, and cockles and winkles for me.

The girls went off with Mrs Frew and Cress, and I expect they were told all they wanted, for Kiri came down and said she was sorry if her father had been a nuisance.

'Looking for you, he was,' I said. 'How is a father a nuisance?'

'He can be much more,' she said, looking at a letter. 'I don't want him here again.'

'Hard, hard old words,' I said, looking at a real frown. 'Are you heartless, girl?'

'No,' she said, quietly. 'But I know him. You do not. I have no mother. She died because of him. I do not forget. I would like, but I cannot.'

I thought of his tears, but I kept my nose from her business, and Cress saved the moments in a jingling tea tray, and Val came running with a letter.

'Look,' she whispered. 'An uncle I never saw just left me a lot of money. Queensland. I never heard of the place. Isn't that marvellous? All right. Now, then. Huw-ee, how about a strictly business deal? You see, yesterday, I had to think twice about buying that car. Now I don't even have to think about offering to buy the cottage up there, and let's say, enough land for a garden. How do you feel?'

'No money passes between us,' I said. 'Use it as long as you like.'

She shook her head, the slow and sure ways that were rock in her character.

'Business deal or nothing,' she said. 'Kiri's coming in halves with me. We'll fix it up for living in, and we'll have the office in the cowshed. But no gifts. I wouldn't rest. It's got to be *ours*. You with me, Kiri?'

'With you,' she said, another obstinate one.

'Very well,' I said. 'If that's what I've got to do to keep you here? I'll have Douglas up, and a surveyor. It's yours at their price.'

Val jumped at me to kiss, and Kiri put an arm about my waist for a soft of lips on the cheek, and very good, both.

'Well!' Val said, and clapped her hands, turning in little rings. 'What a lovely day it's been, hasn't it, Kir'? Wonderful drive up, and Mini purring away there, like a real blue. Then this letter, and just to put the bonnet on it, these two perfectly sweet Galahads'll be here in just about an hour.'

'Galahads,' I said. 'Are they coming to dinner, then?'

'Oh, I told Mrs Frew we were going to have dinner out,' she said. 'I'm happy about it. I was getting to feel like Matilda, sans waltz. The back of a car'll feel like going home.'

The point of that knife I felt go in, and stay in, and troops of guanaco galloped on soft hooves between my ears, but I was sure no Indio ever had a flatter face, or less in the eye.

'Good,' I said. 'Go you.'

The newspaper was a fair excuse while they dressed, and I heard the cars turning in the drive while they were coming downstairs, and Cress opened the door, and Val in a black trouser suit went to meet a young man with long curly hair, wearing a sheepskin.

'My new friend, Glyn Harris, Mr Huw Morgan,' she said. 'Kiri's friend's Joe Campbell, Mr Morgan. We shan't be late, and have a lovely dinner without a couple of nuisances to bother you. Good night, Cress. 'Night, Mrs Frew. See you soon. Huw-ee!'

Kiri's look, passing me, and her smile, strict to the night, were like the sweet my Mama passed to us in chapel to put a bit of sugar in the sermon, but still we had to sit there, and I had to wait till Cress shut the door, and I went in, then, to the drinks tray, but the whisky did nothing except make me cough so much that Cress had to answer the telephone.

'Mr Hooper, sir,' she called. 'Mrs Hooper and him are in the village and they would like to call in only five minutes, and off, yes?'

I nodded, and coughed more, and told Mrs Frew to see if she had enough dinner for three. I just had time for a wash and brush, and Cress opened the door, and Ella gave me a kiss, and Sam looked about.

'Well, I'd heard about it,' he said. 'But seeing's different, isn't it? What a lovely place, eh? El', this is the old Swansea. Remember what I was telling you about? Here it is, look.'

Cress brought the tray of glasses.

'Mrs Frew says she has got poached salmon from the Wye this morning, and her own mayonnaise, and new potatoes,' she said. 'Lay for three, sir, yes?'

'Yes,' I said, and looked at Sam. 'You haven't got a word to say!'

'Thank God!' he said. 'I love salmon!'

I knew he was far from being there for drinks, and salmon, Wye or not, and I was sure when he looked at me in light of the match held over the cigar.

'Huw, we have a hell of a problem!' he said. 'The country's in a bloody uproar. Miners, railwaymen, the lot. A lot of us, I mean, people like you and me, we're on the sidelines. But we've got a bloody sight more to lose. What do *we* do?'

'Is there anything?' I asked Ella. 'I've always felt people like us are helpless. We've got work to do. Isn't it why we pay the politicians to look after the rest of it?'

'Look after it?' Sam said, and filling up from the bottle.

'I like that. I like that *very* much, I do? Listen, if I ran my business the way those buggers run the rest of it, d'you know what'd happen? I'd be flat on m'bloody arse!'

'Sam!' Ella said. 'Your language!'

'I don't mind one bit,' I said. 'A man has got to have more than a gentle word to say, sometimes. Who can he talk to if not a friend? But away from old talk, what is to be done? I've heard this before, not only here. But what is there to *do*? What can *we* do, sitting here?'

Sam looked at the cigar, and over at Ella, and smiled.

'I got a bite!' he said, and sat up. 'Huw, let me set it up for you. I do most of my business in London, Birmingham, Liverpool and Manchester. Everywhere I go, especially in the past few months, I've had dozens of people like us talking to me about a new party. First of all, I didn't pay much attention. You know how it is? It's been tried before. It's failed. You've got a Conservative, and a Labour, and a Liberal party. God made them on the seventh day, and never had the energy to do anything else. He gave up. Now, there's a lot of us'd like to tip it all over. Before the unions do it for us!'

'A job,' I said. 'How will it be done?'

'Some new ideas, new men and women, and money, and more money,' he said. 'The money's no problem, so far. The ideas certainly are. Nobody's got any. Or they're so far out, they sound like comic books, know what I mean?'

'So what is the use?' I asked him. 'Without ideas, what use to talk?'

'Well, that's just it,' he said. 'We have to start out on the far-outs. Find out if they have any chance of working. A sort of laboratory. I've got space over in the yard. Do you feel like giving us some space, here? For, let's say, a dozen people to work?'

'First, at what?' I asked.

'Well, about twenty of us got together the night before last,' he said. 'We agreed on three points. First, a broad survey of money, all over the world. What, exactly, money is. How it's manipulated, and who has the handling, gives the orders, and takes the profits, and if it's done with

Government permission, or if banks are a state on their own. Second, where, and how do prices rise and go on rising? And third, what should be the basic wage for all workmen and women all over the world. A political programme based on that might put us well on the road!'

'If all you want from me is a bit of space, you shall have it,' I said. 'The ideas, I'm not sure.'

'What d'you mean, you're not sure?' Sam said, looking at Ella, and to me.

'Well, if you will have it straight, I think you would end in a lot of old paper, and more facts that are not,' I said. 'I don't think that's what we want. Argument, yes, we have plenty, and words more than enough. What we want is something people understand. Ordinary people. Me, for one. But all of us know a bit more than we show. How will you put the new facts into us? If I see a block of print in a newspaper I won't read it.'

'You're so right,' Ella said. 'That's me!'

'Well, I mean, dammit, there are other ways!' Sam said. 'Television's one. That's why we need money!'

'How many will listen to a lot of dry old stuff?' I said. 'I haven't got a television, for a start!'

'Listen, you start talking about money, they'll damn' soon listen!' Sam said. 'It's what goes in their pockets!'

'But no words they won't listen to, and they won't read,' Ella said. 'I turn it off, and I make fires with paper. That's *that*. And there's lots of us!'

'Will you listen to that?' Sam said, nodding at something beautiful in the corner. 'Right in my own house. My help-meet. Listen to it!'

'I'll help you to meet anything or anybody,' Ella said, and I believed her. 'But this political stuff, no. You're going to work twice as hard as you are now, and you'll have twice as many worries, and I'll have you in bed, again. I won't have it. You've got enough to do. You've built a wonderful business. Isn't that enough?'

'Darling!' he said, and I saw he was holding back. 'If it goes on like this I won't *have* a business, Christ Almighty.

111

I can't meet contracts. I've got to put off a lot of men. So I just sit on my arse and take it?'

'There's nowhere else to sit, and you can't do anything about it,' she said, calm as water. 'I think Huw's right. We're suffocated with words. It's a relief to listen to some good music. Huw, that was a lovely dinner. I wish I could think of you with a really nice wife!'

'Me?' I said, gone in wonder. 'I'm too old!'

'Old?' she said. '*Old?*'

'You can take *that* out!' Sam said, and raised his glass. 'You're as young as you feel, and the more you feel, the younger you are. And fuck 'em all!'

'Sam!' Ella said. 'You're impossible!'

'But I'm dead right, aren't I?' he said, and taking her hand. 'Eh?'

'You'll do!' she said, and looked innocent at me. 'You must think we're terrible!'

'No,' I said. 'Come again. Any time you like. What about Gwynaldrod?'

Sam stood, and put his arm about Ella, and I wished I could put my arm about somebody as beautiful.

'We have to talk about it,' he said. 'I think Lys Machen's right. It's no use wasting a lot of time on building if it's all going under water, never mind what you get in compensation. Westminster's got the answer. See what I mean? We've got to change things *there!*'

'It won't be done *here!*' Ella said, with an arm about him. 'Come on, my darling, I'm driving!'

I had plenty to think about, indeed, and when the girls come back, more.

'Just fancy squatting in bars all night and swilling beer!' Val said, looking at heaven. 'No more. We told them we're leaving tomorrow. Did you know this house is supposed to have a ghost?'

'I'd heard, yes,' I said. 'Who told you?'

'The boys,' Val said. 'There was a murder here. Somebody was cut up and buried, so they've always heard. Any details known about it?'

'I haven't got the smallest interest, and I'm not one to

believe in ghosts,' I said. 'If there are unquiet souls about the place, they are welcome to come and go.'

'What difference?' Kiri asked. 'The ghost or the unquiet, it's the same thing?'

'One has got a shape, but the other is only in your mind,' I said. 'So the Indios believe, too. But I am not an Indio, so I don't believe.'

'What exactly *do* you believe?' Valmai asked me. 'If it's not a leading question? Or plain rude?'

'Neither,' I said. 'I believe in spirit. Everything is in, and of, spirit. Without that spirit there is nothing. How *can* there be?'

'I haven't tried very hard, but I can't believe any of it!' Val said, taking a cup of chocolate from Kiri. 'There's no passion in it. It's only a matter of thinking. If you think one way, you do this. If you think some other way, you do that. It's ridiculous!'

'No!' Kiri said. 'It's not, of course not!'

Valmai flourished a hand and nearly spilled the cup from the saucer.

'Here we have the inveterate candle-burner!' she said, in a deep voice. 'She probably has an arsonist gene. We couldn't pass a church, but there she was, rosary and all, giving it a go. That's the one segment of mental activity where we just do not click. I can't see any reason, and more than that, I don't see it doing one dam' bit of good!'

'But if we had more thought like that, we might have a better world,' I said.

'The operative word there, is *might*!' Val said. 'I don't believe it. I don't see any reason for a better world than we have, or for a belief in anything else than ourselves and good hearts.'

'But what made the good hearts?' I asked her. 'If it was not people believing before you were born, and living in that belief?'

'All right,' she said. 'You use that argument to me? Why don't *you* believe?'

'But I've told you!' I said. 'It's what *they* believed!'

'Yes, but it didn't work, did it?' she said. 'I never knew

my Daddy. He died in a crash. So did Mums. I went to live with Uncle Davy's family in Melbourne. Well, just outside. I suppose I've got a lot to be thankful for. But I can't see any candle burning in it. And let me tell you, Uncle Davy and Uncle Owen, and Uncle Iestyn hated everything to do with it!'

'Who *was* Uncle Iestyn?' I asked. 'The only Iestyn I knew married my sister, Angharad. And they had no children. He died in South Africa. Then she married the Reverend Merddyn Gruffydd, and they went from Argentina to New Zealand, didn't they?'

'And their second son was Uncle Iestyn,' she said. 'He died about six years ago. The bottle, and a fight in a bar in the Outback. But he left the family pretty well off. He was very good to me. That's why I'm here!'

'Perhaps it is the candles,' Kiri said. 'They have no voices. They are only a little light. But we light them with a prayer. Perhaps the prayers burn?'

'Enough from you!' Val said, and stood up. 'You're not proselytising me, bambina. I've dragged you to bed drunk too many times, and undressed you, and held you down in the bed. Candles and rosaries didn't help then. Just plain old fashioned thinking, and a *lot* of muscle!'

'I shall go to bed,' Kiri said, and got up in a sweep about of the dressing gown, like the open-and-close of a fan, and looked at Val. 'I think you are not right to speak of this. A friend does not speak against a friend!'

'I'm not,' Val said, comfortable, in the chair, and pointed a slipper at me. 'That's the best friend we'll probably ever have. Give him a kiss, and *go* to bed!'

'No!' Kiri said. 'Good night!'

Val looked at me with a middle finger between her teeth, and I heard Kiri going upstairs, and I wished I could put an arm about her.

'She gets kind of tied up when she's coming up to, y'know, moon time,' she said. 'Sometimes a week. Sometimes just a day or two. But she *can* be a real burn-out. I don't want it to happen here!'

'If it does, nothing will be known,' I said.

114

'For how long?' Val asked, and sat straight, looking at me. 'I was dead-on about buying the cottage. I want it. I want to go out on my own. I said Kiri's in, halves. Well, yes, she is. Theoretically. When her Dad dies, she comes into something or other, and she'll pay me, yes, but I have this doubt. I've seen her in a bad way. More than once. If I hadn't been there, she might have been, what? That's what I asked myself so many times. What?'

'All right,' I said. 'What?'

Val shook her head and sat forward, fist on chin, looking towards the drinks tray.

'Where's that bottle of whisky?' she asked, from far, far off. 'It *was* there. I saw it. Didn't you?'

I had opened the bottle earlier in the evening. It had gone.

'Cress didn't take it,' I said.

Val looked up the stairs in a small staring smile, if fear were part, and bitter patience.

'I'll tell you where it is!' she said, and got up, but climbing mountains. 'I already told you she hits the bottle. She goes mad. I'm sorry for her. But I don't think I want her around me any more. I'll g⸱t her out of this, and tomorrow she goes. All right with you?'

'If the girl needs help, she shall have it,' I said. 'Where will she go?'

'Home,' Val said. 'I'll pay her fare. There's nothing anybody can do. I've tried the past couple of years. These people, the more you help, the worse they get. Feel like helping me?'

We went upstairs, and Val tried the door, and knocked called, and leaned, tired.

But in that house the doors were old as the walls, and a master key fitted all the locks. I got it from the hook in my room, and quietly opened the door.

Kiri stood in light from the bathroom, naked, drinking from the bottle.

Val ran to her, pulled the bottle away and threw it to smash, and pushed Kiri towards the bed, but she was fighting, a terror, with teeth, and screams, and blind eyes

115

through black hair, but she was tripped and flung flat, and Val kneeled on top of her and held the shoulders down, and for moments they struggled in the half darkness, and in sudden white flash, Val's hands came up, and struck twice. Kiri's arms fell, she moaned, and whispered in French, and started the gulps, and sobs, that screamed coming from deep inside. But then she screamed again, and a fight began, and I wanted to help but among the arms and legs I saw nothing to hold to do any good.

'Go!' Val said, half turning to me. 'I can handle it!'

She smacked again, hard, and Kiri's arms went wide again, and Val got off the bed and pulled off the jersey, and started to unbutton her trousers.

'Why don't you go?' she said, fierce, to me. 'Stop those women coming in here. This is the only way I'll get her quiet!'

She ripped off the bra and put her thumbs in the panties, and bent down, and they were off, and she threw herself on top of Kiri.

Well.

I wish I knew by what path my mind went from two girls on a bed to the rock at the top of the Valley I always stood on to meet my father and brothers coming up from the pit. And why think of evening dark, instead of light, though dark or not, I knew them by the shape, and I often took my father's hand without anyone seeing me, and made my brothers give me room to walk with him. Sometimes one of them would pretend a clout, but they knew if I had coal dust on my clothes, my Mama would have more than a little word, and after a bit, they left me alone, and I was always proud to be part of the men climbing the hill to be home.

I am not sure when did we stop singing at those times, or what took the voices from us, but stop we did, and I have tried to think if I noticed the silence, but no, I never did, and I often wonder why. My father and the men of his age had learned to sing from infancy, and so had my brothers, but my father had known the golden age when pay was in sovereigns. My brothers only lived at the end of gold, and

116

the rest in paper money, though it was never the same, and after the strikes, and the hunger, I suppose the will to sing was not in them, and all they wanted was to leave the slave-pit, and go home to bath, and to hell.

It is not the way to sing.

But as a boy I often felt I was being lifted on those voices singing to the rhythm of boots on stone, and I hear them now, formed and disciplined night after night in chapel, with hymns, first and then the choral pieces, and the conductors coming very strict with them in tone to be got, in quality of sound, in balance, in clarity, if not one, then the other, and no arguing, and rehearse and rehearse, until it would push from your ears. But the night must surely come, and we heard ourselves singing as though the Lord God stood among us, and we knew the conductor was right, and earning in blood the Sir we gave him always, after.

Not sure I am of the year, but we won the choral competition for all the Valleys, and the men came back drunk and senseless, and Ellis the Post was in the trap with Lily, the white mare, half the night with him, picking them up and dropping them home, and going back for more, in stumbles and staggers, or sleeping beside the path. I was down at the watchman's hut with a coke brazier, and conducting a choir of us, and over that waving bit of stick, and nice in the use of the other hand, I saw my good brother, Ivor, pointing a finger at me, but he waited till we finish *I Know That My Redeemer Liveth*, and I put down the stick.

'Come you!' he said. 'Mama has been waiting these hours!'

'Ah, well, now, fair play, indeed!' Morris Evan, the watchman said. 'They have been in song as bloody angels, here!'

'They should have been in bed as bloody angels long since!' Ivor said. 'The rest of you, off. Or your Dadas will be here with a belt!'

Well, the scamper of those legs I can see to this day, but I went home with Ivor, and my Mama sitting in the big chair, elbow on the rest, and a fist in the cheek.

'Will you let me go in the grave, then, boy?' she said. 'Where have you been?'

'He had a boys' choir down with Morris Evan the Watch,' Ivor said. 'He was doing the conducting. Singing, yes, like a lot of old nightingales, with them. The young man is not slow to learn, indeed!'

Mama sat up, and something different was in her face, and instead of the strap, she opened the oven and took a cloth to bring out my dinner, and put the plate on the table, and took off the top, and pulled out a chair.

'Sit, now, and eat well,' she said. 'If we have got old conductors in the house, they have got to have something good in them. And straight to bed, then, is it?'

'Yes, Mama,' I said. 'But I had them right in that last chorus, yes, Ivor?'

'Beautiful, yes,' he said. 'But you were too hard on the beat. They have got to have their breath. You were beating it out of them, boy!'

'O, well, it will come better, I expect,' Mama said. 'He only had a jersey on. Were you cold, with you, boy?'

'No, Mama,' I said. 'I was hot with the singing, yes?'

'Go, you,' she said, and a hand soft on my neck. 'Eat, now then!'

How it came in my head at that time it would be hard to say, but those memories were coming closer, perhaps because bowls of daffodils and crocus were growing in the house, and I suppose they made me think of the mountain, and Mama, and all of them.

I remember her with a foot on the fender, and shelling pods, and the peas going in tinny piddle in the colander, and Angharad ironing the Sunday shirts in starch gloss for my father and brothers, and the plaits red-gold about her face in lamp light, and Ceridwen in the corner using shears to cut patterns, with a tongue poking from chewing teeth, and Bron rolling pastry, and shouting coming nearer, and the deep howl of the pit siren, and a woman's scream, Mrs Hughes, two doors up, and Bron looking at my Mama, eyes gone black in a stare beyond the ages, and holding a hand flat as if to keep something away.

That was the night Ivor died, with all the others, and for days I thought the coffins would never stop coming from Jones, Carpenter, and down to the pit, then, and waiting for the cage to come up, and back to the houses, and the screams and crying of women and children, and slow to the cemetery and a long, slow way in a long, long line, between thousands come over from other valleys, but nobody singing, and the houses quiet for weeks after, and the rain crying for all of us.

I don't believe any of us ever saw my Mama smile again. Bron locked herself away for days, and many a time my father had to put his arms about our girls, in tears with them, and tell them to have strength, but what from, except the warm muscle about them, it would be hard to say. Perhaps it was in those days that the Chapel lost the dutiful, and nobody wanted to sing, and so, no more choirs. A few there were, yes, but not as before, and strange it was to see the doors shut, and not even anybody going in to clean.

Only in that, so much was said. Closed then, and warehouses and old shops now.

Well, well.

Such a difference between then, and today.

And so often I have asked myself, why?

If there is an answer, I have never heard it.

Except, yes, in the writings of the Prophets, but they have got too much salt for many. It is easier to shut the Book, and hide it, then, and find a bit of twank on the radio, because enough noise and you will finish to think, or feel, or worry.

In those days we had no twank.

Idris the Post came in the little red van while I walked about the garden in front of Plas Sûs, looking at the new seedlings, and roses in pink sprouts, and late bulbs, and Cress took the newspapers and letters, and looked at me.

'Idris wants the receipt from yesterday, sir!' she said.

'Receipt for what?' I asked him.

'A registered letter from Australia,' he said. 'Cress wouldn't sign!'

'I had nothing from Australia,' I said.

Cress pointed to the table.

'I put it there, sir, and the receipt on top,' she said. 'I thought you had it when I saw it was gone!'

'I'll have to have the receipt, sir!' Idris said, poor boy. 'The postmaster have got a shocking temper with him, see?'

'He'll have to control it,' I said. 'Call in on your way back, will you?'

Mrs Frew, Cress and Mrs Rhodrick went through the house, and I searched the library and my study, but no letter.

'Did the girls leave before or after the letter was delivered?' I asked Cress.

'After,' she said. 'Their clothes have gone, and nothing in the bathroom, either, and the offices have got only tables and pictures!'

'I knew Kiri was leaving,' I said. 'But surely Miss Val was coming back in the next couple of days?'

'Doesn't look like it, sir,' Mrs Frew said. 'You don't need a dozen dresses for a couple of days, do you?'

I began to have doubts, about what, I was far from sure.

Douglas was in Court, but he called at lunch time.

'Something curious about the whole business,' he said, when I told him. 'The father left his name and address, and his bank. I sent my account, and it's come back marked unknown at both addresses!'

'Did you do something for him?' I asked. 'An account for what?'

'Two hours of my time, and drawing a sales contract for the cottage behind your place,' he said.

'First I've heard of it,' I said. 'Valmai was *go*ing to buy, but it never went beyond talk!'

'It's not in the contract, but a price of a hundred and twenty-five thousand was mentioned,' he said. 'That's why I asked for the name of his bank!'

'Either we are both mad, or I have not come from sleep!' I said. 'It's long beyond me. What could be the notion behind it?'

'We'll have to wait,' Douglas said, hands deep in pockets, and moving from foot to foot, anxious. 'Open any newspaper. People cheat and go on cheating. It seems impossible that others could believe a word, but they do, and the Judges are kept busy, and so are we. What the devil the idea is I have no guess whatever. But there must be something, and I'm sure it'll be unpleasant. For you!'

'And the registered letter?' I said. 'Wasn't it theft?'

'No evidence,' Douglas said. 'Anybody could have taken it. I'll ask the Inspector to look into it. If you hear anything, let me know!'

I had not been near the cottage for weeks, perhaps months, because I had little interest there, and a lot to do closer to home, and I have never liked mud. There was plenty in the dip, and more through the lower meadows. But I was surprised to see a stone path all the way, winding about the fields and up, over the rise. I had not ordered a path, and I was sure that I had never paid for it.

At the top of the ridge I saw that a lot had been done to the building. It was almost complete except for scaffolding at the end, and an upstairs window without a frame. Two men worked at the side, and two or three behind came out with wheelbarrows and props.

I knew none of the men. They were there without my permission, and certainly the alterations I had never known anything about.

'Who is in charge, here?' I called.

A man pointed a thumb towards the house, and I walked in. Plenty of work had been done, walls taken out, a wide stone fireplace burned a good log, big tiles in shades of beige, brown, sand and grey went out to a shining steel and glass kitchen, beyond to a dining-room in panels of oak, and a glass door went out to what had once been the cowshed, but now a long, high room, floored with oiled wood, very good to the eye.

A young man sat at a drawing table, under the roof light.

I had never seen him before.

'My name is Morgan,' I said. 'This is my property. What are you doing here?'

'I'm working for the company,' he said, and got up. 'What do you mean, it's your property? It was sold months ago!'

'What time do you finish here?' I asked him.

'When the truck comes,' he said. 'About five, give it a few minutes. Why?'

'I'm going to find out about the company,' I said. 'Who are the builders?'

He gave me a card, and pointed to the name of the architect, and the company. I never heard of them.

'Something is seriously wrong,' I said. 'Tell the other workmen they will not be needed after today. You'll have the Police here in thirty minutes!'

I was too surprised to feel anything. A two-way macadamised path went up to the turning on to the main road, that I had not ordered or paid for, and there was a lot of building material about the place.

I walked back trying to think, and not thinking, but I got Douglas, and he said, leave it, I will take care.

But I should have been taking care.

It was then I felt an old foreigner. The people I once had known were no longer alive. The world where I had lived was dead. Nobody thought as I did. Everybody was turning things, not the way they should be, but the way they wanted, and nothing came right because nothing was truly honest.

When I got back I went to stand in front of the glass.

You bloody old fool, I said. You have lived many kinds of life, but a couple of bits of girls can still put you into hell. What is the matter with you? Have you gone spindly, with you?'

I looked at grey eyes, and grey hair, and still the reddish complect of years in the pampas and up in the Andes, but I felt as a five-year-old shouting for his Mama. A wonderful feeling that is. The disgrace of forgetting what is known. To be a man, and yet a little child.

'It won't take long to explain this,' Superintendent

Alford said, that afternoon, pulling a lot of coloured book-lets out of a case. 'You see, Mr Morgan, you were lucky. Others have been dead unlucky. Now, look. Here, you're a long way from everywhere. There are other places. Look at these brochures. Properties for sale in Scotland. North of England. Lincolnshire coast. Northumbria. Wales. Devon. Cornwall. Home Counties. South Coast. Ireland. Brittany. Basque country. Spain. Portugal. Morocco. Algeria. Tunisia. Spanish Africa. Even a little money buys you a share in one, or in them all. A lot of people have invested a lot of money in all of this. It's a swindle, start to finish!'

'Swindle, how?' I said. 'Am I part of it?'

'Only in so far as you've been used,' Douglas said. 'I've been on to the Australian High Commissioner. I regret to tell you the young lady, Miss John, is unknown at that Melbourne address. About the other girl, of French nationality, nothing is known. For the moment!'

'But look,' I said. 'A lot of money has been spent on property belonging to me. Why?'

'If you look at these, you'll see there are more than forty odd places where investors can sink their money, and remember I used the word *sink*,' Superintendent Alford said, tapping the brochures. 'There are any number of fly-by-night schemes. People have lost millions. Nobody's said anything very much. Most people cut their losses. They don't want to be known as mugs. This scheme's very well done. The cost of printing this stuff's little or nothing. Then you have high pressure salesmen. Everything's planned to the detail. Your place up there's lonely. Very few people get there. So if you build a place you can photograph, you're halfway home!'

He opened a brochure, and the drawing of the cottage was a copy of the framed wash upstairs.

'You see, they can bring people here,' Douglas said. 'Have you heard planes buzzing about?'

'Heard them, yes,' I said. 'I never took notice?'

'Ah, but if you can show somebody a place going up, and at a nice distance, you've probably made a sale!'

123

Superintendent Alford said. 'As far as it's known, there's about a couple of million, or more, lost in this sort of swindle every year. Nobody seems to learn any lessons. I expect you'll have a few angry "owners" dodging about here, soon. Let me know. That's when I get busy!'

'What about the men working up there?' I asked him.

'They've all been taken down for questioning,' he said.

'And what about the cost?' I asked Douglas.

'It's your least worry,' he said. 'It's not the first time a man's been conned by a couple of good-looking girls!'

'Conned?' I said.

'Victim of a confidence trick,' the Superintendent said.

'Listen to me,' I said, and coming angry. 'Two girls, well-educated, come here, one of them pretending to be a niece, and the other a friend. The friend's father comes here and pretends to cry for her. They work upstairs, and over there at the cottage. All for nothing?'

'Certainly not!' the Superintendent said. 'All the time they were here, the gang was making money. The minute they get the word, they're off!'

'But so much old fuss!' I said. 'Is it worth?'

'Well, if they sell a thousand or so shares on that place, how much did they collect?' Douglas said. 'Your name's good in the area. It's supposedly for you, because it's your property. In other words, they spent nothing. The loser's what's-his-name, Hooper, among others. They've supplied. They'll never get their money!'

'Wrong!' I said. 'The work is well done. I will pay. But I still don't understand one moment of it!'

'It's very simple,' the Superintendent said. 'A few crooks get together. They plan a very simple scheme. Lonely estates are photographed, or drawn, and they're printed in these coloured booklets. These people know there's a lot of funny money. The sort the tax authorities would like to know about. People invest, let's say, a few thousand in shares in a number of properties supposedly owned by the parent company. The parent company doesn't exist except in these brochures and false addresses. This goes on in Europe and the United States, South America, and the oil nations, anywhere there's cash to invest. There's one born every minute!'

'I still can't see what would make a man spend his money on a lot of old nonsense!' I said.

'Easy!' the Superintendent said. 'Your money's honest. Honest got, honest paid. But most of this isn't. The people cheated can't complain. They'd have the taxers after them. Or us!'

'And what is to happen now, then?' I asked.

'Refer all callers to me,' Douglas said. 'I don't think we shall have much trouble. Don't let the workmen finish anything up there. You are not responsible. Let us find out who is, isn't it? First, let us trace those two beauties. You'll see them in custody next time!'

'But what sort of idiots can be caught like that?' I shouted. 'How is money made on such work?'

'How?' the Superintendent said, eyes wide and pale blue. 'There's millions in it!'

I had a feeling I was standing in a forest of rough shapes and silly sounds, nothing solid anywhere, and I could almost see the flash of gold and silver guitars, and the hairy masks of sparring dancers, and suddenly I was sorry for everybody.

There was nothing, no, nothing to be done, and my father staring at the kitchen fire was not sadder than me.

Mrs Frew and Cress kept everybody away in that time, friends as well, and only by spicing their talk with mention of the Police. It was a magic. Everybody went as fog. But they took car numbers, and one afternoon the Superintendent came again with a list of names, though I knew none of them.

'Look,' I said. 'I'm tired of this. I want to know nothing more about it, except who the architect was. Because that place is done better than I could imagine. Who was it?'

'Lys Machen,' he said. 'Contracted by another company. They paid her fee for the working drawings. She thought it was for you!'

'Never had a word about it!' I said. 'Is anything owing to her?'

125

'Not that I know,' he said. 'But there *is* something much more serious. This woman Kyrille Brieuc. What do you know of her?'

'Not so much as you,' I said. 'What, now then?'

'Did she come here with a lot in the way of luggage?' he asked, looking at papers.

'Luggage, I suppose, the usual,' I said. 'But plenty of cases with drawing office stuff.'

'Where were the cases kept?' he asked, a dog at scent.

I went to find Mrs Frew, and she took the Superintendent out to the store shed, and up to the drawing offices, and Rhodrick drove him in the jeep up the rise, to the cottage, and he came back in time for tea, and quieter than he went.

'More here than meets the eye,' he said. 'Those cases are twice as many as the furniture, drawing tables and such, would need. Did you ever hear of the movement in Brittany to have their own government? It's close to the nationalist trends in other countries. Here, for example. Among the backers may be the Arabs. They're helping the I.R.A. Did you hear any talk of it?'

I had to think.

'I heard her talk of the Bretons, yes,' I said. 'They were struggling with the French, as we are in a struggle with the English.'

'Struggle?' he said. 'What struggle is this?'

'Well,' I said. 'If you don't know, should I tell you? I know less. Except what I feel!'

'Are you a Nationalist?' he asked me, head down, a hard eye.

'Of course,' I said. 'Am I English?'

'Are you sympathetic to the Bretons?' he asked, putting papers neat.

'To all of us wanting to be free of foreigners, *and* the Bretons, yes!' I said, flat. 'Especially us!'

'Good night, Mr Morgan!' he said, and off, in a slow step for the front door, and Cress let him out, with a tongue behind his back to make me laugh.

But it was no laughing matter.

The cases were taken by the Police, and Douglas was up that afternoon.

'You will have to step delicate as an old turkey,' he said. 'If it's found that explosives came in those cases, you have got a lot to answer for. Did you sign for them?'

'No,' I said. 'They came on a van. Look, Douglas. I am not interested in this old nonsense. Any more, and I will leave the country. Understood?'

'It will be understood differently elsewhere,' he said. 'Don't forget a lot of Nationalist movements are conjoint with each other. Financed by the same people. Many types of madmen are trained to use explosives. Paid for it. If it kills or injures, or not, so long as it does damage. Is that what you want?'

'Never,' I said.

'Careful with the Police,' he said. 'They don't understand how those two stayed here so long, and you know so little of them. Didn't you ask?'

'What, in the name of God, was there to ask?' I shouted. 'The girls were here. They worked. Who can ask more? One thing I can tell you. It won't happen again!'

He put his overcoat on, arms overhead, and I almost saw his mother, all those years ago, putting him into a pair of sleeves in a way he had never forgotten.

'Listen, Huw,' he said. 'You've been severely had. It's wonderful good luck it didn't turn out worse. What I didn't like about it was any smell of a Nationalist inclination. It's all bound up with the I.R.A. and their guerrilla movement generally. In other words, suspect!'

'Not our lot, surely?' I said.

'*Any* lot!' he said. 'There's always hotheads ready and willing. Especially if the pay is enough. Has anybody asked you for a little bit of cash? To help the movement?'

'No,' I said. 'They wouldn't get it, either!'

'Good!' he said. 'Stick only to that!'

Blodwen came on a Friday afternoon, after I finished paying the men, and while we were having a cup of tea, the cheque came on my plate for the full amount of the loan.

127

'I can never repay all I owe you,' she said. 'I'll never want again. And I'll never have to scrape!'

She was more of a woman, steady in herself, but not so nice as I had known her, though why that was, I found hard to tell even myself. But I suppose if you live among the rough, then rough you will be, and it sounds in the voice, shows in the eyes, plain in the way of the hands, in sitting, or standing, and in the walk. I was sorry for another good one spoilt, and again, nothing to be done.

I took her in late afternoon to Gwynaldrod to see her place, and all the way she called out at the beauty of fields, and hedges in bud, and bushes coming to blossom, and the calm of little lakes with only a fish's silver ring to ripple the shadows of trees.

'It's still the most wonderful country of them all!' she said. 'I've seen most of the others. I'll take this. Mama was right!'

Then, it was, I told her about the plan to flood Gwynaldrod, and I thought she would cry.

'It can't be true!' she whispered. 'This dear little place?'

'The English need water,' I said. 'We have got it. They will take it!'

'But who allows it?' she said, looking about. 'Are they mad?'

'No,' I said. 'English!'

'Do you mean to tell me there's nothing to save it?' she almost screamed. 'Nothing to be done?'

'No,' I said, and I heard again sorest echo of those words of so long ago. 'Nothing, no, *nothing* to be done!'

Her face was her Mama's as I remembered her when she was angry, eyes gone in white slits, mouth in small move at the side, nose wide, and a little shake in the body.

'No wonder people are Nationalist!' she whispered, only short of a scream. 'I'll find out about this!'

We drove back quiet, and in the house I told her of Lys Machen, and she asked to use the telephone. I went out for the nightly look at the farm, and found Rhodrick still in the main greenhouse. I had come to trust him for a good one, but I talked to him only about the farm and the

128

markets and what went on in the district, though never about politics, and I wondered.

'What do you think of this Gwynaldrod business?' I said, while he tied back ramblers for planting.

'I don't think of it, sir,' he said. 'I am finished to think. Those buggers will drown the country. Never mind about us, isn't it?'

'Isn't anybody doing anything about it?' I asked his broad, blue canvas back.

'Do?' he said. 'What *is* there to do? They have got us. They can do what they like. Nobody to say a word!'

'How about the Member for the Constituency, in Parliament?' I asked him. 'Hasn't he said anything? Isn't there any local feeling?'

'Well, plenty, yes,' he said, and cutting a tie. 'Will it do any good? *No*. Any more than the last time. Or any more than this time. Or the next. We are chewed in the chops of bastards. We always have been. We always shall be!'

'But why?' I said. 'Why are we so helpless?'

'Look, Mr Morgan,' he said, and turning to me, and leaning against the rail. 'I've got a good job with you, and a shame to spoil it, yes? But I would give everything to be *us*. To have our own government, and *bugger* the bloody English!'

'How long have you thought in such a way?' I asked him.

'O, since I was little,' he said. 'But no use, see? My father, and his father before. No use. That *bastard* lot in London would do as they pleased. We were *shit* under-foot!'

'Why did you allow it?' I asked him.

'I had a family to keep,' he said, and took his cap and lunch box. 'Good night, now Mr Morgan. We will never come better!'

'Why not?' I shouted at him, in the dark.

'We haven't got the men!' he shouted back. 'The brains. They are the servants of the English. The pageboys of the fine talk. When were they other, from the time of their fathers, and their bloody dams? To *hell* with them!'

Well.

I had never thought that Rhodrick, good old boy he was, could have such feeling inside him. How many more like him? How many women? And what, when they made up their minds enough? Marching in the towns and villages would do nothing except make the traffic worse. Burning farms would only be hurt to people thinking as themselves. Blowing up pylons would black their own homes from having heat and light. Wrecking television masts would stop the old ones from having something to amuse them.

Nothing would affect a vote in London.

There, it was, the devils howled.

I saw the use of a Nationalist party, if only to give despair some cleansing vent, and loose the energy of hate too long held in, perhaps not more than a voter's mark on a piece of paper, but worthless or not, no matter.

Sam Hooper called after dinner and said the Police had been with him all the afternoon, with stacks of papers, and a book of photographs.

'I picked out three of them,' he said, and glum. 'The most charming men you could ever dream of meeting. Well. I was wrong. Ex-convicts, can you believe it?'

'But did you take the orders without any money?' I asked.

'Look,' he said. 'It was your place. Lys Machen was the architect, and the builders were local. Where was the possible worry?'

'I don't see how *she* is in this,' I said. 'The two girls did all the drawings!'

'Wrong, again!' he said. 'Lys did the ground plan, and the drawings were all done by the youngster I put in there. Those two girls were a pair of frauds. He spotted it first time he saw them. I talked to Ella about it. She said not to mention it. It might upset you. Let him find out for himself!'

'I gave them too much rope,' I said. 'Let me have your account. If these builders are local men, let them go back to work, and put the young man in charge. That will be a proper finish to everything. The place has become an old ulcer!'

'Don't say that!' he said. 'You've made a derelict into one of the finest estates in the country. You can't help it if crooks snake a way in. I wish you'd see Lys. She blames herself for a lot of this!'

'Tell her, not!' I said. 'I will see her anytime. Will you tell her?'

I went next day to her office, and if she was still far away, and I further, at least I found out how the pair had worked, though I felt no better, indeed. She showed me a report in a trade magazine that Miss Valmai John of Melbourne, Australia, would welcome enquiries for the restoration of old houses in any period, mosaic flooring, wall panels, and woodwork, with a box number for replies. In two later advertisements she gave my address.

'I knew nothing about it,' I said. 'And no further interest!'

'I wish I'd talked to you,' she said, looking out of the window at mist flowing grey over trees. 'The men who came to see me both knew her. They were French, but the man who did the talking wasn't. The Police have the details. Ever wasted an entire morning answering questions?'

'No need to tell me,' I said. 'Sooner forgotten, the better. What, now, with Gwynaldrod?'

'Nothing, until Commons takes a vote,' she said. 'I'm afraid we shall lose. We haven't the power to stop it. Did you read the Plaid reports?'

'No,' I said. 'I felt that nationalisation was only splintering. But now I think it's necessary. Did you have a visit from another niece of mine? Blodwen Tiarks?'

She nodded, smiling.

'Something new for us, a pop pianist!' she said. 'She's lovely. Gave the Plaid a lot of money too. We can use plenty more. If there's an election!'

'When there is, let me know,' I said, thinking of Superintendent Alford, and Douglas. 'We are not very popular, here and there, are we?'

131

'Why should we be?' she said, sharp. 'Un*pop*ular? It's an honour!'

Somebody came in to say that someone was waiting, and I went from there liking her a lot more, and thinking of her in a suit the colour of a new chestnut, and a white blouse, her hair combed straight, only polish on her nails, pale blue over the eyes, but you would have to look, and a gentle way with the pen, grouping thumb and all the fingers about it as if to protect. I wondered what she did when she was alone. I was sorry to think of her, lonely.

As I was.

'Mr Morgan,' Cress said, when I got back from Brecon. 'The Police have been with a warrant – a warrant, mind you – and they have taken every bit of paper from upstairs, and there was plenty, indeed!'

'Good,' I said. 'What else?'

'They wanted to know if the girls had visitors or friends,' she said. 'Mrs Frew told them about the two Irishmen. Remember? Their night out? Irish, they were!'

'Everybody has got to be something,' I said. 'Eskimos or Irish, what difference? They were only with them once. Leave it now!'

'Once?' she said. 'We often saw them together, Mrs Frew and me!'

'Not my business,' I said. 'How about a good cup of tea, with you?'

I could see she wanted to say a lot more, but I was in no mood for old chat, and Mrs Frew stood in the door, a hen waiting for thrown corn, only too ready to join in. But I was ill to think of slyness in those two girls and almost ready to believe they had never been in the house. Nonsense, yes, but it was how I felt, indeed.

Cress had just poured, and Douglas called, and if he was smiling, it was a serious smile, and he no-thank-you'd a cup of tea.

'Huw,' he said, and careful. 'I want you to listen well, now, to me. I am afraid there will be trouble about these two girls. This Valmai and the other, the French lot. She talked to you openly about her sympathy with the Breton movement?'

'What little we spoke? Open, yes,' I said.

'The Police can find no trace of anyone of that description, in France, or here,' he said. 'To work here, they would need a permit. The pair of them told you they had been to the Sorbonne. One passed, Valmai, and the other failed? They are not in the University records, and the French Police can find nothing of them anywhere else. Here, they seem to have disappeared. Could they have gone to Ireland?'

'I don't know, indeed,' I said. 'I only know I have heard nothing of them since they left here. Why?'

He tapped the briefcase.

'It's suspected that they, and others in this area, men, were part of an I.R.A. team,' he said. 'You are known to have Nationalist leanings. Would you have given them and their friends a quiet place to meet? To plan other I.R.A. bombings?'

I have only a few times been in such anger. Any thought that people would talk of bombings in Plas Sûs was like laughing while somebody held the girl and spat in her face.

'Nothing of bombing has ever been here,' I said. 'Nothing of the I.R.A., so far as I know. I would never permit anything of the sort, don't you know that?'

'A lot might have been done behind your back,' he said. 'They aren't fools. All their doings are carefully planned by people nobody would suspect. That's why they happen. It's why they are rarely caught. Here, they had a quiet place. Out of the way. You never had a thought beside?'

'They were always very natural with me?' I said. 'They spoke. Well. Like a couple of girls at home, isn't it?'

Douglas shook his head, took the briefcase, and hoisted the overcoat.

'No,' he said, quiet. 'They had a job to do, and it was well done. Rehearsed, like a play. That's how they go in the darkness. Who could suspect such natural, innocent people?'

'I can't believe it,' I said.

'How do you think they can bomb, and disappear?' he said, holding out overcoat and briefcase in a question. 'Why can't the Police catch them? Why are people having a quiet drink in a pub blown to hell? And no answer?'

Walking about the farm and looking at poultry, and the roosters in a swagger of colour, and the milch herd, and the horses, and then strolling through the garden seemed to cool the mind and ease worry, though not much, indeed, and I was glad enough to talk of ordinary little things with any of the men, and callers were ever welcome, if I had no liking for the telephone. That trrring-trrring always gave me the jumps.

I heard it in the house, and I wanted to run, but I called myself a fool, and went to meet Cress, to tell me Douglas was on the line.

'Huw? Look, boy. In case there are any more impostors thinking of playing a little game, I'm sending you a letter to sign. A copy will go to cach of those relatives you know to be alive, wherever they are. Then we shall know where we stand!'

'What sort of letter?' I asked him, and ready to say no.

'It's an enquiry from this office, acting as your solicitor, asking each of them to state the names of those in their immediate families, with details of their antecedents, and any known relatives, with their addresses. Do you agree?'

'Well, a lot of old fuss, isn't it?' I said. 'Are we better off?'

'By far,' he said. 'We have to remember you should make a new Will, isn't it? All these people will have a claim!'

'O, *diâwl*,' I said. 'I haven't thought of taking the free ride, yet!'

'Free or not, better to leave things tidy, isn't it?'

Tidy, indeed.

Never once had I thought of death. If I had seen it, and been near it, and many times, there had never come any notion that one day, at some moment, I would be dead, and tied to a stallion, and sent into the pampas with a good smack on the rump. Of course, I was thinking as an Indio, and I knew I was coming more and more to think in their way.

I saw no fault in it. Some of the best men and women I ever met were Tehuelche or Mapuche. But it is not our custom to tie a man to his horse and send him into the pampas at night to find his fathers.

We prefer the business of the box, and groans, and leaving the body to worms.

To hell with it.

Well, Mr Prosser came up with the letter, and I signed, and I gave him all the addresses I had, and the names of all those I could remember. A sad little list, too, of all of them I could see and hear with love, and gone, except in my mind, and given a mark with my fist, a pen, and ink, and perhaps, as with so many of us, nowhere else remembered. I have often wondered if that is all so many of us deserve.

Rhodrick came up that morning in a fine blush of sweat.

'No good to go on, Mr Morgan!' he said. 'Months, here, I have said nothing. Pity, yes. But now is enough, indeed to God. She is taking lambs, here!'

'Who?' I said.

'That old thing down in the dip, the other side!' he said. 'Chickens, yes. Eggs, always. But lambs? O, good God above. It have got to stop somewhere, yes?'

'Who is this, now, then?' I asked him. 'Is there proof?'

'Proof, deep in the mud going down there!' he said, and pointing. 'Her, and a couple more. Old poachers, they are. Living at the expense of anybody, and do they care who will have the blame?'

'Come, you,' I said. 'Let us follow the proof in the mud!'

We walked for almost a couple of miles across the farm and the new land I had bought, most in thick mud because the men had not yet got there to drain, and Rhodrick kicked down a thicket gate, and walked uphill on dry turf to an old gipsy caravan, pretty with paint once on a time, patched and nailed to hold together, and a small fire with a pot swinging over. The dogs growled, but they rolled over when my dogs poked a nose at them, and Rhodrick went up the ladder, and hit a fist on the door.

'Out with you!' he shouted. 'I will put a match to the lot!'

The top half of the door swung out, and a woman old enough to be my mother's mother looked up at the sky, two white, white plaits hanging between her arms, mouth open, eyes masked white, and blind.

'Will you have a curse on you?' she whispered, in Welsh, of the old order. 'Go, now, before I will stretch my fingers!'

'Stretch your old legs!' Rhodrick shouted. 'These lambs you have had, with you. Where are the fleeces, you old *pŵt*?'

She turned inside, and came back with a string-sewn rug.

'It will keep me warm till I am steady before the fires of hell!' she said, and in a giggle to send you cold. 'Satanas has blessed me. I am the black virgin. Will you wait for the curse?'

Under the healthy red of his face Rhodrick was pale. I wondered if I was.

'O, Christ!' he said. 'We've got a beautiful bloody case here, whatever. Should I call the Police, sir?'

'Leave the poor old thing in peace,' I said. 'What good will the Police do? She is in misery enough. Come you!'

I called the dogs, and off we went, and she screeched laughing till we were over the hill.

'Who is that one, then?' I asked him. 'How can she live there by herself? What has she got to eat? Where does the money come from?'

'She does a bit of basket work,' he said, and looking over his shoulder. 'She used to weave. Her, and a sister had a house not far, but before we came to the town. I don't know what they did, they lost it. Then she lived in the caravan in places round here, and she came where she is now two or three years ago. She've got the old age pension, see? She don't live rich, no. But stealing lambs, no excuse, isn't it?'

'If she is blind, how can she see to steal anything?'

136

'No need, sir. That pair of sheepdogs she's got there? No good, of course. Only whelps, they are, see? But they will bring the lambs where they are wanted, and sure it is, she is working with a couple of poachers? Salmon and trout from the river, and birds from anywhere. I will bet my time on earth, look!'

'Do you know them?'

'We all know them well,' he said. 'Never any good. Even in their mothers!'

'I'll call the Police,' I said. 'Leave the old woman alone, and I'll have Mrs Frew fill a basket for her. If I know it, nobody shall go hungry. And let our dogs go loose at night, is it?'

Mrs Frew was happy enough to call the Police, and tell me more about the two sisters.

'Elsi and Neges Aravon, they were,' she said. 'They had a farm up there in Treweryn. Well, the English came in and took the house and lands –'

'Wait a moment, now then!' I said. 'What is this, *took*?'

'They flooded it all for the lakes, and had the water in England,' she said, and surprised. 'Didn't you know? Well, I suppose the sisters had a fight for it, but they were taken out by force. They never touched the money they were given. They say it's still in the bank. I think both of them went a bit, well, savage, with them. Tinkling in the head. This one, here, her name is Neges. The other one, Elsi, she has got a shop in Gwynaldrod, poor little thing, yes?'

Well.

I made well sure that Neges got her basket every week, and I went in the jeep to Gwynaldrod, and walked in the shop of Elsi, with more dust than any pampas shed, and less to sell than a child's make-believe.

There was a likeness between the sisters, but Elsi looked with a clear eye and she was clean in person, and the hair was grey, piled, tied with a green plastic ribbon.

'I have an interest in Gwynaldrod,' I said, and no words before. 'I would like to buy your property here, if you agree?'

'No,' she said, soft, and not looking at me.

'I will accept your price,' I said.

'No,' she said, without a move, quiet.

'If I pay for the privilege, would you let me alter the building to come in line with the rest of the village?' I said. 'I want to make it all as it might have been in the tenth century. We have the evidence to show how it could have been, then. Everybody pretends we have no history of our own, haven't you found it so?'

'No,' she said, still no look to me. 'They will take me from here only in a shroud, and they will be cursed every step of the way, and cursed evermore after. Have you heard? Are you finished?'

'I talked to your sister,' I said.

'She is long dead. Go *from* here!'

No sense to go on, and I knew she was tinkled as her sister, but I was certain she should not come to harm, and I called Douglas and told him.

'Hopeless,' he said. 'Cracked as old pots, the pair of them. Wait for them to die. They have got a fair estate. A windfall for the English government. The irony's lovely, isn't it?'

'Could you convince them?'

'Not enough sense between them to smooth a small ball of paper,' he said. 'Everybody says when they were young they were beautiful, and extra-smart. I don't know what happened. They are daft as a couple of old pishies, there. And no sign of better, isn't it?'

'Any news of Gwynaldrod?' I asked him.

'No,' he said. 'And no news is bad news. They'll push it through, you will see. The place will drown. We are not the masters of our own house. We are only the poor pricks with a begging bowl. One step down, and we will be using the leper's clapper. Can you hear it?'

I wondered about national morale if Douglas could talk in such a way.

Rhodrick and the men about the farm were no different, as I knew.

Mrs Frew spoke only of the Bloody English. Cress did. Others did, and no better. But many said, look, leave it,

138

will you? We will have no gain with our lot. No experience, and less authority. Who are we to speak of self government? With what?

In them the voice of almost two thousand years of slavery spoke plain, and loud, in the voice of the slave-owners.

'Yes,' Lys Machen said, that afternoon, pouring tea. 'We are truthfully a lot of slaves, pretending not. But the shackles are on us. How to get them off, God knows. I have tried, but I think the women are worse than the men. Less spirit. They are afraid the English wages and pensions will stop coming. Then what?'

'Vote Liberal,' I said.

'Of course,' she told the teapot. 'Not so English as the Conservatives, but less Nationalist than us. Wanting our own government, good or bad, who is arguing for us?'

'Wait you,' I said. 'Have we got a minister fit to take charge, with us? I mean, anywhere?'

'Of course we have!' she said. 'Who runs the industries and businesses? Universities, schools? We have plenty of brains to do the job. We don't need outside help!'

'How about cash?'

'More than any of the others,' she said. 'And far greater potential. We've got most of the coal. All the tin plate. Iron. Steel. With the oil from the Celtic Sea, we'll have more than enough. There are only two and a half million of us, remember. The pie will cut in far larger slices. For us, for a change!'

I was unsure. By their talk you will know people. Even in the tone of voice you will know them better. Lys, yes, I liked. I knew she had a temper, and she spoke to the point and no old nonsense. She was gifted in her profession, sensible, and from the look of her office, no clutter, no confusion, efficient. But to champion the Nationalists made a sour little note, somewhere, perhaps because I had seen us long before. We were not enough on the ground in Patagonia, though we could, certainly, have voted more representatives to the State, and to the Federal Government, and so kept our influence alive. But not many of us wanted politics, and after the floods, when the country filled up with Basques and Arabs and Lebanese and Italians, and all the others, time was out for us, and the end was not far.

I had a notion that we in Wales were fighting the same type of rearguard battle, and depending on feeling rather than fact and cold reality. Too many times I had seen big healthy businesses taken over by amateurs, and go in ruin from month to month, and governments shaky from here to there, and the value of money losing by the day, and only because nobody knew enough to control, and lack of working knowledge led to blunder.

Wales, of all those two-and-a-half million people, needed breakfast, dinner and tea, and a bit of supper, for at least a year from now, or something more than a few shouts tomorrow and a couple of flags.

But what, only God in his wisdom could tell, and if He had any, well, true it is, we had seen little evidence in all our history, never mind in our own time.

The shaking thump of the shut back door and somebody running across the parquet downstairs had me out of bed, and quick, but before I could get into slippers, I heard footsteps thudding on the stairs, and then knocks on the door.

'Mr Morgan, can Cress and me come in?' Mrs Frew said, in a high little voice.

'Come, you,' I said. 'What, now then?'

They both had faces of frightened children, standing, staring.

'What is it?' I said.

Mrs Frew sniffed a big, big breath, and sighed it away.

'We saw the ghost!' she whispered, and looked at Cress. 'Plain, it was, no?'

'Running, and white, and plain as plain,' Cress said. 'No dream about it, either.'

'Well, well,' I said, to calm. 'I was told about it. I wish I had seen it. Sûs would have loved it. She would know how to talk to it, too. I think a cup of tea would do us all a splendid bit of good, don't you?'

'Not for me,' Mrs Frew said. 'I wouldn't go downstairs

140

tonight again for all the gold in the banks!'

'Me, neither,' Cress said, and shaking. 'O, Mr Morgan, I'm sick with chills, here!'

'I'll dress, and have a look about the place,' I said. 'If somebody's having a joke, they'll find out when to laugh, indeed!'

I went in the dressing-room and put trousers and coat over pyjamas, and took the duckgun from the cabinet, and out I went. As I thought, there was no move anywhere, except the dogs coming up to have a sniff and a scratch of the ears, and off. I found it strange, if there had been something, not one barked, that I heard, anyway.

I was dull.

The house was silent, and again, I had those thoughts of my Sûs, resting quiet with her Grandam, and her Mama, and her sisters – yes! – Lal – in the ripple of the river, and the willows' whisper, and in all this world, no place prettier or more fit to hold the only beauty I had ever known.

That was wrong, too. I had known my own Mama, and my sisters, none lovelier, or with more of beauty than them. How did I forget? I came angry with myself, forgetting so much, and I stopped by the tray, and had a good couple, and they came so well to the teeth, I had a couple more, and looking in the fire, and seeing faces I had known, and others not.

Upstairs I went, and took off my clothes, and went in the bedroom.

At first I saw only the bedside lamp. But on the far side, on the floor, Mrs Frew and Cress were under blankets.

They were both awake.

'I hope you won't mind, Mr Morgan?' Mrs Frew said. 'We couldn't face the thought of sleeping on our own, down there. Only tonight, isn't it?'

'If you are going to sleep, get in bed,' I said. 'There is room in plenty.'

'O, Mr Morgan, we are an old nuisance, here,' Mrs Frew said. 'Leave us, now then, and have your comfort, isn't it?'

'I doubt if any man ever found a woman in bed a

141

nuisance,' I said. 'And two of them, a half of less. Into bed with you, now then!'

They both got in, Mrs Frew on the outside, Cress in the middle, next to me, and I put out the light. Not long, and I felt her warmth. Wonderful, it is, to feel the warmth of a woman near to you. I suppose Cress could feel that I was near, too.

And the next, a hand. Blunt, yes, but knowing.

Mrs Frew snored.

Cress turned, slow, not to make a noise, and raised herself to have the nightdress up, and pulling more, and she was against me.

'Come you,' she whispered. 'If a piece you are wanting, take. I have wanted too long. Tidy, now, isn't it?'

Nobody tidier than me.

Tidy, indeed.

I wonder is a man ever tidier than in a good girl.

I am sure not.

Tidy, yes, indeed to God, and His good mother.

'Huw, what are you doing for the next couple of days?' Sam asked me on the telephone. 'Ella's going to her mother's. Poor old dear's got neuritis. I've got a business trip to Cardiff and Swansea. We could come back on the coast road through Cardigan and Aberystwyth. Lovely country. Been that way, have you?'

'Years ago,' I said. 'Yes. What time?'

'Seven do you?'

Seven chimed, and he was at the door, and Lys, and another girl I had seen in her office, sat in the back.

Well, I was happy about it, and they were happier to see Mrs Frew's luncheon basket, and a box with the wine and glasses grunted in by Cress.

'You always have wine with a meal, Huw?' Sam asked me, driving out.

'Always, since I went to Chubut,' I said. 'Nothing in a chew tastes good without. It is the added blessing, indeed!'

'Beginning to agree with you,' he said. 'Hear the news?

142

The miners are out. General election's in. Poor bloody miners always catch it!'

'More money again?' I said. 'Will they always have to strike for a few shillings?'

'Enough to live on,' he said, nodding at a cow crossing the road, o, a stately one, as if she knew everybody would stop. 'That's against the law. That farmer ought to be fined!'

'Why?' Lys said, quiet. 'There were cattle long before cars. Seniority? *Priority!*'

'Doesn't follow,' Sam said, just as quiet. 'I might have slammed into it, and killed the four of us!'

'And the cow,' Lys said, still quiet, 'Cows cost money. We cost nothing!'

'Ah, come on, Lys!' Sam said, a little laugh. 'This one of your edgy days?'

'But who would give a curse for any of us?' she said. 'Bury us, reckon the wills, and finish. But you would have plenty to pay for that cow, depending on her milk record. Have you got a nice milk record, Sam?'

'No,' he said, no laugh. 'But you're making me feel like a drink!'

'Pubs won't be open for hours,' Lys said. 'Would you like some coffee? Instant, of course. But you'd have to stop the car to boil the water. And the wood is wet from the rain last night. Everything is against us, isn't it?'

'Lys,' he said, chin down. 'Has anybody ever booted you in the arse?'

'Many have wanted, yes!' she said, and both girls laughing. 'They thought better, though!'

'There's too much of this women's lib crap these days!' he said, steady, and chin further down. 'If you want to be treated as men, you ought to get the same treatment!'

'The same as men, no?' Lys said, quiet again. 'As women, yes. Not little dollies, or fly-by-nights, or anything else, except as *us*. Different in form, in outlook, and even in accomplishment. Are we to be kicked every time you disagree?'

'Give over!' he said, harsh, but pretending a laugh.

143

'You've lost many a job by saying too much!'

'Jobs I didn't want, yes,' she said. 'I got those I wanted, though. And without any advice or help, I'll have more!'

Well, you would have to go to the Pole to put your nose in colder air.

'Are you two playing a game, or do you like making people uncomfortable?' I asked Sam.

'We're saving petrol on a business trip,' he said, in a bend of the head. 'She's the architect on a few jobs, and I'm supplying materials. It's no game, believe me. I'll work with no woman again!'

'Good!' Lys said, and put a hand on the door catch. 'Stop here, please. I won't go with you another moment!'

'Ah, for Christ's sake!' he said, but not slowing. 'Lys, grow up!'

'Stop the car!' she said, and a tremble in the voice. 'Or I will throw myself from the door!'

The door swung out, and Sam slowed enough to throw us forward.

'You're out in the bloody blue!' he shouted. 'Hell's the idea?'

'The idea is to be away from you, or anyone like you!' she said, calm as the windless air. 'My love to Ella. Come, Teleri!'

They both got out, with their bags, and stood on the grass verge.

I opened my door and got out, too.

'I can't leave them,' I said. 'Thank you!'

'What about the lunch basket?' he shouted, in real anger.

'Enjoy it,' I said. 'Compliments of Mrs Frew and Cress!'

He leaned on the seat to look up at me.

'You're not blaming me for this, are you?' he said. 'Wasn't my fault?'

'I'll go to your office in Cardiff,' I said. 'Leave a message where to find you, will you?'

I shut the door, and he waited a moment and went, in a screech of tyres that said more than words.

'There was no need for you to follow,' Lys said, and smiling. 'We are safe enough!'

'I'll get a car,' I said. 'If you allow, of course?'

She smiled the wide, thin mouth of resignation, and began walking, though neither allowed me to carry their suitcases, and both had a large and a small. I turned to wave down a car, but he passed without slowing, and the second and third, the same. A tractor turned out of a field in front of us, and I called to the driver, a young man, hair to the shoulder enough for a girl.

'Just up the road here you can have a taxi,' he said. 'Hop up. I'll ride you there.'

A bumpy old ride, too, and I heard not one word of what he was saying over the noise of the motor, and it must have been interesting, because when we turned into the garage and he switched off, he was still saying her throat was slit, and no clues, and not a word since.

'Well, well,' I said. 'A lot more could do with it, no doubt, yes?'

A very old-fashioned look he gave me, and shook his head at the note I offered, and turned out.

'His sister he was talking about,' the taxi driver said. 'Murdered, she was, in England, there. Talks of nothing else. Mad as a bloody hare, yes!'

Going down to pick up the girls, I thought about the morning's strangeness, well, anyway, to me. I am sure, in those years ago, that I remember so well, as a boy, there was less bicker, few quarrels, and a lot more laughing. Plenty of wags were about, and nobody was in want of a joke. But today, everybody seemed touchy, even the most sensible, and ready to fight over the smallest word, or argue any remark that had an edge, only to soothe a hurt in themselves, perhaps, or to have the pleasure of drawing blood in others.

But laughing, no.

In that time we had no radio, or television, or cinema. We had no more space to find ourselves, to strengthen the inner man, and to savour what was spread before our senses.

We were far more ourselves, our own men, and certainly the women were very much their own women, servants of none, and equal sharers in all.

Everything to be heard in this day, it seemed to me, had a bit of the rancid, and what came as jokes on Mrs Frew's radio out in the kitchen, that people laughed at, were not worth a move of the face.

I was puzzled why they laughed, and I asked Mrs Frew, and she said they were supposed to be the comics, and anything they say is funny, so laugh, I suppose? Everybody else is, so you might have missed the words or something, and you don't want to feel others are having more than you, isn't it? So laugh. It does you good, yes? Not much to laugh at, these days, so be thankful for a bit of crust.

Sure I am that my father, and his kind never thought in such a way. If somebody was funny, they would laugh, yes, but if he was not, they gave him the straight face, and silence, and that is worse than a plague of scorpions.

I asked Lys what she thought.

'We are all a bit thick in the skin,' she said. 'Faith, hope and charity, no, no more. We haven't got them, because we don't want them. Faith in what? Hope for what? And who wants charity?'

'Well, you are having a splendid life, then?' I said. 'What is keeping you going?'

'Ourselves, and what we can do,' she said. 'Should we look to others? What for?'

'But others must be necessary, no?' I said. 'Without others, where is the world?'

'You have got to choose,' she said. 'Plenty of worlds, there are. Find yours, and stay there!'

As a rock she sat, staring in front, and I had quick thought of the County Engineer, and wondering what he could have in common with this one.

Speak of the devil.

'I'd like to turn off here,' Lys said. 'I'd like to show you one of the loveliest farms in the country. Probably the oldest. Not so well stocked as yours. Certainly not so well kept. But it's a perfect example of one of our farms in

146

about the fifteenth century. Or long before. It has fourth-century foundations and in a few places I'm asking to dig. But the owner says No. Let them rest!'

'Good!' I said. 'The same it will be with me. No digging, isn't it?'

'So how shall we ever know how we were, once, here?' she asked. 'Everybody thinks we ran in woad. How many know of the speech of Caractacus before the Senate in Rome?'

'Him, I haven't heard of,' I said. 'Another liberal, yes?'

'One of the many, and among the first and best,' she said, and Teleri laughing. '*There* is the very knot of our trouble. None of us know our history. We are a people of shadows. But when did we have our language? Our critics cannot answer. We are as old as Sanskrit. Can the English say so?'

'What, now is this Sanskrit, whatever it is?' I asked her. 'Why should the English worry?'

'No worry,' she said, and laughing. 'It is a root language of mankind. And our language has its roots *in* it. English is an old jumble of everything. Very useful, mind? And practical. The language of the industrial revolution, first. Of a certain kind of scholarship. But it's like a lot of others. It can't always be translated. A language of the machines? Perfect. Of poetry? In one sense, yes. But oblivious to translation. Well, except in the lame, and hop-a-foot-pull-a-foot-back. They are looking for parallels. They forget the warm mouth of those that said it. They look at words. They never think of the stretch of the minds behind, do they?'

It was all nicely beyond me.

That farm was in surety a small wonder, of stone, one long, broad room, slate-floored and raftered, down, with two others half the size, a big kitchen with a brick oven, and an iron stove, and a new bathroom, and four bedrooms upstairs, a bathroom, and above, five attic rooms, and all furnished in nothing less than three-hundred-year-old pieces, all of them beaming in wax polish.

'I brought you here for a reason,' Lys said, cold, apart. 'The owners are burying their mother tomorrow. That's one reason Sam didn't want to come here. So he made a good excuse. For *me*. I would sell everything I've got to make a down payment on this place. They want to sell. But it's more than four hundred acres. I can't meet the price. We're up against the finance companies. They'd buy this place, put in what they call improvements, and sell it to some alien for three or four times their buying price. It's a racket. A tax write-off. Do you want to buy it? Everything in?'

I nodded.

'I'll buy,' I said. 'I'll send Rhodrick to look at the land and livestock. Why didn't Sam want to come here?'

'He's a scout – or a tout – for many of the finance companies,' she said. 'I told him I would show you this place!'

'What finance companies, then?' I asked her.

'They buy properties, and put in a bathroom and electric light and sell for five times what they paid,' Lys said. 'Ten times. A mortgage is good profit, isn't it? For years. The English, or who they are, can take a good tax cut. For them, it's a farm. A farm can bring deduction. Buying and selling these properties has become a profitable business. The heart of the land is being sold to foreigners, isn't it? For solid profit. To moneylenders!'

'First I heard of it,' I said. 'Am I one?'

'Well, no, of course not!' she said. 'But I wish you could buy a few derelict farms and hold them. Kill the price maniacs. The government should be doing it. But they don't. Young people can't get a house. If they can, what's the price of the mortgage? Anything they can afford? This country is solid in debt, Mr Morgan, and nothing to save us, and I'm talking of the *young* people. Not the ones who've had the years to make money in good times, but the young people *now*. How can they have a house?'

'Beyond me,' I said. 'I don't know the market.'

She laughed.

'How many do?' she asked the roof. 'You've got to go to London to find out, yes? How many will tell you?'

'A bright old lot you are,' I said. 'I wish I knew another

country to go to. But I don't believe I'll find a better one than this, indeed!'

'Keep the thought warm with you,' Lys said, and a hand on my knee. 'Make sure, now then. We are the best. If we can scrape the scum. Do you want to see the rest of this place?'

'No,' I said. 'I'll buy!'

'No surprise,' she said. 'Driver, the road to Cardiff, direct, if you please!'

Not a word more till we got to Cardiff, and I dropped them at Ansell's, the builders.

'Thank you, Mr Morgan,' Teleri said. 'I am sorry not to have talked to you. My family are still in Chubut. I am the only one here. Tom Rowlands, Gaiman. Do you know him?'

'O, girl!' I said. 'Good God, now then. I will be back the day after tomorrow. Will you promise to telephone? We will have a cup of tea, isn't it? Of course I know your family. Tom and me were young together!'

'Tom was my grandada,' she said. 'Dafydd is my father, see? He has finished the shearing, and a wonderful clip, he says!'

Only the words brought a homesickness sharp enough to send me back to Patagonia, and I could see the miles of willows, and wheatlands patched with pasture, and the glittering green run of the river, but when I began thinking of the Andes, well, I had to stop or I would have gone, then and there. It was sore to the heart, thinking of fishing rainbow trout in the silence of broad lakes, and salmon on the waterfalls, and riding after the wild boar, and it seemed to me, standing where I was, breathing the stink of a lot of old cars, and listening to a buzz of chat I only half understood, indeed to God, I was wasting good time.

My son, always think well, once again, my father said, and I have never forgotten his voice, and I am glad I heard him, then, for when I got to Sam's office, they gave me a telegram sent on from Plas Sûs. Taliesin, the son of Bron and Ivor, was in London and wanting to see me.

Well, I sent a telegram, and wrote Sam a note, and got

a car back, quick, and all the time, I was blessing my father for keeping me from a stupidity. I wonder how many sons have blessed a father for a good bit of advice so long ago.

Well, from the moment I met him at the station we were two of the same root. He was so much like Ivor, I could have cried, but, O, Bron was in his smile. A big fellow, too, and hair well-cut, and a good bit of London tailoring, damn, I wished he were my son, and the place would never hold me.

Most of the night we talked, and if the names and places were far from me, I listened, and when Valmai's name was said, I stopped him, and told him what had been, and he frowned and shook his head.

'Valmai is a pocket Venus,' he said, raising a hand to about five foot. 'A doll of all dolls. She came to us from Australia about five years ago. Dad used to take her round, and when I had free time I did. She loved animals. She went to Uncle Owen, and got a degree at Northwestern University. Top of the year. Dentistry. I just had a letter from her. She's in Jakarta for the next couple of years, working in the dental lab. She's a research fellow. How can these people get away with tales like that?'

'Because a lot of us are not careful,' I said. 'I should have made enquiries. Where are you in this Plaid Cymru business?'

'Up to the neck,' he said, straight. 'I'm South African. By birth, I'm Welsh. I feel the blood. So did Mama. What do you think of the chances?'

'Here and there, perhaps,' I said. 'Generally, no. It will depend on the young. The old are rotten. Sorry I am to say it, see?'

'My father would agree with you,' he said. 'He came back here some years ago. But he couldn't stand the conditions. He said he was just plain glad to get back!'

'Wait, now then,' I said. 'Your father, my brother, Ivor, was dead long before I went to Argentina!'

He stared at me, and his face went comical with him, and he began to laugh, and stopped.

'I've been feeling there was something not quite on key,' he said. I'm sorry I didn't make this clear. My father's name was Taliesin. He was the younger of Grandfather Ivor's sons. My Grandma was Bronwen!'

I got up, and stretched muscles with a tiredness unknown before, and O, God, the years of age, and weight.

'We live in grey little worlds of our own,' I said. 'We forget. Sleep well. Good night, now then!'

I almost knew why I had accepted Valmai as one of the family. Without thinking, I had missed a generation.

It is enough to know, and regret, and nothing to be done, except go to bed, and try to sleep, and every moment all of them in the Valley coming to life once again, to poke a tongue, and ask if I was going spindly with me.

Not many can forget a generation of the living, and never miss, for one moment, any one of them. Selfish we live, and selfish we always are. But grief is in the wakening.

I began to have my wits with the cup of tea Mrs Frew brought me, and after breakfast we were off in the jeep for a look at the country, and he stopped dozens of times to *oh!* and *ah!* at the lakes and mountains, and the half moon of a white-bearded bay the colour of the sky, but he always pulled up at stands of trees and went to look at them, and talk to the men there, and from their faces I saw they had respect for him as a forester, and I knew well that Ivor and Bronwen were smiling then, somewhere, and well content, as I was. It is something lovely in the spirit to know you have the honour of some of the same blood as a good boy.

We went all the way along the Lleyn, looking at country not much changed in the past couple of thousand years, and showing little of our time, except in the trailer parks, and in the food at the cookshops, and what they call hotels. Nothing was there of the dishes I had known, or of the kitchen of Mrs Frew and Cress.

'Most of it's out of plastic bags or cans,' Taliesin said. 'Mama won't allow it in the house!'

'Good girl,' I said. 'Your great-Grandmama would have laid about with a chopper, indeed!'

'It saves time,' he said. 'If women have to go to work, what are they to do to feed a family? It takes a hell of a time to cook a good meal. I know when Mama goes off to visit her father, Dad and me feed out of cans. We just don't have the time, and Mama raises hell every time she comes back. Lucky my sisters are in school. Gareth's got a practice in Rhodesia. We expect him to be thrown out any day. Or worse. He's more or less a black Plaid Cymru. He doesn't like apartheid. Neither do we. But you haven't got a hell of a lot more here. Have you? With the English?'

I said no word because he had a finger in the wound, and there was little to say, and nothing with sense.

Three days of slow travel we had, and every moment and place a joy on its own, but we were coming to the valleys, and he wanted to see every yard of them, Big and Little Rhondda, and the little valleys in between, but I was trying to think of some way to take his mind from our Valley, that everybody had so often talked about, and his father, until he made that last trip, and went home to forget.

'Couldn't get a word out of him,' Taliesin said, up on the cliff, looking at the proud rock of St David's Head. 'All excitement before he went. Clamp down, after. We often wondered why.'

'Why didn't he write to me?' I asked him. 'How did you know how to find me?'

'First, he didn't know where you were,' he said. 'Second, we had a letter from your solicitor, and my father cabled me to go and meet you. You're the mystery man of the family. And the third millionaire!'

'Who are the other two?' I asked him. 'And how do you know?'

'Simple,' he said. 'Credit ratings. The other two? My father, and Uncle Owen. He's got patents as long as your arm. You older lads had a chance. I mean, to make a bit and salt it. If we make any, the God damned politicians take it away from us. To make a nice living for themselves? They can vote themselves their own money. Who else can?'

152

But he had a map on his knee, and he went everywhere he wanted, and the nearer we were to the Valley, the more I wished he would turn back. But turning back was not in him, and so I knew he was of the blood, and true. The Valley was not marked on the map, but when he turned on the road, I knew it was hopeless because signs were up, and when he saw the first, he shouted triumph, and turned to me.

'We're here!' he shouted, like a little boy. 'I'll cable Dada from here. Only for proof!'

Well, I have always looked for the little miracles, and then was a real beauty, when the engine coughed, and stopped, and he trod hard on the brake and pulled at the other.

'No petrol,' I said. 'Very good, and no odds. You will have a taxi, and go there, and come back, and I will see this one right, and I will wait tidy in that little pub by there, and everything splendid, isn't it?'

'Ah, you're not coming with me?' he said. 'I thought you were going to tell me where everything was?'

'You will find everything under the slag,' I said. 'Only for that, I am not coming with you. Your good father felt the same, no?'

He looked away from me, to the hills that were, and slammed his palms on the jeep door.

'I'll go and find out what you mean,' he said, and walked across the road, and not far, up the hill to the garage. I went slower. But I had noticed a change, when I had time to look.

Strange.

All the houses, both sides of the hill, were in bright of fresh paint, no two the same, and the gardens sang with flowers.

Well, it was something new with us. I had to think when I had last seen flowers in a front garden. Back gardens, generally, were put to vegetables of every kind, with flowers here and there, a few snowdrops, daffodils, crocus, primroses, violets, and roses, all wild and taking their proper time, no old nonsense from anybody.

But these front gardens, not very big, were in song with them, and beautiful, indeed, one after another all the way uphill, as if one had joined in a chord with another, and all were singing, one with a voice next, and a good, strong hymn rising in hope, yes, for a better day.

'What is this, now then?' I asked the garage owner, Howell Williams, with his name on the truck. 'I never remember a flower in the Rhondda. The place is in flowers with us. And fresh paint?'

'Well, yes,' he said, and filling a can from the pump. 'But we have got a royal man, see?'

I looked well into his eyes, and he was a Countryman of mine, and so I knew, and knew well, he spoke good truth.

'What royal man is this?' I asked him. 'It is somebody from the ordinary with us, yes?'

He stared at me, and stopped the pump.

'Well, where have you been, boy?' he said. 'Goodness gracious, everybody do know, isn't it?'

'Who, now then?' I asked him, and coming angry. 'Don't tell me some telly star, or I will hit you flat!'

'Telly star, my arse!' he said. 'Nothing to bloody do with it. The next King, he is. The bloody Prince of Wales, boy. *Y Twyssog*. Ours. At long flaming last, see. The last one, they told to bugger off, yes? But he was bloody right. He gave his royal word to a girl. He kept it. The royal word. *That* is the difference. The royal word is *not* to be broken. He will have everything taken away. Except his word. His word is *there*. Naked. *That* is the royal word. It is what we have got, yes?'

'If we have got it, good,' I said. 'But what is it, now then? What can he *do*?'

'Well, what he told us he would do,' Howell Williams said, letting the last dribbles of the pump echo song in the can. 'In two languages, yes? English, and ours, isn't it? No room for doubt. *Two* languages, the same. Will he break it to us?'

'But what did he say?' I asked. 'I was away from the country. I never heard it.'

'O, damn!' he said, and impatient. 'I thought everybody
154

knew. Everybody round here, anyway? We knew what he was going to say before he put it to the winds. For that we had the paintpots, and the flowers, and the smartening up. If you are going to be looked at, you will smarten, isn't it? And he came here. Passed in front not two yards from us, now. I had bloody flags all over. And he saluted us. Yes, we had the salute, *here*. O, a beautiful boy, yes? *Ours!*'

'How do you know?' I asked him. 'They have all been saying this and that?'

'Not this one,' he said, and screwed the top on the can. 'This one is a royal man, look. We have got the royal word. For us, it is enough. In the banner, we trust him!'

Well.

I filled the tank and walked down to the crossroads, and looked at the houses and shops, all in a shine of paint, and flowers in window boxes, new with us, and the gardens splendid with them.

Funny how we forgot to use our eyes, though now I knew, I saw the sign of a royal man everywhere, and strangely wonderful it is to think that any human being in this day can still bring down a miracle, whether in the spirit, or in the very stones of the streets.

Taliesin's car turned into the garage, and he got out with a little dark man talking with both hands, even while he slung a bag over his shoulder, and walking towards me.

'Mr Singh,' Taliesin said. 'We're giving him a lift to Ponty. He had the hard luck to be born in Uganda!'

'Not hard luck to be born there, but very hard luck to have an Army fellow as a chief of government,' Mr Singh said, late thirties, I expect, and as if speaking through clenched teeth. 'Uganda is a place for civilised life, very happy, very peaceful. Now it is a crawling, howling warren of savages. Thugs. We thought we had taught them. But taught them what? How to steal? Pillage? Rob? Rape? Murder? We are all lucky to be here. They were all supposed to be Christians. Well, certainly, they acted as if they were. But how do we blame them? We were unprotected. We all had English passports. Did it do any good? The more we showed the passport, the more we got kicked and

155

robbed. Did the English do anything? They put us all in a camp. Always they are putting people in camps. Now they are going to send many of us away. Me and my wife. They said we were always Indians. Why? Is it a crime to be a Hindu?'

'Be what you like,' Taliesin said, with breeze blowing his voice. 'In this country they can't touch you. Do you have a business here?'

'Yes, I have got a restaurant,' he said. 'You are invited. My wife and her mother know how to cook. It is the best curry beyond Bombay. We also have other specialities. But we curse in our minds for what we have lost. We have no appeal. How do we know what is to happen to our children? They can be taken by the roots also. And raped, pillaged, and kicked and robbed?'

'Beginning to sound like us,' Taliesin said, over his shoulder to me. 'It's a god damned shame!'

'It is not our god,' Mr Singh said. 'We have no god. How shall we do more than pray our knees to blood in no skin? We have no more theological idiocies. We are ourselves. We live and we shall die. Cooking curry to live. But that fat one, Amin, will not escape the curse. He lives his fat in a curse. It surrounds him. He will not escape. He, nor his. He is doomed. Make a bet!'

'When?' Taliesin asked him. 'I'd be happy to win a few rands on that!'

'When you hear he is sick,' Mr Singh said, and pointing. 'His fat will save him nothing. He will die rotten. In our curse. The next turning, please. And that sign. The Star of Asia. There!'

Taliesin pulled up outside a little shop, with a sign, and a menu list, and the door opened and a girl in Indian dress ran to hold him, and very pretty to see them, and hear another language, unknown, though meaning is in the voice, too, and we saw in their hands, and heard, love.

'Come in, come in!' Mr Singh said. 'My wife will cook for you the best of every good meat and vegetable. Ask for what you want. But you are not English?'

'Hell we are!' Taliesin said. '*This* is our country!'

'Please, please, my mother will go on spiffingly at me for letting you go without a sign of thanks for bringing my husband home!' Mrs Singh said, talking English as Mr Singh, perhaps late twenties, breathless, smiling, black over her eyes, a little red spot in the middle of her forehead, and hands that could fly away, so delicate. 'We have got lamb fresh this morning. Nothing so tender. *Tandoori*. In the clay oven. Please!'

'We must be in Cardiff for an appointment,' I said. 'But on the way back, I will call in, be sure, isn't it?'

She took my hand.

'Please,' she said, soft. 'You promise? *Promise?* How many people are kind? Kind to us? We like also to be kind. But how many times can we be kind to people? How many do we meet?'

'Aren't the people here kind, then?' I asked her. 'Don't you like us?'

Her eyes were in sudden big lakes of salt, and shining.

'You, yes,' she said, in whispers with her. 'How many are *you*?'

They waved after us, and we went miles down the Rhondda before to talk, and every yard I saw the paint, and the flowers in gardens, and a royal man spoke plain, and a people spoke plainer, yes, of him.

'Christ, what a mess, eh?' Taliesin said. 'Everybody the same. Why *should* people be fucked about like that? Who's got the right? The astronauts got the correct idea. They saw it all on a ball, down here. Spinning round. We're all on it. So some bastard comes up to you, and taps you on the shoulder, and says *Out!*'

'Authority,' I said. 'The brute, and the bullet, isn't it?'

'Not here,' he said. 'The last place!'

'Careful, you,' I said. 'We are not at the end of history. The brute is still well with us. It *can* be here!'

'I'll wait for it,' he said. 'You don't intend going back to those two, do you?'

'Well, certainly!' I said. 'I promised. What would they think of me if I didn't?'

'Is what *they* think important?' he asked me.

'More important,' I said. 'They are a couple of lonely ones in a strange old country. Can't they trust the word of only *one*? What sort of life have they got?'

'Jesus Christ!' he said. 'People certainly have to suffer to live. The black boys here. In the mines. It's a bloody sight worse for a lot of the blacks in South Africa. Their skins are black. These lads can soap themselves white!'

'Why do you allow it?' I asked him.

'Why do *you* allow what's going on here?' he said. 'Incidentally, I don't want to make a big ta-ra-ra out of it. What's this about the valley? You told me it was terrible. Nothing of the sort. Finest stretch of landscaping I ever saw. It's beautiful!'

'What is this, now, then?' I said. 'What landscaping?'

'If it's the place you told me about, you're wrong!' he said. 'Go there and have a look!'

'Very well,' I said. 'I am tired to think. I will go back to those two, and then I will go to the valley, and we shall see, is it?'

But to say is one thing and to do is another.

To give every word its proper weight, I was afraid to go back to the Valley to see what I had seen, and hated. The ugliness I saw was insult to them I had known, even if they had lived to create it, without knowing, only to earn enough to live.

You know NOT what you do! I heard Mr Gruffydd's voice, yes, more than a good lifetime ago, but nobody took notice. We were blind in the pits, blind in the kitchen, blind in the pubs, and blind in the pews.

Blind, and feeling about for what?

Because whatever it was, it was nothing.

Strike, and strike again, and for what? A few pennies or shillings. And when the shillings had no more value than pennies, then go for pounds. But the poor pounds no longer had a proper value, and so strike again. Stupidity on stupidity, and no end except in another strike.

We saw the pickets on the way down, some of them warming tea cans at braziers, others round fires of scantling and small coal, but no children, anywhere, in case a fight would start, and I knew that behind all those closed doors men waited to join their brothers, ready and willing for blood.

'Wouldn't take long for this whole place to blow up,' Taliesin said. 'It's in the air. I can smell it!'

'Pray to God it won't,' I said. 'They are not little boys to be pushed, and there are plenty of them. *And* the women, don't forget. They are every bit as dangerous as the men!'

But I was coming tired of seeing from the sides of my eyes all the little houses sliding past in ribbons of colour, knowing well how they would look inside, and in a quick moment I wanted to be home, and in peace, and I told Taliesin to take the jeep on for as long as he pleased, and left him at Treforest, a bit sad, but a youngster in a jeep on his own can do more than with some old fool with him, and well I knew it.

So did he.

I went the long way back not to go near the Valley, and Plas Sûs looked better even than I remembered, everything blooming or in bud, and inside, a wonderful quiet and lovely thought of Sûs – *YES!* – for she was never far from me. I had a touch on the cheek from Mrs Frew, and a bit more from Cress, so happy they were that I was home, and a good cup of tea, then.

'Mr Gough has been on and on,' Cress said, pouring. 'Very important, it is. Will I get him?'

'Huw!' he bellowed. 'Thank God you're back. Superintendent Alford wants to talk to you. Urgently. Shall I bring him up?'

'To hell with the telephone,' I said. 'Come, you!'

I just had time for a look at the farm, everything in order, of course, and Rhodrick and the boys crating eggs, and the girls potting out in the greenhouses, and Cress came running and off I had to go.

'Here's the situation, sir,' the Superintendent said, when we sat down. 'You see, this isn't simply a local matter and this isn't the only Police Force concerned. Everybody is, Secret Service, down. I'm dog biscuits, so I have to get the answers dead right. Now, why did you take those two girls in?'

'Well, I thought Valmai was a relation of mine,' I said. 'She asked if she could bring a friend, and I said yes. That's all, isn't it?'

'Neither of them gave a correct name,' he said, opening a cardboard file. 'What sort of man was the father? Save you some trouble. Is this him?'

I looked, and remembered.

'Yes,' I said. 'Kiri's father, is it?'

'Pretended to be,' the Superintendent said. 'He escaped from prison not long ago!'

'But why should he come here?' I asked him.

'You were away,' he said. 'He had the chance of a look about the place. To see if anything of any importance had been left behind, perhaps? Well, something had. Quite a lot. Do you do any business with quarries?'

'Quarries?' I said. 'No, indeed.'

'You know there are quarries round about?' he said. 'Dynamiting?'

'We hear them all day,' I said. 'Sometimes they will even shake the windows.'

'If you have no business with them, why should there be drawings of quarries here?' he said, and unrolling a plan. 'Especially of areas where explosives were kept?'

'Well beyond me,' I said.

'Three nights before they ran, two quarries were robbed of gelignite, detonators, and the mix,' he said. 'We believe they ran, finally, because of a letter from Australia, which made it plain that someone calling herself Valmai John was an impostor. I have a copy of that letter. May I read it?'

'My solicitor is sitting next to you,' I said. 'Let *him* read it!'

'*Read*,' he said. 'And not good reading, either. Did you meet the men they were going out with?'

'Once,' I said. 'They never came again.'

'A good look over the place, and no further need,' the Superintendent said. 'Same with the so-called father.'

'But he *cried*!' I said.

The Superintendent stared, wide, at me.

'These are trained actors,' he said. 'They rehearse till they've got it right. He cried, and he was left alone? What better chance to examine anything in the room? Was anything left? He'd take it. I mean, anything incriminating. Have you a radio set here?'

'Yes,' I said. 'Mrs Frew has got one in the kitchen.'

'There's no transmitter here?' Douglas said, leaning forward.

'Transmitter?' I said. 'What is that?'

'To send messages,' he said.

'Go on, boy,' I said. 'You know there isn't!'

'Well,' he said, and taking an envelope from his brief-case. 'Here is a Post Office report that messages are being sent from this area. Your property!'

I had to think.

'Let them come here, and search inch by inch,' I said. 'They will find nothing not known to me!'

'I'm sorry,' the Superintendent said, but not looking it. 'We found quite a lot of evidence that the mix has been made in the shed beyond your turkey lanes. *This* place!'

He pointed to the map.

'It is news to me,' I said, cold. 'Did you ask Rhodrick?'

'He knows nothing,' the Superintendent said. 'But he is a Nationalist. So are you!'

Our eyes were locked, as in hot iron, beaten in.

'Go to hell!' I said. 'Be sure I am a Nationalist. In your own language, *fuck* yourself!'

He got up and put the papers together.

'You'll regret this,' he said.

'I can leave the country at any time,' I said. 'I don't give a damn for you, or anybody like you. Be *sure*!'

'Wait, now,' Douglas said. 'No need for this!'

'All need,' I said. 'What is this about a mix? A mix of what?'

'Explosives,' Douglas said. 'It's thought that many bombs used in Ulster were put together here, or somewhere near. The same with the book bombs. Huw, we are a land at peace. We have got a long coastline. We could make bombs, and sail them over the Celtic Sea. They could use them in Ulster, or anywhere, yes?'

'But this is altogether different, and something I don't understand, and certainly I am sorry for,' I said. 'If I thought anything to do with me had been used to blow the legs off girls, or blind, or kill, you make an enemy of *me*. If you think this place has been used to help that type of bastard, tell me, and I will help, be *well* sure!'

'I hope so,' the Superintendent said, files in the case, and ready to go. 'But I'd like to know how those two were able to stay here all that time, and go to Ireland, or to France as and when they wished, and you knew nothing of it?'

'I was the host,' I said. 'Why should I put my nose in their business? Every time I went up there, I saw nothing. Both were drawing or painting, or Valmai was typing. Nothing of bombs, or old nonsense, isn't it?'

'There's nothing of nonsense about those hundreds of dead and maimed, and all that damage,' the Superintendent said. 'Mr Morgan, I'd like your permission to bring a squad here, and search every inch, as you told me, of this house, buildings and land. I make it formal on the urging of your solicitor. I should tell you I wouldn't have let it go beyond today. I already have the warrant!'

I took the keys from my pocket, and put them on the table.

'Go, you,' I said. 'Search!'

'Thank you,' he said. 'Now I want you to make a statement to Inspector Lewis, detailing your movements since you left this house on the tenth.'

'I shall see that the questioning is in order,' Douglas said.

I sat and talked, and Inspector Lewis wrote. Lucky, I had all the hotel bills, and the garage slips, and the restaurant checks, and then, it was, I remembered a promise not kept.

I had forgotten the Star of Asia.

'I have got to go back somewhere in the Brecon road,' I said.

Inspector Lewis looked over his glasses.

'Where?' he said.

'I don't know the name of the place, but I can go there,' I said.

'You don't mind, I'll come with you,' Inspector Lewis said.

'Come, you,' I said.

'We'll go in my car,' Douglas said. 'Save time!'

Well, of course, I forgot exactly where it was. All those streets in the valleys look the same, and one town goes into another, hardly a brick different in any house, all the houses the same size, even the shops looking the same.

'Hold tight,' the Inspector said, after the fourth or fifth wrong guess. 'Turn here, and stop on that corner, sir, if you please?'

We stopped outside a Police Station, and in moments the Inspector came out with a piece of paper, and we went back the way we had come, and turned left, and there was the Star of Asia, and Mr and Mrs Singh came out with open arms, and you might have thought we were the three wise men come again. Mrs Singh's mother came from the kitchen, and a lovely smell of cooking, and a young woman stood shy in the door, and we sat, and drank scotch and soda.

'I'm glad it turned out like this,' Douglas said. 'The Inspector thought you might be meeting a few of your Irish friends. Didn't you, Inspector?'

'We have to make sure,' he said. 'Job like this, if we miss a trick, we can get thrown to the cats. Not our idea!'

'But look,' I said. 'What makes you think about bombs? We have never had bombs in this country. Have we?'

They both went on eating away.

Douglas broke a piece off a *chupatti*.

'Huw,' he said. 'We've had people doing time for bombing. A couple are in now. In the past few years we've had the Free Welsh Army. A couple of other movements. We've had men blown up by their own bombs. *Here.* Make no mistake. We have *got* to think about bombs and

163

the people who make them. They are a danger, day and night, isn't it?'

'I never heard of them,' I said. 'It's not my idea, certainly.'

'But, Mr Morgan, *does* your idea matter?' the Inspector asked me. 'There are people making bombs. They are to be used for destruction. Of people, or property, or for peace of mind. They earn good money. If from the Arabs, or anybody else, the same. Our job is to find them. Simple as that, yes?'

'Everybody thinks we are a pastoral people,' Douglas said. 'Living in the crags. They forget there are nearly three million of us. It is convenient to forget. What shouldn't be forgotten is that all of us are not rotten with television. A percentage of that three million want freedom from the English, even at cost of their lives. If they can help the Irish, or the Bretons, or the Basques, or the Kurds, or the Greeks, never mind who, they *will*. They are as prepared to die for their own freedom as for the freedom of others, and nothing will stop them. And as the children grow, it will get worse. The English have had their day. If only the silly buggers would realise it!'

'It will be many a long year,' the Inspector said, and looking about. 'Could we have a bill, please?'

'No bill,' I said. 'You and Mr Gough are guests!'

'No,' he said. 'I am nobody's guest. My bill, please, I have got to get back!'

'I am sorry,' Mr Singh said. 'This gentleman is invited, and so are his friends. We are open only because of him. Otherwise we are opening only at six o'clock?'

'I *can't* be anybody's guest,' the Inspector said. 'I want a bill, and I want to pay, d'you hear?'

'I have got very good hearing,' Mr Singh said. 'But I shall not open until six o'clock, British Standard Time. Until then, I am not in business, and therefore, no bills. Only guests. And guests pay nothing!'

'Look,' the Inspector said, and coming a bit rough, with him, 'I'm a Police Officer. Now, let me have my bill, will you?'

'I have met many officers,' Mr Singh said, o, quiet, and looking through the lace curtains of the window. 'Police, Army and others. A lot of thieves and pillagers. Rapers of women. I scrape dirt on their memory, as cats scrape dirt on their droppings. We are from Uganda. We are victims of a fat fraud. Are you also of the same droppings?'

'Just a moment,' Douglas said. 'We've had an excellent lunch. Don't let's spoil it. Mr Morgan and ourselves are your guests. Is that it?'

'It is, exactly,' Mr Singh said, and put an arm about his wife, leaning againsst him, hands gripped under her chin. 'We are glad to throw open our doors to a kind man. We accept no money!'

'That's plain, and that's all,' Douglas said. 'The food was delicious!'

Mr and Mrs Singh put their arms about me, and old Mrs Singh came from the kitchen wiping her hands, and carrying packages, and the shy girl stood again in the doorway.

'We are happy you came,' Mr Singh said. 'Please come again. Kind people are not many. We were afraid you would forget. Another wound is little to us. But a promise kept is a rare marvel. A bandage to hold in the blood. You know where we are. *Please* come again!'

'A variety of sweetmeats,' old Mrs Singh said. 'Remember us while you eat, please!'

We said nothing much, going back, except that Indian restaurants in the country were about as many as the Chinese, and how many Welsh restaurants we would find in China or India, or indeed, how many Welsh restaurants we would find in Wales, and Douglas said we had lost ourselves. There were none there, and none here.

I thought so, too, because when Mama was in our kitchen we had many dishes I have never tasted since, though Lal had them from her Mama and cooked a few of them, and so did Sûs, and Mrs Frew had some, and Cress knew others, though not as I remembered them, or the good smells that stayed in the age of the head, either. Instead, we had the French in the restaurants – as they call

165

them – all flour and frip, or else English, of frozen beef or mutton called lamb, a pudding here, a pie there, desserts from packets, all tasting the same, and God help the poor vegetables. A plastic bag, with Duck à l'Orange, is only mortuary fodder, indeed to Christ.

Everything to stuff the belly, nothing for the mouth to water, less to remember, and to hell.

'Why worry?' the Inspector said, after a bit. 'It all drops in the hole just the same?'

'So do we,' I said. 'In a cathedral, in marble, or our bones, on the pampas. But it will depend on what went before, certainly that will be remembered, isn't it? What will be remembered of us? A lot of old nothings. Not even our *own* food? What *are* we? A kitchen forgotten? That's the history of a people forgotten, isn't it? What you eat makes you what you are. If you eat what is foreign, who are you?'

'Well, of course, a supermarketeer,' Douglas said. 'What the hell else *are* we? Dragged in by politicians and bloody bankers. Profits the easy way. Slaves, follow. Or feel the whip. Europe forever. Who the hell are *we*? Who the hell *were* we ever? Since the time of the bloody Romans?'

But all the lights at Plas Sûs stopped the talk. It was dark of evening and it looked like patchy morning. Lamps were alight about the house and among the farm buildings, and all the way down in the fields.

'What's this?' Douglas said.

'The search,' Inspector Lewis said. 'They've found something. The hounds are in!'

Superintendent Alford met us, and pointed to the lounge.

'Mr Morgan, for the moment, please, you will remain there,' he said. 'Later, I shall ask you to come with me to a number of places on this farm to verify certain findings. Do *not* attempt to leave, will you?'

'I shall accompany Mr Morgan at all times,' Douglas said. 'Is there a good drop of scotch there?'

Cress brought the tray and I could see she had been crying, but I said nothing, though when the police whistles

166

blew, with a lot of shouting from far off, she pulled a breath, and ran, poor girl, and a good bawl before the kitchen door shut.

'They had found something,' Douglas said. 'They probably had a tip. It's beginning to look serious, yes?'

'Beginning?' I said. 'Police in the house is always serious, isn't it?'

I hated the notion of Plas Sûs coming under the boots of policemen. I thought I heard her giving them a real Tehuelche rant, there, somewhere, and I laughed to think what she might say.

'Well,' Douglas said. 'Your idea of serious is very far from mine, indeed. Is there a nice joke I have missed?'

I was going to tell him, but the Superintendent pushed open the door, and stood a moment, not looking at us.

'Mr Morgan,' he said. 'I want you to come with me for the purpose of identification. A body has been found in that caravan down there. Are you ready?'

Douglas came with us in the Police car, but all round the other way, to a path going up. I could smell death when we stopped. Dead humans have a different smell from dead animals. Both the dogs were dead under the caravan.

Lights and policemen were all about, and the Superintendent pointed to the steps.

'Tell me if you know who it is,' he said. 'Don't touch anything, will you?'

I went up, and looked in the little room, in wreck, as if somebody had smashed and torn.

The body lay staring at the roof, and eyes, and two front teeth shining in the light.

One look.

'His name I don't remember,' I said. 'He was the County Engineer, yes?'

'Correct,' he said. 'Gilbert George. We'll go back to the house, and I'll take your statement. Any objections?'

'What have I to do with it?' I asked him.

'You own the land,' he said, going to the car. 'This way!'

'Wait you,' I said. 'Where is the woman who used to live

here? The witch they called her, yes? The one who stole my lambs. The silly one, poor old thing?'

'Wait, you, again,' Douglas said. 'I will supervise the deposition of Mr Morgan. Let us go to the house and have everything in order. First, I will insist on finding the owner of the caravan. Don't you know where she is?'

Well, that week would defy the Devil and all his clerks to hit a bit of shape into any of it. I was at the police station, and the Court, and the County Office, and with Douglas, and the solicitors of interested parties – they called them – but as to understanding any of it, I was dull.

'Leave it to me,' Douglas said, and I left it.

I felt I was being thrown, one to another, like an old football, but I said nothing until Taliesin came back, that night, and I told him.

'Well, good God,' he said. 'Are they making a mark of you?'

'I don't know, indeed,' I said. 'I'm not sure what is going on anywhere.'

'I'll bloody soon find out,' he said, that night, but next day, he seemed not sure, and later that morning he was out before Douglas got there.

'We seem to be in a bit of a mess,' he said. 'They can't find the sisters. The one in the caravan down below here, and the other one in Gwynaldrod. They can't find Lys Machen. She might be in the United States. They can't find out what the County Engineer was doing in the caravan. He died of a knife wound. They can't find the knife. There are no weapons in the place. Poison killed the dogs. Who killed him is the mystery. So far. We'll find out the rest from the Coroner, isn't it?'

I went through those days as if I was an Indio, feeling everything, knowing all, but showing nothing. Police were about the place through the hours, but only God knows what they were doing. I had no interest. I walked about, and nodded to Rhodrick, and he raised his cap to me, and so did the other men, and the girls in the potting sheds smiled at me, and I raised my hat, and that was all.

We all felt the weight.

A dead one.

It was in the air.

Christians, I suppose, we were, and murder, to us, was only horror, that last, deadly, brutal sin.

I knew it was Sunday because the wind was right and I could hear the people down in the Chapel singing *The King Of Love My Shepherd Is.* Why I was not with them is a puzzle, indeed, but after a bit of life, I suppose we come out of habit and go on our own, and never for the best, I am sure.

Standing there, I was, and thinking of them in the Valley, and hearing their voices, and us going two and two from Chapel, and Mama and Dada last, and Sunday dinner smelling lovely, indeed, and bringing spit to brim, yes, a smell not with us today, and grief that is, too. Often I have wondered when did people stop to cook something good to the nose, as well as the mouth, and why. I am sure my Mama never had any money to throw away, or any thought of it, because the old tea tin was always on the mantelpiece, and any coin come spare was sure of a good welcome. But whatever little she spent in the small shops up the Hill, she gave our family the food I still remember, though nothing of luxury was in what she used, or any of the wonders in the shops today, but only what came from the farms over the mountain, or our own gardens, and with Ellis the Post.

Mind, with Mrs Frew and Cress in the house, I was least to grumble. Our kitchen was good, no doubt, but not in compare with my Mama's, or with some of the houses down in Patagonia, whether in Trelew, on the Atlantic side, or with others over in the Andes. There was reason for that, too. Twice, floods took everything of a lifetime of work, house, animals, and stores, out to the ocean, never to be seen again, and a salting of miles of good land was no great courage to cook anything for anybody, and it was too simple, in the pain of the heart, to light a fire of branches, and spread the red ash, and hang the sheep on grill irons, and wait for them to be cooked, and eat, then, with half a loaf of good crusted bread, and a swallow of wine, and give thanks. From the first to the next, and the next, was a following of days, and presently the grace of the kitchen was only memory, something of other times, another place, a thought in past life, long, yes, long ago, in the love of Grandam, and the grace of Mama.

But it was funny to think of tens of thousands of sovereigns, and half sovereigns, and guinea pieces, all in gold, piled in the tea boxes of all those houses on the Hill, the same as ours, and nobody ever dreaming of touching, much less robbing.

We were the innocent, and honest, because of Chapel, and the Book.

It is not now.

Not the Chapel, not the Book.

I heard the doorbell sound in the pantry, and Mrs Frew came to say Miss Rowlands of Gaiman would like to speak to me, and in I went, for a pretty shock, too, yes, indeed, a pretty one, in National dress, and the hat worn over a lace cap, and the silk ribands in a bow not quite under her chin, and white stockings, and shoes with big silver buckles.

Well, well.

She made a little curtsey, holding out the skirt.

'My Mam's birthday,' she said. 'We always dressed National on a birthday. Mr Morgan, a message from Lys Machen. She has got serious trouble!'

'Tell me,' I said.

'Only she will say, and I have got to take you there,' she said. 'Not far, but the road is rough.'

'Mari Fach, the jeep,' I said. 'Come, you.'

Not far it was, but the road was rough enough, a path full of the ruts of years and soft with the leaf falling in many a lifetime, and Mari was in four-wheel gear all the way from the main road we turned off, and through a forest, across fields, over small brooks, and at last we came in the open meadows, with sheep from my flock, and cattle from my herd, and even the poultry were of mine, and the ducks and geese, as well.

I wondered.

The cot was fresh painted, white, with green shutters and a red door, a bit of a change, and a garden in splendid order and full of everything, from roses to olives, and all in hearty song, and Lys at the door and coming down the brick path to meet us.

But she was wrinkled with misery, and only a small smile.

'Thank God you have come,' she said. 'I am going mad, here!'

We went in a front room beautiful with the treasures of cabinet making and porcelain, and a girl came with the tea tray as if she had been waiting. Lys sat on the edge of a Queen Anne armchair, and began to pour.

'I will go off, now then, is it, Miss Machen?' the girl said, and Lys nodded.

She poured a cup for Teleri as if she knew two spoons of sugar were enough.

'Sugar, Mr Morgan?' she said.

'Two please,' I said. 'A lovely place you have got here. How did you find it?'

'Hywel John, a smallholder, died, and his wife sold to me,' she said. 'I remodelled, and I use it for weekends, or when I've got a big job, and I need to think. I have got to think, now. I am afraid I've got a murderess in the house. Her accomplice is her sister. They are aunts of mine. They are both dotty beyond recall. I don't want to give them up, poor old things. They have gone back to being children. But ugly, to seep verdigris in your heart. They came to me for help. I have always helped them. Must I give them up? Or keep them here?'

'Ah, have your wits, girl!' I said. 'The Police are after them. You know that, don't you? If you help, for only a moment, never mind shelter, you are an accomplice, too. So is Teleri. So am I. Will you have us shut in jail? Come, you. I'll get Douglas Gough, and he'll see Mrs Soper Reynolds, and we'll have them somewhere safe. No more of this. Be sensible, girl, will you?'

I walked out, to the passage, and looked at the rooms downstairs, and up, to two bedrooms, and nobody, but in the third, at the back, the two were on the floor, asleep, and dirty to turn the stomach of a beast. Dried mud, poor things.

I locked the door, and went down. Lys was crying, and Teleri had an arm about her to soothe.

'Come,' I said. 'Those two need good care. You are putting yourself in reach of prison bars. Out, quick, now then, is it?'

She came at me with claws, and screaming, a fury from beyond, and I knew madness was in her, and I shifted my head from the hooked fingers, and went under, and hit to the plexus, an uppercut that took her breath and put her soft on the floor.

'Take her shoulders,' I said, to Teleri, crying now. 'Out to the jeep. Come, you. Hold her tight on the way, not to fall out.'

I got them back to Plas Sûs and we carried her in, and put her on the couch, and I telephoned Douglas, but he was at the Golf Club, and I had to wait.

'All right, Huw,' he said. 'I will have the Magistrate there, and the Superintendent, and we will have the lot, dear God, committed. I'm not sure what got into Lys, indeed!'

'She is mad as those she has tried to protect,' I said. 'For her own sake, put her away. For a time, anyway. She is not with herself, or with us!'

Well, the house came full of police, and men and women in long linen coats, and cars and ambulances outside, and then, nobody, and we were quiet, except for a sergeant putting small two-way radios in the lounge, the bedroom, and in the jeep, all on police net.

But then Mrs Frew and Cress were in hat and coat, and standing in the door.

'Mr Morgan,' Mrs Frew said, as on the morning of the First Day. 'We have had enough. We had everybody – and everybody – talking. But now, the Police are never out of the house. And ghosts. And a murderess. What will be next? No. Our money, please, and we are out!'

'Good,' I said. 'Mr Gough will pay, and give you your

cards. You shall have a good reference.'

'Not needed,' she said. 'We have ordered the cab. Sorry I am I was ever here. It will always be against us, see?'

'Go, you,' I said.

But a sad moment, too. Two good ones off, and nobody in. People have got their own way to think, and nothing to be said by the rest of us.

'Never mind, Mr Morgan,' Teleri said. 'I will stay here. I will look after you. No trouble, see? I am finished with exams, and I am free. I think you are in bad luck with this old nonsense. Now you are clear of them. I will never have them near, no. Half-English, they are, *Ach y fi,* indeed!'

'What have you got against the English?' I asked her.

'Nothing,' she said, flat. 'Except, leave us, and go. We shall do well on our own!'

'How long have you been of Plaid Cymru?' I asked her.

'Since I was born,' she said, with the clear eye. 'That was with my Grandada. He hated the English. I have tried not. But they have done nothing to help us, yes? A lot of old fools, and greedy for what we have got. How can they tread us down? Why do we let them?'

Well, it was like having Sûs back again. If the other two could cook, Teleri was truly a mistress of the kitchen, and when Sam and Ella came that evening, he said I was putting on a bit of weight, and Ella said it was about time. Teleri had gone shopping in the jeep, so I got the drinks tray.

'What the hell's this about Lys Machen?' he asked me. 'They've got her in the loony bin? I couldn't believe it. But you know something? It doesn't surprise me. Ask Ella. I always said she's cracked. Couple of days ago I found out. Her office staff didn't get their money the past couple of weeks, so somebody called Anstruther came to see me. He's the chief draughtsman. Didn't take me long to get the story. Listen to *this.* I always respected her as an architect because of her drawings, prints, quantity surveyals, you know? The job?'

He sat back.

'It was this man, Anstruther. He was sent to prison for

173

corruption and this and that, years ago. Bribing civil servants, and all the rest of it. Well, anyway, I took him and most of the staff on. He's a *real* architect, and he'll be a wonderful help to *me*. So I asked him how she got away with it, and he said, cheek. She had enough grey cells to give him a job, and he took on the staff. She was good looking. She got the contracts. Don't ask me how. He did the work. This house, and the cottage up there? *His*. All the others? His. I asked him why he didn't own his own business. He told me convicted criminals aren't much good. One enquiry, they're finished. I think it's a shame. Losing a good brain doesn't do anybody any good. So I've got him, and the people he's trained. You watch me grow!'

'But the poor girl?' I said. 'What about Lys?'

'There's a bit of a mystery, there,' Ella said. 'There's a lot of talk she's been working for the I.R.A. From the stuff they've found. Every quarry robbed of explosives, she's got the drawings. Pinpointing the sheds. She's had a cabin cruiser at Aberporth for the past five years, anyway. Easy to cross to Ireland. They say Gilbert George was an informer, and they did him in!'

'I find it hard to believe,' I said. 'What was he doing in that caravan?'

'But they've found it's a place they made bombs in,' Sam said. 'The traces. Didn't you hear? Don't you read the papers?'

'No,' I said. 'Traces, what?'

'Where they brought the stuff to make bombs,' Ella said. 'Stolen from the quarries. Of course, they can't do any stealing, now. The game's up. But that caravan was perfect. Lonely. Out of the way. I don't think she was cracked, at all. She's like the rest. Well trained, and *very* well paid!'

'I don't like to think that about her,' I said. 'She tried to save a couple of old aunties. I suppose I would do the same?'

'You'd have to find out why,' Sam said, lighting a cigar. 'Why did that old biddy stay in that place in Gwynaldrod? Why did the other stay in the caravan down on your place? Why? They've both got bank accounts in six figures. That's only what's known so far. Lys Machen's got a lot more. Where from? *What* for? Northern Ireland? The Irish Republicans? Ulstermen?'

'Well beyond me,' I said, 'I think we are all gone daft. Nothing to be done, isn't it?'

'Nearly a thousand dead, and thousands more mutilated, and tens of thousands in agonies every day, and not a proper night's sleep for anybody, nothing to be done?' he said. 'You're giving the game to bloody murderers. Assassins. How long before it happens here?'

'Never here!' I said.

'Come on, Huw,' he said. 'We've got the same type of bloody idiot. Plenty. For money, anything. What the hell, you know that as well as I do. It'll begin here if we aren't very careful. The Army trains soldiers by the thousands. And if they leave? They've got a job, haven't they? Doing exactly what they've been trained to do. Any doubt about it?'

'I don't like to think that,' I said. 'I don't like to think bombs were made here, either. I'll ask Douglas about it!'

But he was worse.

'Look,' he said. 'If I hadn't done a lot of talking this long time, you'd have been in clink before this. You're lucky you've got good, solid men out there. Rhodrick, and the rest. They're loyal to you. Their evidence counts. Plus, that you keep yourself to yourself. But that caravan could have been a facer, indeed. It's lucky it's in what's always been known to the locals as the Witch's Field. Nobody ever went there. Lucky again it's never been put to plough because of the marsh at the foot. Useless except for geese and ducks. But the furthest quarry is only six miles away. The nearest is less than two. They could hide the stuff there, and then take it over to Gwynaldrod when it suited them, isn't it?'

'Suited who?' I said.

'Whoever wanted explosives, of course,' he said. 'They've found all the evidence they need. In your place, in the feed shed, in the pantry of the barn, in the cottage, up there in the ridge, and in the caravan. The only reason you are free today is they can't connect you with any of it. They've had your servants, the first two, and the last, the two I sent you, under questioning for hours, there. All they have got is about hippies. And a niece of yours. We've got some of her cassettes. We like her. She plays beautiful piano, yes? A treat to listen, indeed!'

'What do I do?' I asked him.

'Sit tight by there,' he said. 'Let them all go to hell. I shall always be here!'

There is nice.

I felt like an old bandit on the run.

Rhodrick laughed when I told him.

'Look, sir,' he said. 'We've known about Lys Machen since a girl. She was always a bit funny in the head. It's in the family, no? Cracked, the lot. But clever, like the father. A furniture dealer, he was. Died of drink, yes. The mother made jams, and pickles, and all sorts, to send them to school, and she sold the rights for a lot of money a few years ago, yes, and went to live in France. A suicide. Like Lys. For weeks, no trouble. Then off she would go. We never liked to talk about it. Bad luck, see. And a witch in the family, O, Jesus, who wants such a blessing?'

'But did you know they were mixing whatever-it-is here?' I asked him.

'No, indeed,' he said. 'There was building going on about the place, see, these months, and builders are always making a mess, here and there, isn't it?'

'They could do worse than have a look at some of these builders, then,' I said. 'Did you know any of them?'

'No,' he said. 'They were from outside. Not local men, yes? From Mr Hooper, isn't it?'

'I'll have to talk to Mr Hooper,' I said. 'Now, what about my animals and the poultry up at that cot?'

He stared out of the door, a light of pale blue, and nothing to say what he was thinking, except stillness.

'Mr Morgan, please have good quiet while I tell you,' he said, and in a shift of the feet. 'We knew what was going on, from the start, isn't it? We didn't know you, then, see? But you remember I took you down to the

176

caravan? You saw her. Well, when I told the wife, she bounced off the wall. We will have the curse on us, she was shouting, there. O, damn, I had no peace for days, here. So I didn't say more. But no doubt everything up there is yours, and no doubt the old witch had them up there, yes? That's how people saw her at night. And they are afraid of her, mind? Afraid, yes!'

'So I lose?' I said.

'No, no,' he said. 'But don't bring them back here. The curse is steady on them. It won't go, never. You would be asking for real trouble *here*. Better ask a butcher from outside to make an offer for the animals and poultry, and take them away. Let *him* do it. Don't go near!'

'Right,' I said. 'See to it, and take the jeep, *now*!'

He looked at me, a big man, and steady, in pale blue blaze of fright.

'O, Mr Morgan!' he said. 'Not up there, is it?'

'The butcher,' I said. 'Go, you, and no more about old witches!'

But I knew too much from living among the Indios to blame him, poor old boy. No doubt some humans have got another gift. Some turn it for good, and others for evil, and both will work, and I have seen both, but more of evil, indeed, because good, to some, is dull, but evil is a jump of devils, and lovely, and they will bath in it, and use it as others use soap.

Sam shouted when I told him. He never had workmen about the place. He supplied materials, but the workmen were Lys Machen's. He delivered, but no more. I telephoned Douglas, and he said I might have a break, and he would call the Superintendent.

Well, the place came full of old Police again, and asking this and that, but nobody knew anything about names and addresses, I, the least, though how a lot of men can work on a job for weeks, and not be known, is strange to me, indeed. But they were not my men, and I was not paying them, and so noses were not put in, and we knew nothing, and we looked a lot of old fools, there.

But after eleven o'clock, and coffee, Rhodrick came in

the cattle stalls while I was strolling, and smelling the ancient rich of milk, and walked with me out to the hay ricks' sweet whiff and he looked over his shoulder, and whispered that most of the Machen men were known Nationals, or Free Welsh Army, and everybody was afraid to say a word, in case of a funeral or two.

I turned and walked away.

The King Of Love My Shepherd Is, Whose Goodness Faileth Never.

But there is a beautiful mess we make of things down here, indeed, without help or even trying, and who, yes, *who*, is the King Of Love? And what has He to do with the Free Welsh Army?

There is lonely, and forsaken, so many of us are.

Except we find a good, good girl to put our arms round, who are we? Where?

I was all the happier to see Taliesin back again with a good one, about six foot of lovely sunburned South Africa, a real old beauty, Daise, he called her, and both flying home together, and marrying in Pretoria. She had been visiting an uncle in Cardigan, so I knew why he went off so tidy in the jeep. He knew where he was going. They called in to return Mari Fach, and have a look at the farm, and lunch, then, with steak, kidney and mushroom pudding, young sprouts and new potatoes boiled with a sprig of mint, and if I never move from by here, the best I ever smacked my chops at, and Daise had a double helping, but Taliesin had three, with black plum pie and cream after, and a splendid cup of coffee from our own espresso machine, and a good friend that was, too. I often wonder why the English, so famous for the coffee house, can bear the old wash they call coffee today. Even the tea is not what it was, and Teleri had to order special to have a real cup, because Sûs, unused to drinking tea, and knowing nothing about it, put up with what she got, and I said nothing, for what is the use?

Well, off they went, as Daise said, groaning in the Nelly-Kelly, but she had the pudding recipe from Teleri, and I never saw a finer couple. I promised to see them in South

Africa if I went there, and Teleri said it must be nice to fly all that way, and see so many new places, and be married. If I heard a little shift in her voice, or not, but she was gone before I could ask, and then, it was, I wondered why such a fine girl was running loose and why all the men she must have met were so daft to let her.

It took me time to find the one really daft, but I would never have guessed, indeed.

Sam and Ella came over to or three times a week for a drink, or dinner, and I went down to them, and often Douglas and his wife came with them from the Golf Club, but his wife, Emily, a nice girl, was always in a wander to be back with the three children, and picking at him to go, even if his mother was with them, so there was rest in the house only when they were gone, and we could talk.

'I suppose you know that poor old lot in Gwynaldrod's dead?' Sam said, that night. 'The other one's not much better. Lys is supposed to be in a bad way. In, or out. She's got charges to answer. I hope they find her barmy and put her away. Mental home's better than a prison. We can nip up and see her sometime. Take her things, y'know, books, tidbits. We're going up there at the weekend. Want to come?'

'Certainly,' I said.

'Late night final,' he said, and standing to go. 'Have you had any threatening letters? Telephone calls? I mean, saying if you give evidence against her, you'll be waking up dead?'

'No,' I said. 'I would take no notice. And what evidence can I give?'

'You'll have to,' he said. 'You're mentioned on the list. If you get anything, letter or call, whip it through to the Police, won't you?'

Well, I had to think of Teleri, and so, when I waved them off, I went in and double-locked everything, and opened the alarm system in the cabinet, and switched on all the little blue lights, so pretty, that turned to red when somebody came in, because then all the bells rang everywhere, and the siren mewed how-how-how, and the alarm signal went to the patrol cars.

Well, *Iesu Mawr,* what a wonderful way to live.

And the poor North Irish had it, day in and out, and nobody, and nothing to give them peace, or comfort, God love them every moment, our brothers and sisters, and nothing, no, nothing to be done.

That morning, Mr Anstruther called with a message from Sam Hooper, that the Machen cot, and the Gwynaldrod shop were up for auction, with other small properties in the hills, and I called Douglas and told him to buy. But he was far from wanting.

'There is a curse in this,' he said. 'It will never be forgotten!'

'Ah, for God's sake!' I said. 'Enough, now, is it? You are an officer of the Court, yes?'

'Yes,' he said, quiet. 'I am also human. And my wife is frightened to death. What shall I say to her? Did you know that in the curse, children are first to suffer?'

'To hell,' I said. 'Give the job to somebody outside. I want those properties. Enough?'

Mr Gammons came to see me about the sale, and I asked him to nominate a bidder.

'I will get you a shrewd one,' he said. 'Matt Lewis. Usual commission, is it?'

'Yes,' I said. 'Why not Lys Machen's man?'

He half-closed one eye, put the tip of his tongue on the lower lip, and made a tight o with his mouth.

'Not with her any more, see,' he said. 'Used to work for me. A fiddler. Fiddler? He's a bloody orchestra on his own. Matt's your man. But Mr Morgan, I must warn you. It's common here. They say those places are cursed. Nobody ever went there. I happen to be a Roman Catholic so I'm not a bit afraid. I mean, to handle the sale. But indeed to God, I wouldn't go there, yes?'

'Not my idea,' I said.

But it was. I had seen enough to know the power of evil, and I was last to scoff at thought of a curse. Even so, I knew how to cure it. I went in Mari Fach that afternoon to the Church of the Immaculate Heart, and I found Father Herlihy doing a bit of gardening.

A young man, he was, and cheerful to welcome, but he came serious soon enough.

'I agree,' he said. 'It's a deadly business. All right. When the properties pass to you, let me know and I'll deal with it. But *don't* go to *any* of them without me, will you?'

Yes, well, I was careful of that, too, and when Mr. Gammons came up to say I had bought the lots for not even a song, I went to early Mass, and burned candles for Lal and Sûs, and for all of us, and a good prayer against Satan and all of them, and Father Herlihy said he would be ready that afternoon with a Server and the Sacristan, and I asked them all to lunch, but he told me he never had a meal on Sunday, and Tereli had to put most of the Beef Wellington she had cooked, and splendid with her, in the ice box, poor girl, though never mind, cold it was every bit as good, and a blessing to the buds, yes, so no loss.

I went down to fetch them, and Father Herlihy carried the Book in a red baize bag with gold-lace binding and black cords to knot, and the Server carried something in green baize, and the Sacristan had long candlesticks wrapped in linen, and somebody else had a package all corners, and I thought we were a fine lot to go out to beat the Devil, and to Hell with him, too.

We got up there, and I will say I never saw anywhere more beautiful, in pasture, or trees, or wildflowers, and we stopped on the path near the house.

'Please stay here, Mr Morgan,' Father Herlihy said, and got out. 'Come in when I have finished my work. I'll let you know. If you hear a lot of noise, it is natural, and take no smallest notice. I am in charge!'

I got out of Mari Fach and went for a walk on my property, seeing a careless touch everywhere. Eggs had not been gathered, and rats had been at them. But what caught my eye was a limp of animals, yes, and poultry. I made well sure with a cow, a sheep, a goose, and a hen. Beyond them, I was sick to look.

They had all been cut at the tendon to make them limp. It has to be done with a knife.

Even a poor hen.

A goose, yes, a duck. A poor duck, made to limp? Who is so cruel?

When I heard the first screaming I am not sure. I was a fair way from the house, and I ran back, through pasture, to the farmyard, and even the poultry seemed to be hiding underwing, and still the screaming, as if many scraped a throat in horror, scaled, yes, the ear's limit, that made a wreck in the head, and a blindness in the eyes, and a phlegmy lump in the lungs, and there was no breath, and no hearing, and no sight in the eyes, no light, and I was a little one, alone, in a dark old world, and brought to the knees to pray for help.

If the hot breeze passing me was something or nothing, no odds, but I felt a sudden push that threw me off where I stood, and the screams were louder, and then gone, and quiet, in a small moment, and trees whispering, and birds talking, and men's voices in chant, and a bell rang, a clap to pain in the ears, and again, and I thought I heard the echoes of screaming but I stood in sunshine, in a silence of grass, and shrubs, and the innocence of birdsong, and I was lifted to be with them all, and I could hear Sûs.

'Go to the horse, boy!' she was shouting. 'He has no guile, but only his own temper, and beyond that, clean!'

But five good horses there were cut in the tendon, and they limped.

Father Herlihy came from the door, carrying the Book, and he sweated silver drops in the light, and the server was clipped pale in the gills, and not wanting to look me in the eye, and swinging the censer, and Father Herlihy put a hand on his shoulder.

'A bad one,' he said. 'I think it is done. But give me permission to come here a couple of times a week for a month or so. I don't want *you* to come here *at all*. Do you hear me?'

'Very well,' I said, watching the boy swinging the censer. 'Who will feed the animals? Or milk the cows?'

'Ah, yes,' he said. 'Nobody about the place?'

'I've seen a girl here,' I said.

He shook his head, and went on wiping the sweat.

'I'll see if a man in the parish needs a job,' he said. 'I'll send him to you. Now we go to Gwynaldrod?'

Thank God the village was quiet, not even a dog about the place, and no street can look emptier than without a dog. I stopped outside the shop, and Father Herlihy got down.

'You might take a little walk,' he said. 'When I'm ready, I'll touch the siren. Is there any water in the place?'

'There is a well at the back,' I said. 'Best water in the world. Till the English flood it!'

He looked away, and nodded the others to the doorway, and took the keys from me.

'I'll hang on to these till I'm sure that all's well,' he said. 'As to the flood. One of these days, those blatant English are going too far. They've played the all-powerful ass for too long. They'll be made to learn!'

I walked away from there, and thankful, and turned at the crossroads towards Blodwen's place. The garden was overgrown and the roses needed a prune, but the stone-work was clean, and I could see that young Evan Williams had been doing a good job. But there were fresh tracks of mud going to the back door of the largest cottage, and because the habits of years never die, I used my bit of Indio tracking to go along the path as far as the brook outside the village. Two people had crossed, both wearing leather shoes, not so heavy as boots, and one had followed the other, and the one leading had taken his time, and twice he missed his way and went back, and struck more than a dozen matches to find the back gate.

But there had been no tracks at the front, neither on the step, nor on the flagstone path.

I heard the screams and other sounds, but distant, while I left the place to trot down to the telephone kiosk, and I called Douglas, and he said, Right, the Police would be there in ten minutes.

They were outside the house in much less, two good

boys, indeed, and no old nonsense, they went to the door and knocked. The shutters were closed. While they were going round the house, another car stopped, and Superintendent Alford and Inspector Bennett got out with two more uniformed constables.

'That's enough, Roberts!' Superintendent Alford said. 'Force the door!'

Well, the Sergeant took out a bunch of keys, and turned one, and they were in.

I walked away, along the street, that long, long street, so short, when every step was penance, but I heard no sound, either from Blodwen's place behind me, or from the shop coming closer, and the Sacristan came out as I got there, putting the candlesticks in Mari Fach, and the Server came to put in the green baize bag, and Father Herlihy locked the door.

'Not quite *so* bad, but bad enough,' he said, and pocketed the keys. 'That's all for one day. I'll hold service for the others tomorrow. Don't let anyone go near until they are thoroughly cleansed. That type of wickedness has a nasty habit of sticking!'

'You believe it, Father?' I asked him.

He looked down the street.

'You *heard* it,' he said. 'You didn't see what we *saw*. Yes. I believe in evil. As I believe in good. Would there be darkness without light? Or why am I in this business? For money? There isn't any!'

'I would like to pay for what you are doing, indeed,' I said. 'Only let me know, isn't it?'

'No charge,' he said, abrupt, for him. 'Mother Church has no charge when it's a matter of her bounden duty. We are here to expunge evil. That's all. If you care to subscribe to the repair of the church roof, of course, for quite other reasons, that's different!'

'You shall have a new roof,' I said, and I could hear Sûs's *Yes, Yes!* and I knew I was right, and a good feeling that is, too.

She was always with me.

In a hand's touch, my beautiful was with me.

184

I told Teleri nothing about the afternoon.

To see her, I was glad that other life was in order, in capable hands, and nothing wrong, or in lack. I was coming to have a warm feeling for her, and I knew she had good feeling for me from the way she helped me off with my coat, and put a chair to the fire, and tea, then.

My real worry was the Police, though Douglas told me to sit quiet and let him handle everything, and indeed to God I did. But I was sorry for Valmai, whoever or whereever she was, and for Kiri. They were both good ones, I knew, and if they were doing what they believed in, I found it hard to think badly of them. They had been wonderful to me, though it is easy to be anything if it serves an end, but I was sad to think that Plas Sûs had been misused, or that a couple of girls had made a fool of me. But a thought of Kiri's beauty was only a knuckle's length from my mind, and if Cress, in her way, had been a soothe, it was no more than any other woman could give, if only with the body's heat, but never with the tender touch of love, that I missed from Sûs.

Missed, yes, in heart, mind and soul, though what is the difference in the three, I am not sure, or perhaps they are three in one, no matter, but they hurt the same, and often I had to walk about the place, only to forget, or to try to warm that numbness in the heart that never came to thaw, far less to melt.

My beautiful girl had gone from me, and nobody, no, nobody, to take her place.

Taliesin had his Daise, and others had theirs, but I had to go back to an empty house, and only an electric blanket for warmth.

Yes, it is comfortable, but not the same.

Sam and Ella came in that afternoon with a greengage tart.

'Thought you'd have your own cream,' Sam said. 'El's got a smashing idea. There's a circus coming here next week. How about taking all the Sunday School kids for a bunfight? Poor little bastards never have anything much, do they? I thought we'd take the place for the afternoon,

185

lay on a couple of buses, get what's-his-name, the caterer, to lay on the tea and cakes, buy them some chocolates, and Bob's your uncle. How about it?'

'Fair enough,' I said. 'Fifty-fifty, you and me?'

'Carve it down the middle,' Sam said. 'Dead right. Huw, I'm sorry I've got to say this. I've just heard you'll have to lose Gwynaldrod. They'll flood it. I got tipped off this afternoon. I had the trucks down there a bit sharp, getting the stuff out, bricks, blocks, cement, whatnot. That's been paid for. By you. I think it's a bloody shame!'

'Nothing to be done?' I said. 'How about the public?'

'All right, the public,' he said. 'What can *they* do? Come out in the streets? Smash windows? Get you anywhere? D'you want some sort of I.R.A. job? Bombs in cars? Shops? Bullets in the back? No. Let the swine have their God damned water. I hope it poisons them. And I'd put the poison in!'

'It's all our fault for having the water,' Ella said. 'I suppose they'll take our oil, too?'

'Why not?' Sam said, lifting the bottle. 'They've taken the coal, and everything else. They've got the votes, haven't they? What more do they want?'

'No way of beating them, then?' I asked him. 'It is only cowardly, or something, yes? Sitting down and let others do anything they like, isn't it?'

'Get your Nationalist thirty-odd members elected to Parliament, first,' he said. 'They'll form a bloc with the Scottish Nationalists. Together they can tip any Parliament out at a moment's notice. *That's* how. But you've *got* to get the votes!'

It was plenty to think about. I was more than worried about Blodwen's property, and if she would have something for it, or if the English would take, and tell her and me, to go and scratch. I sent her a telegram to the address in America she had given me, and a couple of days later, I had one back to say she would soon be in to see me, and love.

Solva's monthly letter came that I always looked forward to, but this time nothing to raise a lark singing in the heart.

'O, Huw,' she wrote, on blue paper, so that I knew she had been to Buenos Aires. 'I am in depths to know how to write. Not about us, here, but about the poor country. We have got terrible men loose here. Kidnaps and blackmail day after day and nothing to stop. Millions in ransom, and poor women going mad to know what is happening to their husbands and sons. Everybody afraid to go to work in the morning in case not to come back at night. It is not a life even for dogs. Oracio says the Army must take over, yes, again. They must shoot to kill, because there is no longer civil law. Everything is sixes, and no sevens. Down here, we have no trouble, because everybody is known, and movement of strangers is seen, but my husband says it will not be long before the rot is with us. There is too much money to be got only for hiding some poor man until somebody sends enough to let him go. We are come to the time of anti-Christ. We are a lot of old savages and the decencies of the Law are not enough. My husband says that animals have got to be trained and we are only animals. The farm is beautiful, indeed. You would never believe the change. Last year we planted trees all over the hill, and the garden all round the house would take your heart. The flocks have given a record clip, and they have gone back to the Territory, fat. The herd has multiplied by almost five, and every one of them is like old satin, so glossy. Butter and cheese we are sending to the local market and to Bahia Blanca, and next year, Oracio thinks we shall have good markets in Mar del Plata and Buenos Aires. It only wants transport, and now we have got the airline. When are you coming here? We are out of patience to see you. A big kiss. S.'

Well, I had to give it a good think, yes.

I wanted to go back.

I saw the Chubut running green in shadow of the willows and whiskers of froth about the stones and little islands, and my lovely girls sleeping gracious among the flowers in that wide silence of the pampas. But I thought of my Mama and her sisters, and all the good ones of her time, and Ivor and many another of his age, and my father, and the fathers of how many other men, buried in the Valley, and reburied, under the slag of the pits that piled by the hour on the cemetery, and the houses they had lived in, and the streets they had climbed to come from work, and all they had known to call home.

Even in death, they were not their own.

Jesu, Lover of my soul.

There is kind we are to each other

Let me to Thy bosom.

I hear the prayer rising from the buried voices, and they will never come to be silent.

They will sing through time, through the stones of the cemetery, and they will come in royal thunder from the slag, and those with a heart to hear shall know they live, now as then, in a fullness and goodness not in this day, and surely not in days to be.

We have not got the Book, and the Word is no longer our Bread of Life, or of Heaven.

Our chapels are shops, and old warehouses, with us.

When did we give a heart for a lump of slag? A few coins? Thirty pieces bought Christ.

We have sold for far less.

The clowns were riding one-wheel cycles, and hitting each other silly with long balloons, and tearing their clothes when they got off, and getting caught again when they got on, and ripping trousers to rags, caught on saddles, and the children in stitches with them, and one little girl near me crying-laughing and falling helpless to the floor, and her Mama lifting her, and crying, too, and everybody helpless in a shout, there, but the clowns seemed to know when enough was a gate to shut, and they were off, and elephants were trumpeting, with little gold houses on their backs, and feathers, and the children shouting in a different voice, so pretty, so strange.

Rhodrick stood at the end of the row, waving to have my eye, and I nodded to Sam and Ella, and went along to follow him down the steps, out.

'Miss Teleri sent me, sir,' he said. 'Some poor girl is at the house. She is asking for you. I am not sure who, or what she is asking for. So I came. Did I do right, sir?'

'Good, you,' I said. 'Home, is it?'

Well, no need to ask.

The one I had known as Valmai.

But thin, with bones, and the lines of worry, and hair piled from a bath, and Teleri's morning towel gown, and slippers, and going back from me, frightened.

'Let me tell you, please,' she whispered. 'I know I did wrong. I had time to find out. Kiri got away. She's back home. I couldn't go. I didn't have the French. Look, Mr Morgan. I'll do anything. Anything. Would you lend me enough to get back to Australia? A ticket on Qantas. Sounds like paradise to me. *Please.* Please?'

I felt I knew how Mr Parry, Deacon, thought with poor Meillyn Lewis, in front, for judgement.

Helpless, in tears, there, and I go back in the years and put my arms about her.

'Why did you come here as Valmai?' I asked her.

'We tried it,' she said, back in the chair. 'It worked. It's worked before. People like to know they've got relatives. We'd read you up. I was at school with Valmai. We tried it. It came up, didn't it?'

'Making a fool of me, yes, it did,' I said. 'Did you make bombs on the property?'

'Prepared them, yes,' she whispered. 'Here and up in the cottage. The raw stuff went to the caravan. Then to that village, over there. That's where the detonators and fuses went in. Then on the boat. Worked smoothly enough in that time. I don't know what went wrong. We could have gone on. What did?'

'Did what?' I asked.

'Go wrong,' she said.

'Is that really how you can think?' I asked her. 'What went *wrong*? What went wrong to stop the murder of a lot of innocent people? Poor families homeless? Men having a drink in a pub?'

'Lives mean nothing,' she said. 'We want a United Ireland, that's what. When we've got it, we'll have peace all round. Do the same thing here, you'd have your own

189

government quick enough, wouldn't you?'

'On those terms, no,' I said. 'I wouldn't lift a finger.'

'No guts,' she said, and slid further down in the chair, pulling the gown apart. 'Come on, Huw'ee. Take a bite. Here's the apple. I'll start earning that ticket. Or do we go upstairs?'

The alarm button on the Police radio net poked from under the arm of my chair, and I pressed three times, long, and no sound in the house.

'Little use in that,' I said. 'You are having no ticket. My house is dear to me for a reason. You and the others made a stables of it. Apply to your Arab friends. Won't they lend you the money?'

'You don't seem to understand,' she said in whispers, and putting hands together. 'We can't move. We'd be picked up. We couldn't get a mile out to sea. The Navy's everywhere. We can't go anywhere here. The coppers are just waiting to grab us. That's why I'm here. There's nobody else I can turn to, is there?'

Appeal was in her eyes and voice, and in the young body, and I wondered, if she was a Welsh Nationalist with the excuse of self-government for killing and maiming and destroying, whether I would help her, or us, or we, or any of the others, and I shook my head.

'You say us and we,' I said. 'Are there more of you here?'

'That's neither here nor there,' she said, and standing, gown apart, and showing herself. 'Come on, Huw-ee. Let's go to it. I'm feeling like it. Don't go old on me!'

Anger is not the word for what I felt. Yes, I was angry to hear what she said, and in sorrow she should behave in Plas Sûs as a whore in a seaman's brothel, and shame that she would think me so weak, and I was in disgust to be there, and so many ways to feel, and no words to say, and suddenly, in light, I saw those animals and poultry up at the cot, all in a limp from the knife of a brute, and I was in a limp with me, and dumb, yes, as they, and no word to speak.

With no sound, Superintendent Alford came in from the back way with four constables, and she stood, in a turn of the head, forearms holding back the gown, eyes wide, mouth in a gape, and they ran at her and she began the kicking and screaming, but they each had an arm or a leg, and out she went, face down and showing her rump.

'You recognised her, Mr Morgan?' the Superintendent said.

'That is a woman known as Valmai John,' I said.

'Her real name's Dolours Colum, or let's say, it's one of them,' he said. 'Do you feel like coming down to make a deposition in front of the Magistrate? Better if you did? Get it over with. I want her in a cell!'

Teleri brought clothing in a shopping bag.

She was calm, but a bit pale, and I kissed her hand.

'I won't be long,' I said. 'Ask Rhodrick and the men not to leave till I'm back, will you? I don't want you alone here, yes?'

I went down in a Police car, and the Sergeant took me to the lobby of the Magistrate's Court, and the Clerk led me to Mr Soper Reynolds. Well, he might be a nice little fat man outside, having a drink, but behind that long, shining table, with all the red books behind glass along the walls, and a picture of the Queen behind him, indeed he was somebody else, and no smile, and I had some idea of the strength of the Law.

Well, when I had answered all the questions, and everything was in writing, and I had signed here and there, Mr Soper Reynolds sat back and crossed his knees.

'We have got a problem, here,' he said. 'I have always been fond of Ireland, and the Irish. Poets, musicians, intellectuals, whatever, and the ordinary people are wonderful, indeed. What has happened to them is locked in the heart of Satan, himself. They are killing their *own* people. Their *own*. Never mind Catholic or Protestant or anything else. Every one of them is *Irish*. The property they destroy is *Irish*. But I'm very worried when somebody they threaten is *Welsh*. That's *you*, Mr Morgan. And I am considering how to protect you, further. Because, from what we know, you will need it!'

'A surprise to me, indeed,' I said. 'For what do I need protection? *From* what?'

'From those, all right, let us say, serving the same cause as this woman,' he said. 'They are without reck, or honour, or anything else for human life. If they can kill their own, they will kill you, no trouble. No trouble at all. And so, how to guard you?'

'Why should I need a guard?' I said. 'I am well capable of guarding myself, surely?'

He looked at the pen, and to me.

'Mr Morgan,' he said. 'I am not sure you know what nonsense we are trying to prevent, or circumvent. We are up against an implacable, and serpentine enemy. They are being paid big money from outside. What can we do, except defend? And how? *How* are we to defend?'

'Well, your Honour,' I said. 'We will do our best, indeed, yes?'

'But *your* best, and *my* best, and everybody's best, is not enough,' he said. 'The rat will always come through. And these people of low cunning, are rats. They call them guerrillas, and terrorists, but they *should* be called rats. *Rats!*'

'They go back to the hole, yes?' I said.

'Whichever hole they go into, we will try to make certain they don't come out to devour *you*,' he said, and smiling. 'There will be a twenty-four hour guard on you until we are more or less satisfied there is no longer need. I doubt you will see evidence of it. We try to do things discreetly, yes? Mr Morgan, go home, and please to be at peace. You are being watched over, and very carefully. Go you, with God!'

Well, I went, but I was thinking about Teleri.

I had no fears for myself, but for her, yes. She was hours alone in the house. She slept upstairs from me, on the other side. Anybody coming in from the back way could do what they pleased up there, and I would never hear a sound, and so I asked the driver to put me down at the turning, and I walked up, trying to think I was dead, and looking with new eyes.

A fine, big place it was, and I was well proud to think it was mine, and a good girl had put her beautiful heart in it, yes, and it showed, in the green glebes, and the milch herd grazing down by the river, and the sheep on the long rise, and the geese nibbling in the bulrushes, and the ducks over in the pond, and the poultry in more colours than Sheba's court, and all the trees in noble leaf, and every flower in a shout to be seen and kissed.

But it was a long way from anywhere, and lonely.

Lonely.

The alarm button could bring a Police car in a few minutes.

A shot can be fired in a moment, and a rat can go for its hole in the next.

Teleri was alone for hours in the day. It kept thudding in my mind.

I would be responsible.

I went into the house, spacious, in gleam of beeswax and silver polish, and called Douglas.

'I want three men by day, and three by night,' I said. 'I want men I can trust. They shall have dogs and shot-guns. But they must be of the best, do you see? At least a six months' contract, good wages to be decided by your-self, food and drink supplied, yes?'

'Leave it to me,' he said. 'I'll get a few pensioner Royal Welch Fusiliers. Nobody's going to do any buggering about with them. When do you want them?'

'Now,' I said. 'Tonight!'

'I'll see what I can do,' he said.

Half past six, and the first three were at the door. I gave them shotguns and rounds, and from the way they fondled, I was sorry for anybody coming in range. We went out to the hides Rhodrick had built from bales of hay to be out of the wind, and they each had two dogs, and after a good plate of steak and liver, they were friends for life, and the other dogs went free, as scouts.

Teleri came in with the tea trolley, and I asked her to sit down to pour, because nothing is nicer for a man than to have a good girl pouring a cup. There is something solid, and good to the taste.

I told her what to expect.

193

'Well, yes,' she said, and calm, no odds. 'We have all known this long time. Rhodrick is asleep, one eye, with a loaded gun, down there. We will worry when it is time, yes?'

I could have kissed her feet, and the knees, yes.

'You are not afraid, girl?' I said.

'Afraid, no,' she said, 'I am in disgust to think I would have to see them. I will scream, mind?'

'Scream, you,' I said. 'Only let me hear. I will be there, quick, isn't it?'

That weekend, Sam and Ella picked me up and we went to the home where Lys had been remanded by the Magistrate during Her Majesty's pleasure, and Teleri and Mrs Rhodrick and a few more were off to the woods to pick mushrooms.

But I shall always be sorry I went.

Down in the dip we saw her in a hospital blue dress, and the Doctor called to her, and she turned to look at us, and her fingers were straight and apart, and her eyes staring, and her mouth open to scream but no sound, and she ran, ran, ran, in the trees.

'Sorry about that,' the Doctor said. 'It'll take the staff a couple of hours to find her. She's very intelligent. She leads them a real dance, at times!'

'What *is* wrong with her?' Sam asked. 'I always thought her a real brain. Well, she *was*. How she get here?'

'Seems to be a family failing,' the Doctor said. 'We don't know enough about it. You can leave those packages at the porter's lodge. She'll get them!'

We were not very happy going back, not even enough to have a cup of tea at one of the hotels, and when we got to Plas Sûs, they said they would rather go home.

'Been a bit much for me,' Sam said. 'We did a lot of work together. She could be a bit of a drag, right enough. I've lost my temper many a time. I'm beginning to understand, now. I'm so sorry, honest, I could bloody cry, y'know?'

'Thinking of a lovely girl like that, yes,' Ella said. 'All that ability, and where's it get you?'

But I was remembering Mr Anstruther, and I wondered, and I called Douglas.

'I see what you mean,' he said. 'Hooper's got a lot of Irish drivers. Of course, the Police keep a sharp eye on the lot of them. I'll let him know that all the building materials you bought have to go back to your place, and I'll have a man up there to check it in. Save time. Any job she signed for, I'll see she gets her proper cut, whoever takes over the contract. Sam's a sharp boy. Did you know?'

'I am lost in the woods, and waiting for robins,' I said. 'Why do you think I called you?'

Teleri came in with the tray, and poured a good scotch, and put it down, and stood.

'Thank you,' I said. 'What now?'

'Mr Morgan, I have found two good girls,' she said, straight, no wriggling. 'They are from farms over the hill, and down, on the road. Everything to be done here, they can do. If I have to go home, they will take charge, no odds. To cook, or make butter, or cheese, or curds, or whey, or bake bread, or cakes, well, they are the best. I would like to bring them in, isn't it? They will help me to scream, yes? We will sound beautiful, no?'

I saw, and I felt, her loneliness.

We smiled.

'Take them, girl,' I said. 'Have them to Mr Gough's office in the morning. Rhodrick will take you in the jeep. Get them fitted with clothes and shoes. Yes. Take charge, is it? And when will you go home?'

She pulled a cotton from the overall, looking through the window, and she reminded me of music, though I am not sure what, indeed, except with a lot of strings and a harp or two, but good.

'I am not sure, Mr Morgan,' she said, steady. 'I have got nothing to do there more than here. Not as much, in fact. As to a job, I will do better here. I love the place. But I love Gaiman. A peace is there. I think we all need peace, yes?'

'Yes,' I said. 'Where is peace not here?'

'Those men going about with guns,' she said. 'The

Police always going past. The dogs. Nothing is in peace with us, yes?'

'Guarding, they are, girl,' I said. 'I am sorry if you are worried?'

'I am worried for you,' she said. 'Not for me. Nobody is looking for me. I will have both the girls with me, then, is it, Mr Morgan?'

'Both,' I said. 'Rooms next to you?'

'Next,' she said. 'And ready to jump. I am only waiting to see some old fool come in. He shall have a welcome, indeed!'

Well, I saw the two, and I was sure. Girls are different today, well, yes, they dress different, but eyes and smiles never change, and if they wear boots with heels like a club-foot, what? They like them, they wear them, and they are the same good girls, nothing in loss.

Betwys and Nest, they were, one from the hill farmers, and the other from below, but not a pin of change between them, big in the bone, enough muscle in the arm for a man, and in good scent of health.

Before the day was out, their fathers came to see me, and I liked them both, with the wrinkles of men grown to the plough, and the hands of giants. I gave them good welcome to bring their wives over to see where the girls were living, and Teleri had them in the barn for tea, and I was called to the telephone.

'Uncle Huw?' Blodwen said, clear as if beside me. 'I'm flying to New York, and home. We've had a marvellous time, but I'm terribly tired, and I need some new ideas. Is my place in any state to be lived in?'

'Well, now, Blodwen, listen well,' I said. 'We don't know when or if the English will flood, do you see? Let us have no ifs or buts about this. A cottage I have got, well furnished, with hot and cold water, and a good kitchen. You could stay there, and I will have a good girl to look after you. Only say when you will be here, no trouble, yes?'

'I wish they made a few more like you,' she said. 'I'll be in touch from Paris.'

'Where are you, now?' I asked her.

'San Francisco,' she said. 'It's all they say it is. *Plus*. A big kiss!'

I asked Teleri to take the girls up to the cottage on the rise, and put everything in order, and indeed, when I went there later in the day, I could have stayed there. Only a call from Plas Sûs brought me down to talk to a couple wanting to meet me.

'I am Meic Gruffydd, secretary of the Royal Welch Fusiliers Old Comrades' Association,' one of them said. 'This is Jim James, British Legion.'

'*Royal* British Legion, if you please?' Jim James said, quick.

'Right, you,' Meic Gruffydd said. 'Royal bloody British Legion, then? Go on with you, boy. Junior to the bloody N.A.A.F.I. you are, isn't it?'

'What is N.A.A.F.I.?' I asked him.

'God knows, indeed,' Meic Gruffydd said. 'Something they have got there, no doubt. I will never put anything past the English, yes?'

'Nothing to do with the bloody English,' Jim James said. 'We have got our own branch. We are *from* them.'

'Meaning coming from them?' Meic said. 'Or away from them?'

'Ah, for Christ's sake,' Jim said. 'When were we part of them? *From* them, of course!'

'What is this N.A.A.F.I., with you?' I said.

'O, well,' Meic said. 'I'm not sure, indeed. Something to do with canteens, I think. Selling tea, and fags, and a sandwich here and there, yes? No, Mr Morgan. What we came to say was this. You have always been good to us, and especially the children. Don't think we are not all on your side. We *are*. Especially the girls. If anything happened to you, we would be in a hell of a mess. You are not somebody from round here. So we have got to be much more careful, isn't it?'

'Come to the bloody point, man!' Jim James said. 'We are here for *what*?'

'Well, all right, without some bugger doing a bit of shouting,' Meic said. 'We have got plenty of volunteers,

197

Mr Morgan. From us, of the Fusiliers, and from them. All the lot are marksmen, and they have all got the crossed rifles, yes? The *badge*!'

'They will all do two hours' sentry, and home, then,' Jim James said. 'But we would like to know if the lads going off could have the jeep. It's a long walk, yes, that time of night, isn't it?'

'They shall have both jeeps,' I said. 'And thank you, all!'

'Nothing, sir,' Meic said. 'For you, anything!'

Well, I thought we would have a lot of old noise with all those men traipsing about the place, but if we heard them, they were only talking quietly for a moment, and the girls said they could turn over and go back to sleep, knowing they were safe, and very tidy with them, and good ones outside there, ready for a fight.

Late on the next Saturday, Blodwen came, in a car piled high with baggage, and she fell in a chair, and I was sorry, because the girl was tired.

'I have been everywhere,' she said, head back, looking at the ceiling. 'I have never been in a house like this. I know you will let me stay here. But I have a favour to ask. Gwynaldrod. Will I ever have the chance of staying there? In my Mama's place?'

'I am not sure, girl,' I said. 'Not sure, indeed. Those louts in Westminster will decide, isn't it? The vote, yes?'

'Are we so helpless?' she said. '*So* helpless?'

'Yes,' I said. 'Helpless beyond the helpless. Since the time of the Romans. We are a people forgotten. Most of us have even forgotten ourselves. If we are not very careful, we are Englished beyond redemption, isn't it?'

'I'm part English,' she said. 'But I *feel* Welsh. That's why I so want Gwynaldrod. Will they pay for it?'

'A Royal commission,' I said. 'They will value, and pay. How much for a derelict village? I doubt if we shall have much, indeed?'

She put knuckles to her teeth, and I knew tears were not far.

'There goes a dream!' she said, in whispers. 'It's not much use trying to be married in a place that's going to drown, is it? No basis for a good marriage. Registry office is all right. But not for Jon. He's strict Roman Catholic. I'm not strict anything. I wish I were. We want children. That's one thing I'll take care of!'

As a knife will flash in light I had the idea, and I heard Sûs's *YES! YES!* and I was sure.

'Look,' I said. 'This house will do splendid for marrying. I have got a good friend in the priest, here. No trouble, girl. Wait you!'

I got in the jeep and went down to the church, and Father Herlihy had a meeting in the vestry, and I waited for them to finish, and he came to me, arms out.

'I got your munificent cheque,' he said. 'More than enough for the roof, and a wonderful help for other things. Is there something I may do for you?'

Well, I told him, and there was no trouble. The house had to be painted, and blessed, and a prayer or two, and all in order. I went back to tell Blodwen, and real tears, then, and we sat for a couple of hours, writing the names of guests, and she put in an early call to catch the London train to tell Jon.

Late it was when she went up, but Teleri came in with hot whisky and blackcurrant for me, and I told her, and she turned half away, and looked through the window at a moon, behind clouds, making the sky pink.

'I didn't know church could be in a house,' she said. 'Is it right?'

'If the priest thinks so, what is wrong?' I said. 'Houses there are all over the world, and no churches. But people have got to be married, isn't it? Now, then. What I will do here, is call the florist, and ask her to make the main wall a screen of leaves and fresh flowers, floor to ceiling. The floor will be thick with rose petals. The desk for the service will come from my study. The Book, he will bring. And the candlesticks, and everything else. But in the house, only candles. No electric light. Everybody will be invited, but only half a dozen in the house. Everybody else will have the barn and the tents. The asado we will grill behind the turkey lanes. You will have a new dress and shoes, and

199

help me in the house. You will do nothing outside, except welcome. You will do no serving inside. Only see that everybody is comfortable isn't it? We have got to give that girl the *best* marriage, yes? She came to us. Can we do less than the best?'

'No, indeed,' she said, and picked up the tray. 'Will that be all, Mr Morgan?'

'Yes, thank you,' I said. 'You are wonderful, Teleri. I don't know what I would do without you. *Nos da, chwi!*'

She nodded, and went out, though it seemed to me that the door closed too quietly, but I had a lot to think about, and I began making a list of what I wanted done, and if it was past four when I went upstairs, I had the bones on paper, and I have never been surer.

I intended that Olwen's daughter should have a marriage to remember, not only for herself, but for everybody round about, as with us in Patagonia, where people spend, and careless, only that guests are happy for the day, with thought in many a good day to come.

Superintendent Alford came in on the afternoon advertised in the local paper inviting everybody with relations in Patagonia, or any of my friends in the County, or outside, to come to the wedding.

'There can be trouble, here,' he said. 'Hundreds milling about, if it's anything like the last time. Now, Mr Morgan, we have got to take measures. Traffic has got to be supervised. They can put bombs in cars. They could plant riflemen!'

'You have no need to go on,' I said. 'Make your own plan!'

'I want to close the approach road, and put up Police blocks,' he said. 'I'd like a Police tent here, where we can supervise who comes in or goes out. You approve?'

'It is a hopeless bloody life,' I said. 'A girl is going to be married, that's all? And what?'

'You have to accept the conditions, Mr Morgan,' he said. 'I've got two daughters. I think of them. But you are under threat of men without conscience. The young woman and the man she is marrying both have a certain

200

notoriety. In this area, I have responsibility. Will you help?'

'Yes,' I said. 'Do what you want, isn't it?'

In those days I watched the Police install what they wanted, and Rhodrick and his lads doing what they had to do, and the caterer putting up his tables when the tent makers had gone, and this one doing this, and that one doing that, and all the time the hens laid eggs, and cows gave milk, and turkeys grew fat, and ducks waddled, and geese nibbled, and a big day, indeed, when the swans came back to the lake. I could hear Sûs. Those beautiful black-necked swans, she loved. I loved them for her.

In the house we were quiet. The florist looked about, and chose the day to start work, and Rhodrick had the carpenters to build the wooden screen for the wall of flowers, and the girls in the potting sheds got the plants ready, and Father Herlihy came in to look about and say where he wanted things put, and Teleri had everything in a tight fist.

A cold wind struck when Rhodrick came to say that talk in the pubs was that strangers were about and asking quiet questions about Plas Sûs. I told him to get on to Meic Gruffydd and Jim James to put word in the air and let the Police know, and I sent down enough cash to let them all have enough to pay for a few drinks.

The time came nearer, and still the farm looked the same, and other flowers out each day, and the marquees up, and the tables, and the barn decorated, and the wood piled for the asado, and all the carcases hung, and a morning came, and Teleri brought in the tea tray.

'Good morning, Mr Morgan,' she said, a tall shadow against the candle, and I saw she was in National dress, in the high silk hat, and the lace bonnet, and beautiful, with her. 'This is the day before, yes? We will be in splendid trouble before it is out, isn't it?'

You have got to wonder when a good girl's words swarm about you as wasps.

I took a sharper look about the place, and I saw where Superintendent Alford could worry, with all that space, and a crowd everywhere, and except for local people known to the Police, nothing to tell one from another.

But when I asked Meic and Jim, they both disagreed.

'Everything is in order, Mr Morgan,' Meic said. 'Nothing left to chance. Standing here, now, please to say how many blinds you can see, and where are they?'

'None,' I said.

'There are fourteen to be seen from here, alone,' he said. 'Thirty-two altogether. Police blocks along the road, no cars allowed up here, local taxis to bring up the guests, everybody questioned at the gate? No. They won't have a chance. And if the lads get their hooks on them, no judge will ever see them, isn't it?'

'Be well sure of *that*!' Jim said. '*Noth*ing more certain. They will bloody murder them, and bury them, then, yes?'

'In quicklime,' Meic said. 'We have got a *beau*tiful pile, only waiting, see, round the corner. Tell the girls not to be nervous, Mr Morgan. No need!'

Yes, well. I had never thought of it in quite that way. Of the safety of the house, yes, and of the girls, yes. But of their nerves, no, or not exactly. Why do we make a fuss of old bricks and mortar, and bodies, perhaps, because they can stand up and do a bit of work, but never of the nerves and feelings inside?

Into the house I went, and found Teleri in the pantry, taking cream from the milk in the slate pans, but in an ordinary dress, and she said she had worn National dress to have a photograph taken to send home to Dolavon.

'I thought it was Gaiman?' I said.

'Well, in between, it is,' she said. 'Nearer Gaiman, I suppose. In the days of horses and traps, yes, a difference. But with a car?'

'Come here, with me, girl, and sit down,' I said, and took her by the hand, out, to the study. 'Answer me straight, now then. Are you ever nervous here?'

She looked down, and did something with a button, and looked up, and nodded.

'Yes,' she said. 'I am. They have blown up some other poor little place, again. It is in today's paper. Terrible

202

damage. People shot every day. Why can't they stop it?'

'Can you stop the rats in these buildings?' I asked her. 'Now, look. When the wedding is finished, and everything quiet, I was thinking of flying to Buenos Aires, and Trelew, to stay in Maes Corwen, let us say, for a couple of months, and go over to the Andes, and have a look there, and come back to a bit of peace. Come with me, and you can stay with your family, isn't it?'

She looked away from me, head up to the window, and a fine, white neck she had, and a good chin, with her, a lovely old girl, indeed, and putting only the tip of a tongue over her lips, and sitting back in the chair.

'Mr Morgan, a lot of people here have got relations in Chubut,' she said. 'A lot have written to my family. I was going to let the wedding pass, and go back. If you have got Betwys and Nest, you have got the best!'

'Why do you want to go?' I said. 'You shall have fares and expenses return, and still monthly pay. Come with me. Everything is free, isn't it? What is the difference?'

She stood, and put a hand to her mouth, and almost ran for the door to the kitchen, and turned to shut it, and I saw the anguish in her face.

Anguish, yes.

But the telephone rang, and Douglas said that Sam was in Scotland building oil platforms, and his wife would bring Ella to the wedding, and the children would go to the party with his managing clerk, Mr Prosser.

'Huw,' he said. 'I don't think you need another full page advert tomorrow. The entire place is seething, here. Posters are up inviting everybody to the free dance and show at the hall tomorrow night. The children's party is at three. The wedding is at six, and the Chubut grill at seven-thirty. Why attract more attention? Newsprint can be read even wrapping fish and chips. May I cancel?'

'Right,' I said. 'All this, for a few Irish?'

'They *aren't* Irish,' he said. 'My Dad was Irish. Only suggest harming a woman, and he would split you to the chin. No. Swinepest they are, and until there is a drive to kill out the swine, exactly as we have to do here, and slaughter by thousands, nothing will be right!'

'You are sounding very bloodthirsty with you,' I said. 'Thousands slaughtered? Time of Cromwell again? The new Romans come back? Have we forgotten all about the Book, now?'

'Listen, Huw,' he said. 'The only reason we have got a Book is because the Romans gave us a solid basis of civilisation over centuries. The churches have built on it, to this very day. How many give a damn about it? Does swinepest? Well, now. Wait you. I am sad to say Miss Rowlands, at the house, has asked me to put her documents in order for a flight on Saturday week to Buenos Aires. Did you know?'

'Not so plain as that,' I said.

'Pity to lose her,' he said. 'See you tomorrow, is it? O, yes. Do you want a replacement?'

Heart was not in me to answer.

I went about the farm, glum as an old boot, in scowls and wrinkles of age, with me. How to keep her, or what to offer, I was lost to think, because I knew well that if a girl like that has made up her mind, you can all go and scratch, or push a thumb, or both, as it suits you, no difference.

The catering staff carried stores in the service tents, and the carpenters were finishing all the tables, and placing chairs, and Rhodrick and his lads were shovelling gravel in case of rain, and the florist finished the screen with leaves, and very pretty.

'The flowers are in ice till tomorrow,' she said, a good little girl. 'They will be finished by twelve, and we will carry it in the house. There is pity it is not for you, isn't it?'

I looked at piled braids, and some green over the eyes, and a coffee-coloured smock.

'For me?' I said. 'What, for me, now then?'

'Well, marrying, of course!' she said, and laughing small white teeth. 'Why somebody else, and not you?'

From the mouths of babes and old sucklings, yes.

In pretence of no hurry, I was in the house, and shouting, but Betwys said Teleri had gone shopping with Nest, and back in a couple of hours.

A couple of hours can be a lifetime.

I was into Mari Fach, not yet dry from a coat of white paint to bring the bride from the cottage on the rise, and down that road, as if the Devil had both cloven hoofs on my coat-tails, and I went to all the shops in town, and I found her in a lane in the supermarket, hair in a long braid, thick, beautiful indeed, shining, and a man's cap, flat on the head, no tilt, mine.

'Miss Rowlands,' I said. 'Please to pardon an interruption. If you had to marry, would you have to ask permission of your good father? Down there in Gaiman, Dolavon, the Chubut, whatever?'

She looked at me, big eyes, brows up, but frowning.

'Well, no, indeed,' she said. 'I am well beyond that, yes. Am I a child?'

'But that is *not* what it was in the old days, is it?' I said. 'Well, let us say, in the day of your father?'

'No,' she said. 'And I am old enough to remember. But once we are in the world, we are only by ourselves, no? What has he to say?'

That voice, quiet, among the rattle and jingle of cash registers, and people talking, and babies left in prams and crying, brought to me the lonely thoughts of a girl, and if they scream at you, or spit in your face, or only smile for what it is worth, it is the same. In some lonely place they are frightened to be alone, and so, and often, so many of us, yes, *we* are. And with all the loud denials, and waving of fists, and long after all the shouting and fighting, we are still small boys crying for Mama, and pretending not.

A beautiful thing it is, to slip an arm about the small warm waist of a good girl, and know, beyond the seven seals of Solomon, she trusts.

'Teleri,' I said. 'Are you a Roman Catholic?'

'No,' she said. 'I am nothing, isn't it?'

'Good,' I said. 'Neither am I. And we are the best Roman Catholics of the lot. May I ask if you would marry the worst of them? I put forward my claim. Nobody can come near me for worst. Will you marry me, girl?'

She came close, yes, beautiful to feel a girl close.

205

'Yes,' she said. 'Roman Catholic, or what, yes, but no need to tell anybody, no?'

'Every need,' I said. 'Shall we be married in the dark?'

'I will have to get a dress,' she said. 'Where, now then?'

'You have got one,' I said. 'The one you wore this morning. Will you wear it for fools taking photographs, and not for me?'

'For you, anything,' she said.

'Right, now then,' I said. 'I am off to the priest. Take care to be back safe, isn't it?'

Father Herlihy I found in the church piling books, and a lot of girls and boys taking them out to the car.

'We're preparing for the wedding,' he said. 'I'll be there for a rehearsal at above five. Is that all right?'

'Very good,' I said. 'I wonder if I could ask a question?' He nodded.

'I would like to marry Teleri Rowlands,' I said. 'We are not Catholics. She was born in the Welsh Colony in Patagonia. I lived there many years. I was married by a Roman Catholic priest, the first and the second time, so I am no stranger, yes?'

'It's a little late to speak of catechism, isn't it?' he said, and smiling. 'Can you show me the certificates?'

'Both,' I said. 'And the birth certificate of my son. He died with his Mama.'

'Do I understand that children of the marriage will be brought up in the faith of the Roman Catholic Church?' he asked me. 'If I can have that clearly stated by yourself and the bride-to-be, then yes. I'll marry you!'

'Thank you and God,' I said. 'We will be waiting!'

'Do you wish the service in the language of the Country?' he asked me. 'Should it be English?'

'Never,' I said. 'As with the other two. Latin, please, isn't it?'

He smiled.

'More beautiful,' he said. 'I agree. *Latin!*'

I was off back in a sea-mewl of impatience, and I was in the house just after Teleri.

'You and the two girls, get into your Nationals,' I said.

'We shall have a rehearsal for tomorrow. Off, now then!'

I went out to the barn and found the florist with the girls among the plants.

'Put in the flowers!' I shouted, and they must have thought I was mad, and they were right. 'A bridal bouquet, one for the matron of honour, two for the bridesmaids, and white carnation buttonholes for the groom and groomsman. Four-thirty, ready!'

I called Rhodrick from the long field.

'Go you, and tell Mrs Rhodrick to dress in her National, and you change to Sunday clothes,' I said 'Rehearsal for tomorrow!'

He was off, no questions. I told the men to be ready for a drink, and went in the house to pour one for myself, and upstairs, then, to bath and change, because nothing is better than a good drink in a hot bath, and clean linen, then. I thanked Menai for saying about an old stick-in-the-mud, because I had a few suits, new, one grey I had never worn, and that one did splendid, indeed. I was tying a knot, and knocks on the door, and one of the girls helping in the house said the two photographers from the papers were outside and if they could have permission to take pictures.

'All they want,' I said. 'Come back after, and you have a drink, isn't it? And please to ask Rhisiart, out in the barn, to put a few sheep to the coals ready for seven o'clock. About twenty or thirty of us. Sausages, and the rest on the wire grill, yes? Tap one of the barrels, and see there is plenty of bread. Hot, with him!'

'Miss Teleri has already told him, sir!' she said. 'She is out there, now.'

'O, well,' I said. 'Fair enough!'

Downstairs, I found the servers had made the desk into a beautiful altar, all white, with gold edging, and candlesticks, and the little stands for books at both ends, and a gold crucifix on a table behind, and the screen of flowers and leaves covering the wall behind, lovely indeed. Teleri had shown Father Herlihy the small dressing-room next to my study, and I sat down to look at everything, and enjoy.

Strange, it is, that we will crack our bones to make things nicer than they were, nice as they will ever be, but we will never take a minute to sit down, and enjoy what is there, as we will sit to enjoy a good cup of tea.

We never make the best of our time, and it seemed to me, sitting back, then, that I had never even tried to savour the beauty of Plas Sûs. I had lived there, yes, as some old fool of a lodger, enjoying the cooking, and clean sheets.

Not any more.

Little bells rang silver, as lily-of-the-valley, and the altar boys came in with tall candles, and the Sacristan carried the Cross, all of them in scarlet cassocks and white, laced surplices, and the Server walked, swinging a censer, without smoke, and after Father Herlihy, in blue velvet, white underneath, hands in prayer, and Mrs Aeron Rhys played a soft chord on the piano, and they chanted, in Latin, but they wandered about the place to get past the furniture.

Teleri stood over by the door, and I went to her, and took her hand.

'A rehearsal, this is, for tomorrow,' I said, in whispers. 'We will be the couple in front, yes? Will you go upstairs to my room, and look in the old leather box in the small cupboard, and find the gold watch chain, and take off the ring threaded on it? It was my Mama's. The watch chain was my Grandada's, but I always wear the one I was given years ago by Mr Gruffydd. I never found one better. Will you get it for me, girl? Is everything right, outside? The asado?'

'Be sure,' she said, and I was. 'I will have the ring in moments, here, isn't it?'

I loved the move of her skirts across the room, and up the stairs.

Cars coming in sounded loud in silence, and Father Herlihy turned the boys back to the study.

'They'll have to get this entrance right, or precipitate disaster,' he said, passing me. 'We'll come in two or three more times, and find the right way. If it doesn't bother you?'

'If things are not right, they are not worth,' I said. 'If the table and chairs are moved, they won't have to go round, yes?'

'Far better,' he said. 'We'll walk it a couple of times, and then we'll be ready.'

'The complete service?' I said. 'But no hymns?'

He looked at me.

'They know only their own hymns,' he said.

'The service is in Latin,' I said. 'It is foreign to us, yes? But it is also sacred to us. Our hymns are in our own language. But sacred to us, isn't it?'

'Very well,' he said. '*Not* sung in English. Which hymn?'

'The favourite of my Mama,' I said. 'It is much prettier as we sing it. *The King Of Love My Shepherd Is.* Yes?'

'Yes,' he said. 'It will do very well.'

He went on, and Mrs Aeron played the chords, and we came in beautiful. Till then, I had not known Teleri had a deep contralto, or that Betwys sang lyric soprano, or Rhodrick was a basso profundo, and all the others in a voice to shame angels. Teleri gave me the ring, still singing, and Rhodrick was shaking the floor with that voice, and shifting the furniture over to the side.

Teleri went to answer the door, and Mr Soper Reynolds came in with two men carrying a couple of long red books, and a few more behind, all of them Councillors, I knew, and the two photographers with cameras round their necks, and tin boxes. Rhodrick and the girls were all singing, moving the furniture, and Mr Soper Reynolds and the men had the big red books on another table, and Father Herlihy looked out and saw the space clear.

Again the Latin chant began, but everybody still sang, even Mr Soper Reynolds, in a high little tenor coming through like a drill in the coal face, and nothing clear except noise, though in a rough choir it will pass. With us it passed, and the Latin threading through, as silk in a good wool blanket, and Father Herlihy looked at me to come in front of the altar.

I took Teleri's hand over my arm, and we went through the crowd with a bit of pushing from behind, and I thought more people had come in to have a place, but Father Herlihy took no notice, and I heard the quiet voice in words that had come solid through the ages, and our language, solid too, and so much older, lifting it to rest as on a cushion, in the voices of our time, yes, but in the harmonies and words of another.

Jostle at the back, and noisy talk under the singing made no odds. Father Herlihy took his eyes off the book only to kneel, and although I wanted to shout to them behind to behave, Teleri pressed me to her, and her eyes were a joy, of grey in the smile of those born again, and a wonder.

The crush and noise got worse, and I felt a jab in the back, and I looked at a tall man with a silk stocking tied round in a knot on top of his head.

'You got Dolours Column put inside, didn't you?' he shouted, but tiny in the noise. 'This is yours!'

But in a strong move, Rhodrick shoved him off balance from the side, and the gun went off, and bits flew from the walls, and Teleri bent and took off the heavy shoe, and hit him a clout with the steel-tipped heel, and 'the girls were on him, and kicking and scratching and another man came from behind with a gun, but Father Herlihy got in his way and pulled the little barrels to his chest.

'Would you interrupt a sacred service, you faceless devils, you?' he shouted in the noise. 'Would you be shooting a man in Holy Orders? Is that your desire? Are you not the very likeness of every demon in hell?'

'Out of it,' the man shouted, and I feared to kick in case to jolt the trigger.

But he gave just time, and the girls had him by the coat and collar, and Rhodrick kicked a rough boot at the back of his knees, and bent him over, and I kicked at the trigger hand, and again both barrels fired at the ceiling, and leaves and flowers from the screen flew in pretty shower, but he was on the floor with screeching girls on top of him, and Rhodrick took the gun by the barrels and hit him with the butt, and Betwys tore off the stocking cap.

Him, I knew.

The gingery-fair one with Valmai and Kiri, that night.

210

'Over here, Mr Morgan, if you please?' Mr Soper Reynolds shouted through the noise. 'Never mind that one by there. They are both in good hands. Put your signature by here, and read this declaration, yes?'

I was still in a stun and seeing strange lights, but I looked at the notice, though the print was small, and the sun was on the other side, but I signed, and Teleri signed, and the Town Clerk took the notice from me and gave it to her, and we stood together while she read, and she gave it back, and kissed me in front of everybody.

Well, well.

There is nice.

I am not sure how I felt, but Mr Soper Reynolds tapped the card.

'Look,' he said. 'Those two could have killed you, and who else, here? A car was down there with a bomb. It could have blown everything here to hell. The only reason those two got in, the Police were dragging the car down the hill. It belonged to these two. They had a Press pass from somewhere. God knows how, indeed!'

He pointed the pen.

'Go you,' he said. 'The other wedding will be tomorrow, and no trouble. But you two can go now, and think yourselves more than lucky. Stay away for a honeymoon a nice time, is it? We have got to get everything here right, like, yes?'

'Honeymoon?' I said.

'Well, usual,' he said, and nodded at the register. 'As good as the next, yes? That bit of a service over there, and this certificate, you are man and wife, with you. Sign there, again, now then. Or will you deny?'

'*No*, indeed,' I said. 'One day less, isn't it? And one day more where I want to be!'

'Don't go down, yet,' he said. 'Wait till the Police give us the signal.'

'What signal?' I said.

'Well, that the bomb is going off, or not, yes?' Mr Soper Reynolds said, and gave the pen to Teleri. 'Sign by there, Mrs Morgan. And happy life, and everything good to come, isn't it? Now then, Douglas Gough is in charge of everything here, and I am behind him, no doubt. So go you, and make fools of them saying you are under a curse!'

'A curse?' I said, and Teleri held my arm tight. 'Which one is this, now then?'

'Well, the one down by there, at the caravan, and a murder, and the one up at the cot, and the other one by there at Gwynaldrod, yes?' Mr Soper Reynolds said. 'What use to talk? Send out a curse from somewhere, and where will it land? Father Herlihy can blow old smoke and burn candles, and pray. I am *Presbytyriadd,* and we can pray without smoke and old candles. But what, in the finish? Was this, now, in the past ten minutes, a blessing, with you?'

'I will believe when I see,' I said. 'A couple of ruffians, those were, no?'

'Ruffians, and worse,' he said. 'They could have killed both of you, and a lot of other people, here. For what? Isn't it a curse? What goes into a mind? Love? Charity? Is there conscience? I am on the Bench. I have got to give sentence to minor offenders. The worst of them are cherubim and seraphim compared with these. They are the rot of creation. I have never been less than the friend of the Irish. But not now, indeed. How to be a friend to maniacs? Every one of them, in front of me, I.R.A.? Boasting? I give them to a Judge!'

'How about a glass of champagne?' I said. 'Teleri and me are going to have one, now just, when she is changed and ready to be off. Teleri, where are the glasses with you, girl?'

'Behind you,' she said. 'And some smoked salmon, and little bits. Did you think I forgot?'

'Well, there is a beautiful old girl,' I began to say, and the floor rocked and the windows could have come in, and the room filled with pale-blue and lilac and red light, and a candle fell over, and the explosion seemed to last for moments in a *crack!* to hurt the ears, and rolling, rolling then, as a wave, and stones showered on the roof among shatters of glass from the greenhouses.

212

I ran to the back door in time to see earth and clods of grass and small stones in black rain all about, and waited for the air to clear. Over to the greenhouses, then, and down to the potting sheds, but thank God, all the girls were in the storeroom, of brick and a concrete roof, and all of them frightened, but safe.

'Come you,' I said. 'Up to the house for a glass of champagne, and stay for an asado after. I will be going away for at least three months. Mr Rhodrick is in charge. You have got no worries, yes?'

'Will they come back with more bombs?' Bethan asked, from the back of the bulb shed, 'I don't think my Dada will let me work here any more, isn't it?'

'When I go, nothing more will happen,' I said. 'I shan't be here. The Mini-van will bring you from the town, and take you back at night. It won't last long, and a bit of peace again, shall we hope?'

'You can't trust them,' Sian said, a big girl, at the back. 'Before you know where you are, the legs are off you, yes?'

'If my brothers would have their hands on them, they would be in bad luck,' Eirwen said, a little one, and a little voice. 'I like working here. But I don't want the rest of my life on stumps, indeed!'

'Come you for some champagne,' I said, tired with sadness, and no real notion what to say. 'You have done a beautiful job here. I hope I shall find all of you when I am back, yes?'

They followed me to the house, and I went in to put an arm about Teleri's small, warm waist, and she stopped pouring for somebody else, and filled my glass, and I took the bottle from her to fill hers, and still holding her, I touched glasses, all the way up, up, and down.

'This is for us,' I said. 'A good kiss is in every bubble. You are the only girl for me. I will never look at another. I love you, Teleri, do you know?'

'There is nice,' she said, in whispers. 'Ten kisses for every bubble, then. And ten times ten for every kiss. And if there is a curse, I have kissed it gone. What about the wedding tomorrow?'

'Get your coat,' I said. 'You shall buy everything in London, new. Go from the side door. I will meet you at Mari Fach in five minutes, is it? Blodwen and Jon will be married without us. In peace, please God?'

Well, there is a lot to be said for starting another life in a bridal jeep painted white. I had begun a new time on earth after Lal, and again after Sûs, not that I would have chosen, but their going made me. It is not easy to get up every morning to an emptiness, and those other times, when voices are in corners and shapes call in any shadow, and the arms plead to hold somebody, yes, in love, warm, never anybody else to be in her place, or near.

But what is love?

Often I have asked myself, but I never had an answer I could trust, except that if Lal had lived, I could never have looked at Sûs, hard it is to think, and if Sûs had not died, I would have been far from Teleri. Yet, all three had a tenderness only of a woman. Each had her own way to use it, and not one was the same, and for me, nothing to choose between, not any little word to give one more than the other.

Lucky, I was. But a new wife is a new land. You have got to ride long miles to find where you are, where she is, where you are both comfortable with each other, and that land I had to go in with the girl beside me, and she had to be sure as me. At least, I knew where she was born, in the silence of the Chubut Valley, between Dolavon and Gaiman, where the poplars make tall avenues along the waterways, and that quiet of sighing leaves, and breeze in the wheat, is part of them living there, seen in their eyes, heard in their voices, even to be told in the way they walk, in good purpose, without hurry.

But I felt a bit of a stranger. Neither of my beautiful girls, Lal or Sûs, had ever been housekeeper to me, and neither had they ever called me Mr Morgan. I had been Huw from the start.

How to get over that hedge was a bit of a puzzle, but after all, we have got a tongue.

'Well, Mrs Morgan,' I said, in a West rain wind. 'Would

you like a little to eat, with you?'

'No, Mr Morgan,' she said, eyes on the road. 'I have got a gold ring, and a full heart. Where shall I find room for food?'

'*Mr* Morgan, now then?' I said. 'How about some other name? Him you married?'

'My Grandam called my Grandada Rowlands till they died, and they died the same day,' she said, still with her eyes on the road. 'Is there something wrong? She had his name. She had his children. What, then?'

'I will call you Teleri,' I said. 'You will call me Huw. In love, or not. But in marriage, yes. Isn't it?'

'And in love, Huw,' she said, and smiling. 'From the moment. I often think I have been in love from long ago. How often I wanted to go to you, and put my arms round you and rest your head to have that look from your eyes.'

'What look, now then?' I asked her.

'Of the lost, and not knowing what, or where,' she said, and a hand on my arm. 'But not any more, isn't it? I am here. I will never be *from* here. Where you are, I will be. No?'

'Yes,' I said. 'And thankful, indeed. I am sorry I looked such a fool, yes?'

'Never,' she said. 'You had that place in the grasp of your hand. Everybody knew. But why did those men want to kill you?'

'It has become a fashion for some,' I said. 'The poor Irish in the north are living in a hell on earth. Nothing to be done. Nothing. Men of small intelligence. The same here if we are not careful, yes?'

'What will stop it, then?' she asked. 'Aren't the mothers afraid for their children?'

'Well, of course, girl,' I said. 'But what is that to brutes? They kill the children, too. Fathers and mothers? Put a bullet in them, isn't it? Property? It isn't theirs. So blow it up, why not? They bring the name of Ireland to stink down further than the nostrils. It will be generations before it will be sweet. Cromwell is alive again. But on the other side. Satan stuck his warts on somebody else. Evil is with us. What more to say?'

'Good we are going,' she said. 'I won't be happy till we come to Dolavon. I think Europe has gone mad. Nothing is right, here. Rich people, and only old Indios after. Who is careful of Indios? Anywhere?'

'We *could* be better,' I said. 'If they would let us?'

'Who are *they*?' she asked, turning to me, and not gentle. 'Them my Grandada cursed? Them my Grandam dropped salt to hear the sound of the word? English? *Ichabod, Ichabod. How* are the mighty fallen!'

'Well, yes,' I said. 'But they had a *bit* of good with them, yes?'

'Yes,' she said. 'When it suited their pockets. Without? Nothing!'

'It looks as if we have got an old firebrand in the family,' I said.

'Born, and strengthened while I am here,' she said. 'We talk. But to do is beyond us. The same in Chubut. So they do as they please with us. At the end, they have got everything, and us? *Nothing!*'

'Wait you,' I said. 'We are making a black case, here, isn't it?'

'If anything happened to you, I must stand as Mrs Huw Morgan,' she said, eyes on the road, chin well up. 'I will be sad, and proud. What, then, with Gwynaldrod?'

'It will flood, if they say so,' I said. 'In London is the yes or no.'

'Nothing to be done, then?' Teleri said, high, and the rain starting to pelt. 'Only words, and nothing else?'

'Tell the rain to stop,' I said.

But the rain fell in mist across the moorland, and the heather came mauve, or purple, or paler, and gorse rumpled yellow, and the rocks were grey from time long ago, and I saw a sign on the hilltop where the way curved down, and the very road I had not wanted to go along, yes, that one I was on, trucks coming to, trucks behind, cars in between, and nowhere to turn, there I was.

I had to go down into the Valley, that I had long thought the Valley, not of the shadow, but the very place

216

of death, of them dead, and buried again, and them alive, and only waiting for the slag in front, and above, and all around, to fall and swallow them as with the children of Aberfan.

O, Aberfan, the voices of your children sing evermore from the skull of the school that taught them, and buried them, yet they cry day long in the heart. Only the night is kind, with sleep, and silence, but the little ones are gone.

> There's A Friend
> For Little Children
> Above
> The Bright
> Blue Sky.

We came in the Valley on the lower road. I knew it was the Valley because Mrs Tom Harries's house was up by there, on the terrace, and the Chapel was down in the dip. The postman in the red van took letters from the box, and when I stopped the jeep, he was singing with the chapel choir at practice, and in the same place my good father and brothers often stood to sing to have the echo back from the other side of the valley. Though not since I was a boy, and after the slag piled up and up, and shut the echo, and us, out.

But the slag was gone.

Gone.

The mountain behind our house, gone.

In front, gone.

The rail lines, the sidings, the tips, all gone.

Even the slag was gone.

I free-wheeled in the quiet, down to the postman's van, and stopped, listening to him singing a glorious tenor in a phrase here and there, against the choir, only to listen to his voice coming back, and again I was with my good father and my brothers, and hearing them singing, with Dai Bando, a hard-edged baritone, and Cyfartha, high tenor, and Ellis the Post, baritone again, and Mr Gruffydd, basso, and me, soprano, high above everybody, and the voices coming back from the other side, crystal cut, and everybody out on the terraces to listen.

But the terraces were all buried.

Most of them listening, then, were buried.

Twice buried. Once in the ground, and again under the slag.

A lovely lot we are.

I waited for the postman to have his breath from singing.

'Excuse me,' I said. 'I know this place. But there has been a bit of a change, isn't it?'

'A bit?' he said, a good old boy, curls below his ears. 'They have taken out a million tons of rubbish by the bull-dozers. They have shaped new. The river is running clear as glass down the middle, look. Trout is in there. Next year the salmon will be jumping. Change? Good God, another world it is? And the grass is growing, and the trees are planted. Since a boy, I never saw one. No. Not one. Not a single tree. And now, look, thousands. All little ones. Give it five years. What, then? A bloody miracle, yes?'

'Yes,' I said. 'How do you know trout is in the river, now then?'

'Well, good God, I've caught them,' he said. 'And tickled them. Yes. Between one rock fall and the next. Pools, there are. Beautiful, and clear. I don't think we know what we have got, yes?'

'Only a little of what our fathers had,' I said. 'But they had to give it all away, no?'

'Well, yes,' he said. 'To live, isn't it?? Good-bye, now. I will be late, and no excuse.'

But I looked at the valley, and I took Teleri's hand, and kissed the wedding ring.

'Look well,' I said. 'Here I was born. My Mama and Dada are down there, under a couple of hundred foot of rock. A good feeling? That's why I never wanted to come here. They lived, and they were treated as slaves. They never were. But that's how they were treated. Not only blacks have been slaves. Others have suffered to be slaves only to have enough to feed a family, yes? We will go now, and catch a train in Cardiff, and go to London, and fly to

218

Buenos Aires, and over to Trelew, is it?'

'Yes,' she said. 'And remember, Huw, everybody buried in my family, up to the last flood, are all in the Atlantic. We have no graveyard. Only the sea.'

'Well,' I said. 'What matter, indeed? When we are gone, we are gone. Is it something wonderful to be under a slab of stone? To be thumbing a nose in a tomb? Do you want to be in a cemetery, taking precious ground? Look at all of them, by there. Silent, at rest, in peace. Nobody knows them. Nobody knows the thousands, tens of thousands, the millions, loved, and honoured, and where are they? All adding to the riches of this little ball we are on. Yes?'

'Yes,' she said. 'I will be glad when we get to Buenos Aires, indeed. Then I will know we are almost home. I want to make a special asado for you. Our style, yes?'

In her voice I heard love, and I heard the love I had known in the Valley, but it was not the Valley I had always known, of the tips, and the slag, and the mountains rising to destroy the school and the cemetery, and the gardens, the houses, yes, and the people.

This was not the Valley I had known.

From other brains another valley had been born. Not the one my father had walked to in those first days, and not, of a surety, the Valley I had known, but another, cleaner, happier, greener, than any since the time of my Grandfather, not, perhaps, as he had seen it, but for us, used to packaged goods and supermarkets, good enough, and far better than what we remembered.

How green was my Valley, then, yes, but green, green my Valley now, all praise and thanks to the Lord God, and his craftsmen, of the gentle pen, and the giant machine, and I can hear those little ones singing through the rock down by there, yes, a beautiful hymn for time to come, and we shall see again the West wind with his comb in the long grass, and daffodils blowing on the mountain, and pray to hear the nightingale – *O, Ceinwen!* – once again.

We pray to Thee, Lord God.

Amen.

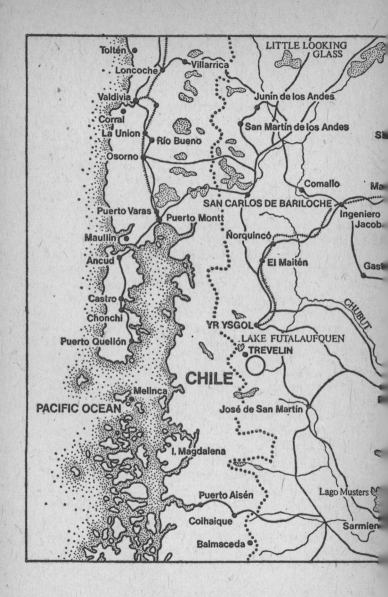

HOW GREEN
WAS MY VALLEY

by Richard Llewellyn

In the beginning were the green mountains and the fertile valleys and the people were happy.

Then below the meadows they discovered coal. And the men of the fields were transformed into people who laboured in darkness. People who fought, loved, drank and sang in the shadows of the great collieries. People who lived with danger and disaster – who had forgotten how green their valley had been.

'Vivid, eloquent, poetical, glowing with an inner flame of emotion . . . To write from the heart, to measure experience in love and sorrow, to bear witness to nobility or the idealism of men – this is not the sort of thing a serious novelist tries to do nowadays. It is what Mr Llewellyn does, however. His story makes a direct and powerfully sustained appeal to our emotions . . . deeply and continuously moving.'
—The Times Literary Supplement

'A work of fiction which enlarges for us the whole bounds of experience . . . I say with all my heart: read it. It is a most royal and magnificent novel.' **—Yorkshire Post**

NEW ENGLISH LIBRARY

NEL BESTSELLERS

Crime

T026 663	THE DOCUMENTS IN THE CASE	*Dorothy L. Sayers*	50p
T027 821	GAUDY NIGHT	*Dorothy L. Sayers*	75p
T030 180	UNNATURAL DEATH	*Dorothy L. Sayers*	60p
T026 671	FIVE RED HERRINGS	*Dorothy L. Sayers*	50p
T025 462	MURDER MUST ADVERTISE	*Dorothy L. Sayers*	50p

Fiction

T030 199	CRUSADER'S TOMB	*A. J. Cronin*	£1.25
T029 522	HATTER'S CASTLE	*A. J. Cronin*	£1.00
T027 228	THE SPANISH GARDNER	*A. J. Cronin*	45p
T013 936	THE JUDAS TREE	*A. J. Cronin*	50p
T015 386	THE NORTHERN LIGHT	*A. J. Cronin*	50p
T031 276	THE CITADEL	*A. J. Cronin*	95p
T027 112	BEYOND THIS PLACE	*A. J. Cronin*	60p
T016 609	KEYS OF THE KINGDOM	*A. J. Cronin*	60p
T029 158	THE STARS LOOK DOWN	*A. J. Cronin*	£1.00
T022 021	THREE LOVES	*A. J. Cronin*	90p
T022 536	THE HARRAD EXPERIMENTS	*Robert H. Rimmer*	50p
T022 994	THE DREAM MERCHANTS	*Harold Robbins*	95p
T023 303	THE PIRATE	*Harold Robbins*	95p
T022 986	THE CARPETBAGGERS	*Harold Robbins*	£1.00
T031 667	WHERE LOVE HAS GONE	*Harold Robbins*	£1.00
T023 958	THE ADVENTURERS	*Harold Robbins*	£1.00
T025 241	THE INHERITORS	*Harold Robbins*	90p
T025 276	STILETTO	*Harold Robbins*	50p
T025 268	NEVER LEAVE ME	*Harold Robbins*	50p
T025 292	NEVER LOVE A STRANGER	*Harold Robbins*	90p
T022 226	A STONE FOR DANNY FISHER	*Harold Robbins*	80p
T031 640	79 PARK AVENUE	*Harold Robbins*	80p
T027 945	THE BETSY	*Harold Robbins*	90p
T029 557	RICH MAN, POOR MAN	*Irwin Shaw*	£1.25
T031 241	EVENING IN BYZANTIUM	*Irwin Shaw*	75p
T021 025	THE MAN	*Irving Wallace*	90p
T022 897	THE PRIZE	*Irving Wallace*	£1.00
T027 082	THE PLOT	*Irving Wallace*	£1.00
T030 253	THE THREE SIRENS	*Irving Wallace*	£1.25
T020 916	SEVEN MINUTES	*Irving Wallace*	90p

Historical

T022 196	KNIGHT WITH ARMOUR	*Alfred Duggan*	50p
T022 250	THE LADY FOR RANSOM	*Alfred Duggan*	50p
T017 958	FOUNDING FATHERS	*Alfred Duggan*	50p
T022 625	LEOPARDS AND LILIES	*Alfred Duggan*	60p
T023 079	LORD GEOFFREY'S FANCY	*Alfred Duggan*	60p
T024 903	THE KING OF ATHELNEY	*Alfred Duggan*	60p
T020 169	FOX 9: CUT AND THRUST	*Adam Hardy*	30p
T021 300	FOX 10: BOARDER'S AWAY	*Adam Hardy*	35p
T023 125	FOX 11: FIRESHIP	*Adam Hardy*	35p
T024 946	FOX 12: BLOOD BEACH	*Adam Hardy*	35p
T027 651	FOX 13: SEA FLAME	*Adam Hardy*	40p

Science Fiction

T027 724	SCIENCE FICTION ART	*Brian Aldiss*	£2.95
T030 245	TIME ENOUGH FOR LOVE	*Robert Heinlein*	£1.25
T029 492	STRANGER IN A STRANGE LAND	*Robert Heinlein*	80p
T029 484	I WILL FEAR NO EVIL	*Robert Heinlein*	95p
T026 817	THE HEAVEN MAKERS	*Frank Herbert*	35p
T031 462	DUNE	*Frank Herbert*	£1.25
T022 854	DUNE MESSIAH	*Frank Herbert*	60p
T023 974	THE GREEN BRAIN	*Frank Herbert*	35p
T015 270	THE WEAPON MAKERS	*A. E. Van Vogt*	30p
T023 265	EMPIRE OF THE ATOM	*A. E. Van Vogt*	40p
T027 473	THE FAR OUT WORLD OF A. E. VAN VOGT	*A. E. Van Vogt*	50p

War

T027 066	COLDITZ: THE GERMAN STORY	*Reinhold Eggers*	50p
T020 827	COLDITZ RECAPTURED	*Reinhold Eggers*	50p
T020 584	THE GOOD SHEPHERD	*C. S. Forester*	40p
T012 999	PQ 17 – CONVOY TO HELL	*Lund & Ludlam*	30p
T026 299	TRAWLERS GO TO WAR	*Lund & Ludlam*	50p
T025 438	LILLIPUT FLEET	*A. Cecil Hampshire*	50p
T018 032	ARK ROYAL	*Kenneth Poolman*	40p
T027 198	THE GREEN BERET	*Hilary St George Saunders*	50p
T027 171	THE RED BERET	*Hilary St George Saunders*	50p

Western

T017 893	EDGE 12: THE BIGGEST BOUNTY	*George Gilman*	30p
T023 931	EDGE 13: A TOWN CALLED HATE	*George Gilman*	35p
T020 002	EDGE 14: THE BIG GOLD	*George Gilman*	30p
T020 754	EDGE 15: BLOOD RUN	*George Gilman*	35p
T022 706	EDGE 16: THE FINAL SHOT	*George Gilman*	35p
T024 881	EDGE 17: VENGEANCE VALLEY	*George Gilman*	40p
T026 604	EDGE 18: TEN TOMBSTONES TO TEXAS	*George Gilman*	40p
T028 135	EDGE 19: ASHES AND DUST	*George Gilman*	40p
T029 042	EDGE 20: SULLIVAN'S LAW	*George Gilman*	45p

General

T017 400	CHOPPER	*Peter Cave*	30p
T022 838	MAMA	*Peter Cave*	35p
T021 009	SEX MANNERS FOR MEN	*Robert Chartham*	35p
T023 206	THE BOOK OF LOVE	*Dr David Delvin*	90p
T028 623	CAREFREE LOVE	*Dr David Delvin*	60p

Mad

S006 739	MADVERTISING	70p
N766 275	MORE SNAPPY ANSWERS TO STUPID QUESTIONS	70p
N769 452	VOODOO MAD	70p
S006 741	MAD POWER	70p
S006 291	HOPPING MAD	70p

NEL P.O. BOX 11, FALMOUTH TR10 9EN, CORNWALL:

For U.K.: Customers should include to cover postage, 19p for the first book plus 9p per copy for each additional book ordered up to a maximum charge of 73p.

For B.F.P.O. and Eire: Customers should include to cover postage, 19p for the first book plus 9p per copy for the next 6 and thereafter 3p per book.

For Overseas: Customers should include to cover postage, 20p for the first book plus 10p per copy for each additional book.

Name ....

Address...

....

....

Title ....
(NOVEMBER)
